The Mother at
Number 5

BOOKS BY JILL CHILDS

The Mother at Number 5

JILL CHILDS

Bookouture

Published by Bookouture in 2023

An imprint of Storyfire Ltd.
Carmelite House
50 Victoria Embankment
London EC4Y 0DZ

www.bookouture.com

ISBN: 978-1-83790-028-2
eBook ISBN: 978-1-83790-027-5

This book is a work of fiction. Names, characters, businesses, organizations, places and events other than those clearly in the public domain, are either the product of the author's imagination or are used fictitiously. Any resemblance to actual persons, living or dead, events or locales is entirely coincidental.

For Ilkley

PROLOGUE

At first sight, it could have been a giant puppet, slumped and lifeless, carelessly abandoned on the kitchen floor.

The body's limbs are twisted awkwardly, bent under its weight as it slid to the floor. One foot sticks out at an unnatural angle. Fingers that once offered love and care are frozen now into stiff, rounded claws. And those eyes. Wide, glassy and staring sightlessly upwards towards the newly painted ceiling. The panic and shock captured in them mirrors the horror of the distorted mouth.

This was not a peaceful death. No tearful, bedside visits at the end of a life well lived. No disguising the fact that death has come with violence and force. The extravagant arcs of splattered blood tell their own story. They draw broken patterns across the pristine kitchen counters where they have caught the edges of cupboards, pooled, congealed and hardened on the carefully mopped kitchen floor.

Later, much later, questions will be asked, by friends, by neighbours, by detectives, by lawyers.

What passion could have driven someone to seize that knife, and plunge it so deeply into another person's flesh that only the handle now protruded? Who else might have watched, might have remained silent, watching this horror unfold? And, perhaps the biggest question of all, how could such wickedness be possible, in this close, caring community?

So many questions. Every one of them too late.

1

ROS

'It's a hard life.'

Ros turned to see who'd spoken. The woman on the next sunlounger had a neat, dark bob. She gave an ironic smile as she lifted her glass. It was brimming with a coconut cocktail, decorated with a curly plastic straw and a paper umbrella. A single plump cherry floated on the surface.

'But someone's got to do it, right?' The woman winked. Her lips closed around the straw. They were artfully painted with bright red lipstick and formed a perfect O.

She wasn't much younger than Ros – mid-thirties probably – but in better shape. Long, slim legs streaked out from a slinky robe. Her dark, even tan was set off by a skimpy bikini.

Ros hadn't worn a bikini for years. Certainly not since she'd been pregnant with Sophie. Frankly, if she stopped to think about it, she didn't expect she'd wear one ever again. But she rarely stopped. Life was too busy.

She shifted her buttocks on the chair, conscious of her stomach and thighs. *You're perfect, Mummy*, the girls told her. They were still young enough to be adoring and she was enjoying it while it lasted.

'Absolutely. It's hell, isn't it?' Ros smiled back. She lifted her plastic beaker of juice and gave a mock toast in reply. She and Adam always brought their own snacks and drinks down to the poolside, to save money. She'd seen the prices on the bar menu. They'd burn through a fortune if they ordered everything from there.

Sweat pooled between her breasts and Ros shifted her position on the sunlounger, angling herself more fully into the shade thrown by the parasol. She liked heat but the cloudless glare of Majorca in August was challenging, even for her. She spent half her day smothering the protesting girls in sun-cream and shoving wide-brimmed hats on their heads.

She shielded her eyes with her hand and watched them now. The early afternoon sun shimmered on the moving water. Sophie and Bella were screaming as they splashed each other in the shallow end of the hotel pool. It was happy shrieking, but she liked to stay alert: every now and then it tipped over into fighting.

She looked up as the waiter headed towards them. He stopped at the other woman's chair and set a platter of fresh fruit down with a flourish.

Ros peered across. Artfully arranged slices of pineapple and kiwi fruit, banana, a knob of lime and a few slices of a fleshy dark orange fruit she didn't recognise, served with a tiny fork. It looked amazing but it was an awful lot of money. You could buy a pound of fresh fruit at the local market for the same price. She could imagine some of the school mums at home snapping a picture and posting it online, just to make their friends' mouths water and, well, yes, to show off a bit too.

The waiter gave the woman a smile. His eyes were all over her. She didn't seem to mind, just smiled her thanks, sat up, gathered her robe closer around her body and lifted up her sunglasses, perching them on the top of her head.

'I know it's decadent,' the woman said, mischievously. Her

blue eyes sparkled at Ros. 'But what the heck. Only live once, don't we?'

Ros realised she must have been staring, grinned an apology and turned away. She considered picking up her paperback again, but she hadn't really got into it. Normally, Adam was there too, but he'd taken himself off for a round of golf on the parched course on the waterfront. He deserved a few hours to himself. He really needed this vacation – he worked too hard – but so far he'd spent most of his time in the water with the girls, throwing them, squealing, into the air, or letting them dive off his shoulders. She smiled to herself.

'Try some.'

The woman's voice pulled her back. It was thick with a mouthful of pineapple. She picked up the lime and squeezed the juice over the orange fruit before spearing a piece with the small fork.

'Here. The papaya's amazing.' She pushed the plate across the table between their sunloungers, closer to Ros.

'No, thanks, I'm fine.' Ros instinctively waved her away.

'Yes! You must!' The woman held the fork out to her, the fruit clinging precariously. 'Go on!' It hung there between them. 'Before it falls off.'

Ros had never tried papaya. It wasn't something she'd think to buy. She reached out and pulled the fruit off the fork with her fingers. It dissolved into a messy mush as she dropped it into her mouth. She licked off her fingers. For a moment, she couldn't speak. Her mouth was too full. The flavour hit her with a punch. 'Oh, my goodness,' she said at last. 'That is amazing.'

'Isn't it?' The woman grinned and forked up another piece for herself. 'Come on, tuck in. There's far too much for one person.'

'Are you sure?'

In answer, the woman pushed another piece of papaya into her own mouth, then speared a second piece for Ros. Ros was already imagining the way she'd tell Adam about it later. She'd build it up into a story and make him laugh. Adam was a good audience. He always joked that he couldn't leave her alone for two minutes without a stranger telling her their life story. And it was true. She was a good listener, a people person. It was useful at work and, most of the time, it served her well outside it too. It was something she was always telling the girls: it never hurts to make new friends.

Eventually, they cleared the plate, leaving a shallow stain of juice. The woman set down her fork, dabbed her lips with a folded napkin and reached out a hand. Ros wiped her sticky fingers hurriedly on a towel and they shook. It was an oddly formal gesture for a poolside chat, but Ros rather liked it. She felt as if they were sealing a deal. A vacation friendship deal.

'I'm Ros,' she said.

'Lotte.'

'Is that—?' Ros was just about to ask more when she was interrupted.

'Mummy!' Bella chose that moment to come running, wailing and dripping, along the edge of the pool, her elbows tucked in at her sides and shoulders hunched.

Ros reached for a large towel and held it open as her four-year-old approached, her face blotchy with grief. Ros wrapped the towel around her daughter's thin body and gave her hair a brisk rub. 'What's wrong, poppet?'

Bella cast a venomous look back at the pool where her big sister, Sophie, was doing handstands in the shallows, studiously avoiding looking across at them. 'Sophie ducked me.' She could barely get the words out for indignant fury.

Ros tutted under her breath. She didn't want to take sides, but she believed Bella. She'd caught Sophie a few times that summer bullying her little sister. She didn't know what the matter was with her. She pulled Bella closer and gave the lumpy towel-encased shape a rough hug. 'How mean.' She dried off her daughter's face and planted a kiss on the tip of her nose. 'Poor Bella.' She patted the space beside her on the lounger. 'Why don't you stay here with me? We can play cards, if you like.'

Bella shook her head, spraying her mother lightly with chlorinated droplets, then shrugged off the towel, took a deep gulp of air and went running back along the pool edge to where her sister was waiting. A minute later, she'd climbed back into the water and the pair of them were cavorting again, their quarrel resolved.

'How old are the girls?'

Ros spread the damp towel out to dry. 'Sophie's eight and Bella's four, nearly five.' She shielded her eyes again and peered at them, keeping a watchful eye. 'They get on pretty well most of the time. Well, when they're not trying to kill each other.'

Lotte grimaced. 'Put them in Kids' Club. That's what I do. Otherwise, it's just childcare in the sun, isn't it?'

Ros turned to her. 'You've got kids?' She realised she was surprised. Lotte was too poised, too well put together. Not to mention the flat stomach.

'Just one. Caitlyn. She's four too.'

'Right.' Ros fiddled a bit more with the damp towel, turning her face slightly away from her new friend. She wrestled with her own disapproval. Four was pretty little. She didn't think a kid that young should be left in a club all day. She argued against herself in her head, trying to be reasonable. Who was she to judge? She didn't know the first thing about this woman and her daughter. Maybe Caitlyn loved it. Maybe Lotte needed a break.

She paused. She really needed one too, actually. She was happy, but it was hard work at the moment, trying to get her own business off the ground along with all the rest of the things she had to do: the shopping, cooking, cleaning, washing and childcare.

Adam was brilliant with the girls, especially with Sophie. They had a real bond. Now she was a bit older, he was always taking her off walking on the moors, or cycling. It was good for them both to have some one-on-one time now and then. But, even so, she was the one who rustled up costumes with no notice for World Book Day and end-of-term plays. She was the one who bought and wrapped presents for endless friends' birthday parties and ferried them to and from swimming and gymnastics and piano and Brownies, then hurried back to stand in the cold waiting for them to come out again.

'Have you read this?' Lotte picked up a glossy paperback from beside her and held it out.

Ros stretched a hand for it and glanced at the blurb on the back. 'Any good?'

'I don't normally go for thrillers but I saw this at the airport and, honestly, I couldn't put it down.' Lotte batted Ros's hand away when she moved to give it back. 'Keep it. I've just started another one.'

'Thanks!' Ros opened it up to the first page and sampled the first paragraph. She was about to comment on it when Sophie and Bella came running along the side of the pool, their small feet slapping wet footprints on the hot tiles.

Ros sat up, attentive at once, and reached for their towels. 'OK, girls?'

'Did you see?' Sophie, pushing past her younger sister, arrived first. 'I swam all the way from one side to the other, underwater. I didn't come up ONCE. Did you see?'

'Wow, well done.' Ros shook open a towel and handed it over. 'A whole width?'

'So did I, Mummy.' Bella panted up too and sat heavily on the bottom of Ros's lounger, making it bounce.

Ros moved her feet to one side to make room. Both girls were running with water, making small puddles around their feet. She said vaguely: 'Mind where you're dripping, girls.'

'No, you didn't.' Sophie turned on her sister. 'Liar.'

'I DID.' Bella stuck out her jaw. Ros saw her bottom lip start to tremble.

'Girls!' She rummaged in her voluminous bag for something to distract them. 'Please!' She tutted to herself, feeling her way past a bottle of sun-cream, packs of tissues, Adam's book.

Sophie, not finished yet, said: 'But she *is* a liar.' She turned back to Bella and pulled a face. 'Liar, liar, pants on fire.'

Bella dissolved into noisy crying just as Ros found the crackers in a far corner and brought them out with a flourish. 'Stop it, both of you. Sophie, give your sister a cracker and then you can have one too.'

Sophie hesitated. 'Can we have an ice-cream?'

Bella magically stopped crying and looked up, her tear-stained face suddenly hopeful. 'Can we?'

'Maybe later.' Ros had bought them ready-made cones from the freezer in a local supermarket the day before. They were twice the price at the pool bar.

Sophie snatched the packet with bad grace. 'You always say that.' She pulled out a cracker and tossed the packet into Bella's sodden lap. 'Here.'

'Sophie!' Ros shook her head. 'Gently, please.'

Sophie plonked herself down further up Ros's lounger. 'What can we do now?'

At almost the same time, Bella, munching, said: 'I'm bored.'

Ros took a deep breath. Beside them, Lotte had settled back on her own lounger, one knee bent elegantly, her sunglasses back on and her next paperback book open in front of her face.

2

ROS

'Hello again!'

Ros opened her eyes against the sun and squinted up into hard whiteness. A shadow came over her face. She struggled to sit up.

Ros blinked. Lotte was there on the beach, staring down at her, blocking out the sun. She looked amused. She was wearing a black baseball cap and a swimming costume under an unbuttoned cotton shirt. A canvas bag was slung over one shoulder. She was holding up her sunglasses as she looked down at Ros, as if she were lifting a veil.

'Oh.' Ros, boiling in a pool of her own sweat, marvelled at how fresh Lotte looked. 'Hi.'

It had been several days since they'd chatted at the poolside over Lotte's platter of fruit. Since then, Adam, Sophie and Bella had decided the beach was 'way less boring' than the pool and the whole family had made camp on the sand each morning.

Ros had glimpsed Lotte once or twice around the hotel complex, but they'd never been near enough to speak and had limited themselves to an occasional smile or cheery wave. She had never seen her on the beach.

Ros shielded her eyes and peered up. 'Still enjoying your vacation?'

Lotte nodded. 'We're heading home tomorrow. Back to reality.' She pointed to the sand. 'OK if I join you?'

'Of course!' Ros tidied the family chaos of towels and discarded clothing, righting the beach bag that had tipped on its side. She brushed off a sand-encrusted bottle of sun-cream and popped it back inside. She felt as if she ought to straighten cushions and do some dusting, as if she were at home and Lotte were an unexpected visitor on the doorstep.

Lotte took out a folded towel from her bag and sat on it, her knees drawn up, her sunglasses back in place, shielding her eyes. She slipped off her sandals and pushed her toes, with their brightly polished nails, into the loose sand. 'How are the girls?'

'Loving it.' Ros turned to watch the two short figures on either side of Adam in the shallows. He was holding their hands and they were playing a game that involved jumping over incoming waves, then kicking up foamy sand and firing it at each other from their toes. The girls' shrieks were just audible, shimmering through the heat.

Ros had raised the idea of Kids' Club with them after she'd met Lotte. Sophie had looked thoughtful, but Bella had put her hands on her hips and said with a withering frown: 'NO, Mummy!' as if she'd suggested something unconscionable. Adam hadn't been in favour of it either, and Ros hadn't mentioned it again.

'How about you?' Lotte took out a tube of sun-cream and started applying it to her long legs. The smell of coconuts wafted across. 'You here much longer?'

'Saturday.'

'Really?' Lotte considered. 'Into Gatwick?'

'Leeds Bradford.'

'Ah.' Lotte paused in her creaming. 'Yorkshire.'

'That's right.' Ros already had Lotte down as a southerner,

from London or the home counties, judging by her accent. She wouldn't be surprised if she'd never been north of Watford. 'We live near there.'

Lotte just nodded, her eyes on her legs.

'Ilkley.' Ros paused. 'You know, Ilkley Moor. It's near Leeds.'

Lotte said vaguely: 'Right.' She moved onto her arms.

They sat in companionable silence for a moment. Ros watched the girls splashing through the surf as Adam chased them. Nearby, a young couple, hand in hand, waded into the waves, hesitating as the rushing sea water reached for them.

'Are you allowed out?'

'Sorry?' Ros thought the sounds of the beach – the soft crash and drag of the waves, and the calls and cries of children, which hung always in the background – had made her miss what Lotte had said.

'I just wondered' – Lotte was staring intently at the sand – 'do you fancy a few drinks tonight, after dinner maybe? I've got a babysitter booked. A sort of girls' night out. Nothing too heavy. I'd love some company. You know, last night and everything.'

'Well,' Ros hesitated, embarrassed. She and Adam had developed their own routine in the evenings. An early dinner with the girls, then, after they'd put them to bed, they sat together on the balcony in the warm air and had coffee and chatted. 'It's just that—'

'It's fine,' Lotte said, quickly. 'Sorry, I shouldn't have asked. It's one of those sad single mum things. Forget it.' She smiled but her lips were tight. 'No big deal.'

Ros thought for a moment. When was the last time she'd been out in the evening with another mum? She was on vacation, for heaven's sake. *Why not?* Just one or two drinks. It might be fun. 'I'd need to check with Adam. But, well, if he doesn't mind holding the fort, then sure, I'd love to.'

Lotte lifted her head, beaming. 'Really?'

'Really!'

The two of them giggled at each other like naughty schoolgirls.

Lotte said, 'Do you think he'll say yes?'

Ros considered. 'I think so.' She looked out at Adam, careering about in the foam and felt a sudden rush of love for him. Of course he'd say yes. He was always encouraging her to do new things. 'In fact, yes, I'm pretty sure he will.'

'Brilliant.' Lotte jumped to her feet and grabbed her bag. She slipped her feet into her sandals, then leaned over Ros, blocking out the sun again. 'I've got to go and pick up Caitlyn. Look, let's say we meet in the lobby at, maybe, nine?' She pulled a mock tragic face. 'If you're not there by quarter past, I'll go on my sad and lonely way without you.'

'Deal.'

'See you later, then. And if you can come, the first drink's on me.'

Ros shielded her eyes and watched Lotte pick her way between the tourists, her figure erect, her pace determined. She couldn't imagine being a single mum. It couldn't be easy.

'Mummy!'

She shifted her gaze. Bella and Sophie were racing up the beach towards her, kicking up sprays of sand. Their arms pumped like pistons at their sides. Their cheeks and noses shone red with exertion and sun. Adam followed more slowly behind them.

Ros waved, then reached for the girls' towels, carefully shook off the sand and held them out, ready.

3

ROS

Ros stood on the balcony, her hands pressing down on the top of the railing, looking down at the tourists below as they strolled past the empty swimming pool towards the main building and the brightly lit dining room there.

'I won't go. This is silly.'

'You wanted to, half an hour ago. What's changed?'

'I don't know.' Ros felt her stomach clench. She turned round to face Adam.

He was sitting on a hard plastic chair in the corner, one ankle crossed over his knee, a book in his hand. He'd been trying to read but he looked up, listening, patient.

'I don't know why I said yes,' she blurted out. 'I don't really know her. I was just, well, sorry for her, I suppose. Because she's on her own.'

Adam shrugged. 'Well, you don't have to go if you don't want to. But you said you liked her. Maybe you'll enjoy it.'

Ros smoothed down her dress. It was tighter than the one she normally wore. She'd gone overboard with her make-up and changed into her new smart sandals. 'I could always bail out early, couldn't I? If I wanted to.'

Adam nodded. 'Yes, you could.'

'I doubt we'll be going very far.'

'Probably not.'

'You're sure you don't mind?'

Adam set down his book and got to his feet. He put his hands on Ros's shoulders and looked into her eyes. 'Stop worrying. Go out there and have fun. Everything's fine.'

'OK.' Ros leaned forward and kissed him lightly on the lips. 'I won't be long.'

Adam smiled. 'Be as long as you like.'

She tiptoed into the darkened bedroom and bent low over the girls on the sofa bed. Sophie's leg was caught up in the sheet and she carefully untangled it, then covered her up. Bella had drifted sideways, her head right on the edge of the mattress. Her straggly hair hung down like seaweed. Ros lifted her gently back onto her pillow and watched her snuffle and settle again in her sleep. She put her lips to her damp forehead, breathing in the residual smell of salt, sun-cream and raspberry shampoo, then took a deep breath and crept out.

Lotte was already in the lobby. Her eyes must have been on the lift: she jumped to her feet as soon as Ros stepped out.

Lotte looked fantastic. She was effortlessly chic in a sleeveless cotton dress with a plunging neckline. Her skin was glowing, her blue eyes blazing. Ros felt lumbering by comparison.

'Look at you!' Lotte, looking her up and down, grinned. 'Don't you scrub up well!'

Ros felt herself flush, still uncertain. 'You look amazing.'

Lotte slipped her arm through Ros's and drew her towards the main doors. Ros was engulfed in her perfume, something spicy and expensive. She felt a final pull back towards Adam, towards the sleeping girls.

'Is Caitlyn OK?'

Lotte raised her eyebrows. 'Caitlyn is fast asleep and perfectly fine. And that,' she raised a warning finger, 'is the last time you mention children this evening. Understood?'

The automatic doors slid open and they stepped out into the humid night air, thick with the scent of brine, frying oil and sap. All around them, in the scrubby grass, cicadas chattered.

'Right, missus.' Lotte hummed with energy. Ros felt herself loosen. The rhythmical clatter of their heels along the tiled sidewalk, the feel of Lotte's arm in hers, the brash music blaring from the bars and restaurants they were passing, the sense of being on show, of unseen male eyes watching them make their way through the darkness, it all rekindled distant memories of a time, years ago, before she was married, when girls' nights out were a regular fixture.

Lotte stooped to check out Ros's sandals. 'Can you dance in those?' She laughed. 'We'll see. Nearly there.'

'Where are we going?'

Lotte didn't answer, just quickened her pace and hurried them on. They reached the beach front and turned a sharp right. The street was heaving. Ros felt her confidence ebb as they weaved their way through the crowd. *Everyone was so young.* Muscular young men with bulging biceps and lithe young women in strappy, stiletto heels, their taut stomachs flashing under crop tops and bottoms poking out of teeny, tiny shorts. What was she doing? She must stick out like a sore thumb.

She opened her mouth to say something, but Lotte pulled her suddenly sideways, across the flow of the crowd and through a gateway. A pink flickering neon sign of a giant flamingo buzzed over the arch. A thick-set guy on the gate looked them over but didn't try to stop them as they strode past. Dance music, hard and tectonic, hit them like a wall.

Lotte seemed to know exactly where she was heading. She took Ros's hand and pulled her through the milling, strutting crowd of young clubbers to the back where they climbed a narrow spiral staircase to a mezzanine area above the dance floor. Here, there were far fewer people, and the assault of the music was less intense.

'You been here before?' Ros asked.

'Let's just say, I did a recce.' Lotte laughed and her teeth flashed in the strobing light. She pointed to an empty booth. 'Grab that, will you? I'll get some cocktails.'

Ros slid along a plastic, cushioned seat and peered over the balustrade to the revels below. It was another world. All the time she and Adam had been pottering by the pool and sitting quietly on their balcony, this place and dozens like it had been pulsating in steamy darkness with young, raw energy. She wasn't sure she belonged down there, in amongst the action. But Lotte had chosen well. This view over the dancers from above was perfect.

Lotte reappeared with two large frothy cocktails, adorned with paper umbrellas and twizzle straws. Ros didn't dare ask what they'd cost. No doubt she'd find out soon enough when it was her round.

'Get a load of these!' Lotte set them down on the table and slid into the opposite seat. The booth was so small that their knees bumped underneath the table. 'Hope you like it...'

A waiter, looming behind her, lifted another two glasses of the same cocktail off a tray, added them to the table and disappeared.

'Because,' Lotte continued, 'I ordered us two each.'

Ros leaned forward as Lotte did, pursing her lips around the end of the straw and drinking deeply. She spluttered. She'd expected it to be mostly fruit juice with a trace of alcohol buried somewhere deep inside. In fact, it blew her head off. 'Blimey!' She gasped. 'What's in that?'

Lotte laughed. 'Oh, a bit of this, a bit of that.'

'And a bucket load of the other.' Rum, definitely. And

maybe vodka too. And a dash of coconut.

'Cheers!' Lotte clinked glasses. 'So, off you go. Give me the lowdown.'

Ros raised her eyebrows. Already the alcohol was kicking in, racing around her body, numbing her fingertips. 'On me? Nothing much to say.'

'Oh, come on.' Lotte leaned forward, her eyes intense. 'Alright, I'll go first. Strictly between us, right?'

'Sure.'

'So, I've just been fired from my job. Again. And Caitlyn's supposed to start school next month and I'm not even sure where we'll be living. Oh, and, before you ask, her dad's not in the picture. He did a runner as soon as I found out I was pregnant. At least, I think he was her dad. That's what I told him. Truth is, I wasn't totally one hundred per cent sure.' She raised her glass. 'Here's to honesty.' She sucked on her straw and swallowed. 'Your turn. Let's hear it. Spill the beans, girlfriend.'

'Did I miss something?' Ros laughed. 'What happened to small talk?'

Lotte grimaced. 'Small talk's for losers. I only do big talk.'

Ros took another draw on her straw. 'Well, I'm Ros,' she said. 'Married to Adam for eleven years. The girls are both—'

'No, no, no!' Lotte leaned forward as she interrupted. Her breath was heady with rum. 'That's no good! No sweet-talking me about your darling hubby and your adorable kids. I want to hear the truth, raw and ugly. Really. Tell me. What keeps you awake at night?'

Ros shook her head. 'Nothing much, unless it's Adam's snoring.' She saw Lotte's face. 'What? Don't look so long-suffering.'

'I've just bared my soul to you, that's all. I thought, you know... ! I thought we had a connection.'

'We do.' Ros hesitated, not sure for a moment if Lotte was actually offended or just teasing.

Lotte grinned. 'Well, there's no one else here. Come on, dish the dirt. I won't tell.'

'What keeps me awake?' Ros thought about it. 'Worrying about the girls, I suppose.'

'Why?'

'Well, about Sophie. She's, she's sort of going through a strange phase at the moment.'

'I thought I'd banned talk about the kids this evening!' Lotte shook her head, then shrugged and made a show of relenting. 'Still, if it's keeping you up at night, I suppose... Go on, then.'

Ros hesitated. She didn't want to talk about it, not really. But they were such a long way from home, and she'd never see Lotte again and she seemed so interested, so genuinely willing to listen. 'She's been having nightmares and, well, it's embarrassing at her age, but she's been wetting herself. I know, it sounds ridiculous. She's eight. But it's happened several times in the last few months. I even wondered about talking to the doctor, but she's made me promise I won't. She's so embarrassed. It happened in school once, in front of all the other kids. Imagine.' She hesitated. 'I shouldn't really have told you. You won't—?'

'Don't be daft. Of course not.' Lotte's smile was sympathetic. 'Go on. Get it off your chest.'

Ros sighed. 'She's just not herself. She hit Bella the other day, really hard. Made her lip bleed. It was about nothing at all – some stupid argument about Bella touching her book. I've never seen her flare up like that before. They've always got on really well.'

'So, what do you think's going on?'

'I'm not sure.' Ros shrugged. 'Maybe schoolwork? They push them very hard at St Stephen's – her school. Maybe too hard.'

Lotte looked thoughtful. 'It's a funny age, eight. Sort of between one stage and another.'

A couple of young men in tight T-shirts paused as they passed and looked them over. One, with tousled blond hair, locked eyes with Ros and grinned, showing even white teeth. He looked barely thirty.

'Easy, tiger,' Lotte said, amused, as the guys moved on. 'So what else? Apart from the kids.' She settled back into her seat with a mischievous look. 'You must have a few skeletons rattling about in your cupboard, surely? Doesn't everyone? I've told you mine.'

'Well, my business is struggling. Does that count?'

'It's a start. What sort of business?'

'Recruitment.' Ros shrugged. 'I used to work for an agency in Leeds, but I left when I had Sophie. Last year, I set up on my own, working from home.'

'Cool.' Lotte seemed impressed.

'Well, not that cool. Not yet.' Ros sipped some more of her cocktail and her eyes watered. 'It's only Adam that's keeping us afloat. I'm still, you know, building it up.'

'Well, it takes time. It's good to be ambitious.'

'It is.' Ros thought about the rush she'd had when she'd first registered the business, carving out time to do the paperwork while Bella was in nursery. She just hadn't expected it to take so long to get off the ground. 'But there's ambitious and then there's going bankrupt.'

'How do you find clients?'

'Social media, mostly.' Ros spent an hour or two a day online when she was at home, chatting up people on local websites and, now and then, slipping in a mention of her services. 'And word of mouth. Ilkley's a small place. So far, a lot of my clients have been school mums looking for local jobs. It's all part-time, though, and not that well paid.'

'Still, good for you!' Lotte drained her first glass with a sharp slurp, pushed it to one side and moved on to the second. 'Come on, you're getting behind!'

After that, the drinks just seemed to keep coming. Afterwards, Ros couldn't quite remember how many she'd had. Every time they reached the end of a round, the waiter reappeared with more of the same. Lotte waved away Ros's protests about the cost and pushed back the cash she kept offering, insisting that Ros was doing her a favour and she'd be sitting there on her own otherwise.

Ros felt her lips grow rubbery as the alcohol numbed her brain. She had to open her eyes wide to focus on Lotte's flushed, grinning face. The seat and table hummed with sound as the music pumped into the night. Below, the crowd was becoming ever more tightly packed, a mass of writhing, gyrating bodies, hands raised above their heads, bare flesh shining with sweat and oil.

At some point, Lotte slipped away for a few minutes and, when she came back, slid in beside Ros, pushing her a little further along the seat. Her leg pressed firmly against Ros's thigh.

'So, Missus Married-Eleven-Years,' Lotte said into her ear. Her breath was warm. 'Have you strayed much?'

Ros blew out hard. 'Strayed?' Her brain was suddenly glacially slow.

'You know, played around. Nothing to be ashamed of. Everyone does it.'

'No!' Ros reeled. 'I would never—'

Lotte shrugged. 'What about Adam? Come on, I won't tell. He must have had a few, you know, indiscretions along the way —? Or does he always cover his tracks?'

Ros shook her head. The darkness spangled, making her nauseous, and she stopped, waiting for it to settle. 'He's not like that.'

'Really? I thought they all were.' Lotte looked amused. 'What's he like then, in the sack?'

Ros was struggling to focus, her head thick with alcohol.

'Well.' She hesitated. 'It's fine. I mean, we're parents. We're both shattered most of the time, what with work and the girls and—'

'Wait!' Lotte's eyes gleamed. 'Don't tell me – he's withdrawn his services, hasn't he?'

'I didn't say that.'

'You didn't have to! Look at your face! How long's it been?'

Ros looked flustered. 'I never said—'

'It's true though, isn't it?' Lotte laughed. 'Don't look so panicked. Tell me. What's going on? Or rather, isn't going on.'

Ros felt herself flush. 'I shouldn't have, I mean, he's just had a really tough time, recently.' She didn't say any more but she felt her mood shift as she thought about her husband. Adam hadn't been himself recently. She suspected it was linked to the sudden death of his older brother, Charles, earlier in the year, from a massive heart attack. The two men had always had such a strange relationship, and she'd learned from bitter experience not to ask Adam about it: it was one of the few issues which always seemed to spark a row. But, although she hadn't dared to raise it, she sensed that the news of Charles's death had hit Adam hard.

Lotte looked thoughtful. 'So it's him, then. He's the problem. Not you.'

Ros didn't answer. She didn't want to talk about their sex life, it was too intimate. Adam would be mortified. She should never have said a word. Lotte was just so good at picking up on things, at reading her face.

They sat in silence for a few moments.

'You know what?' Lotte shifted along the seat. 'How about we hit the dance floor?'

'Good idea!' Ros did her best to sound enthusiastic. Her body was overloaded with alcohol and throbbing with noise, but she was glad of the distraction. 'Just for a bit, then I'll head off.'

'What?' Lotte gave her a look of mock-horror. 'You're not

bailing out on me that soon! We've only just got here.' She tugged at Ros's arm. 'Come on! I've got my eye on a couple of Spanish studs down there. Look.' She pointed over the balustrade at the dancefloor. 'See, those two? Blondie's asked me if I'd put in a word for him. And now I know about...' She hesitated. 'Well, put it this way, I think he's exactly what you need.'

Ros struggled to focus. 'Those two?' They were the young men who'd paused at their table earlier in the evening. 'Well, I don't really think—'

'Oh, don't be boring.' Lotte pouted, then reached for Ros's hand and tried to pull her out of the booth. 'Come on, let's go down and say hi. At least dance off the booze.'

As Ros tried to stand, the floor tilted and swayed. She put out a hand to steady herself and Lotte grabbed it, pulling her forward.

Ros didn't know how she ended up downstairs. Coloured lights bounced and strobed overhead. Sound crashed over her like a tsunami, throbbing through her bones. She held tightly to Lotte's hand as they threaded through the hot, sweaty bodies. The two young men turned, grinning, to make space for them as they approached. The dark-haired one reached for Lotte and drew her to him.

The blond flashed his teeth, then lifted his bulging arms and closed in on Ros. He placed firm, hot hands on her hips and started to move her with him, twisting to the pounding beat. His body, against hers, was hard with muscle and slippery with sweat. He felt alien, so different from Adam, his flesh firm and unyielding.

She closed her eyes and concentrated on staying upright, fighting down nausea, and surrendered, letting her body follow his, mesmerised by pulses of bright light shooting like meteors through her head.

4

ROS

'Mummy.'

A small voice whispered inside Ros's head. Her mind tried to make sense of it. It needed her. She must respond, somehow, rouse herself. She lay still, deafened by the throbbing in her temples.

'Mummy.' She knew that voice. *Bella?* Was it her? She was whispering but her tone was more urgent. 'Mummy, are you OK?'

Ros tried to open her eyes wide enough to see. Light spiked in, painful on her eyeballs. She let them fall closed again. She tried to get her bearings without actually moving. She was lying, face down, on something soft. It creaked as she shifted her weight. Her stomach convulsed. She stiffened at once, tasting bile, and held her body deathly still, praying for her stomach to settle.

A door opened. *The bathroom door?* Shoes squeaked across the polished floor.

'What did I tell you?' Adam's voice, lowered too, sounded stern. 'Get your towels, girls. Leave Mummy alone for now.'

Ros lay still, pretending to be asleep, wishing they would

just leave her alone. She couldn't move, not yet. There was shuffling in the room and a stifled giggle, then muffled whispers and, finally, the click of a carefully closed door.

Sophie's voice echoed from the corridor: 'But why, Daddy? Is she sick?'

Footsteps faded. Ros made out the distant swish of the lift doors and the hum of cables as it departed. She let go again and sank into the mattress. Her head felt as if it were exploding, pain shooting outwards into the rest of her body.

What had she done? She cringed with pain, with humiliation. The girls had seen her like this. They'd remember. The shame of it. She struggled to remember. Lotte, smiling, her lipstick lips around her straw. The cocktails. As she thought of them, a bilious taste of coconut rose in her throat. What was she thinking, at her age?

That guy. The young blond one with the hard, workout body. Had she...? No. Surely not. They'd danced, that was all. Wasn't it? She didn't know. She couldn't remember. Somehow, she'd made it back to this room. Somehow, she'd ended up naked, there, under a sheet. But how? She had no idea.

Strange noises came and went as she tried to sleep. Banging doors. Loud voices, calling in German down the corridor. A rumble of suitcase wheels, as sharp and hard as shrapnel to her brain. Sun pressed in through the closed blinds and hurt her eyes. The contours of her body pooled sweat in the hollows of the mattress.

Water. She needed water, badly. Her mouth cracked dry. She tried to think through the pulsing headache. There was water in the bathroom. She imagined the running tap, the trickle into the glass, the feel of it against her teeth, her tongue.

She opened her eyes. There on the bedside table was a glass of water and, propped beside it, a blister pack of paracetamol. *Adam. Thank you.* She almost cried with relief. Slowly, inch by inch, she lifted her head, then her shoulders, until she could prop herself on one elbow. She popped out two tablets and drank off the water. It sat heavily on her stomach. She fell back against the hot bed again and dissolved, head pounding, into oblivion.

Later, much later. The sun against the blinds was kinder, softer.

Someone was in the room. She heard light, quick breathing, close to her face and snapped open her eyes.

'Mummy?' Bella was peering into her face, her forehead screwed up in concern. 'Are you feeling better? Do you need a doctor?'

From somewhere behind her, Sophie said: 'Daddy, she's awake!'

The bed creaked and shifted as someone sat on the other side of the mattress. Adam appeared and smiled down at her.

'How are you feeling, party girl?' He didn't look mad; he looked concerned and slightly amused. 'More water?'

'What time is it?' Her dry tongue filled her mouth. Her stomach was delicate and very empty.

'Just after four.' Adam gave a wry smile. 'In the afternoon.'

Ros kept very still. She'd lost a whole day. Even so, she wasn't sure she could move without being sick.

Adam bustled about the room. A fresh glass of water appeared on the bedside table.

'You've been asleep ALL DAY,' said Bella. 'We've been at the beach AND the pool AND had ice creams.'

Ros didn't want to think about ice cream, not yet.

'Are you alright?' Sophie, peering in over Bella's shoulder, looked disapproving. 'What happened?'

Ros didn't know what to say. She reached for the water. Sophie's moral universe was black and white, and drinking alcohol was distinctly black.

Adam saved her. 'Mummy's had a nasty dose of food

poisoning, Soph, that's all. She might not want to eat much today but she'll be fine tomorrow, you'll see.' He opened the balcony door and ushered them outside. Ros heard the rustle of plastic. *Snack time.* Maybe mini sponge cakes from the supermarket.

Adam came back into the room, alone, and pulled the door closed behind him. The girls' voices receded. He knelt beside her and stroked her forehead, then reached for the glass of water and held it steady for her to drink.

Ros sipped, swallowed, sipped again. 'I'm so sorry.' How could she have been so stupid? 'I don't know what happened. Honestly. One minute, we were—'

Adam grinned. 'Imagine how she must feel. Didn't you say she was flying home today?'

Ros groaned. The thought of travelling, feeling like this, made her shiver. 'I feel such an idiot.'

'It's fine.' He replaced the glass and kissed her sweaty cheek. 'You're just not used to it and it's very hot, that's all.'

Ros settled back against the pillows and managed a wan smile. 'Love you.'

'Love you too.' Adam raised his eyebrows. 'Just a few drinks, eh?'

'Cocktails.' A memory of the thick taste came back to her and she tried to push it away. 'Vicious ones. She kept buying them. Honestly.'

'She sounds like a very bad influence.' He still seemed amused.

Ros closed her eyes. Maybe if she had a little more sleep... 'I'll take the girls all day tomorrow,' she managed to say. 'Promise. You play golf or something.'

'You don't need to do that.' He squeezed her hand. 'Get some rest and I'll take the girls out for pizza. OK?'

'You're wonderful. You know that, don't you?'

'You too.'

An image jumped into her mind of the strobing lights across the dance floor and the hot, wet feel of the young man's sweaty chest against hers as they danced. What the hell *had* happened?

She remembered Lotte's eyes on hers, intent as she asked Ros so many questions. Ros had talked too much. She knew she had. It wasn't like her, just the alcohol loosening her tongue and the fact Lotte was so attentive. She blinked. How much had she actually said?

Fragments from early in the evening swam into her mind.

Adam. She'd told Lotte that they hadn't had sex in, like, forever. How could she be so disloyal? She couldn't look him in the eye. He'd be horrified.

And what else? About her business being on the brink. She groaned. And about Sophie too, wetting the bed and acting out.

She shuddered. Why had she blabbed so much? She was such a fool. 'I'm so embarrassed,' she murmured.

'Don't be.' Adam let go of her hand as he started to move away. 'No harm done, not really.'

But there was, wasn't there? Wasn't there something more, something worse? She felt a flicker of panic. Her mind was still churning, pulling pieces of memory from the haze.

There had been more. Later, much later, Lotte had led her back to that booth to chat some more. Ros had been so drunk, her lips had felt numb.

Adam, crossing the room to the bathroom, called from the doorway: 'Well, you're safe. She'll be on a plane home by now. So, whatever you did, at least you'll never have to face her again.'

'You're right.' She lay, rigid, trying to remember exactly how much of herself she'd given away. So much of the evening was still blank. She steadied her breathing.

But what else had she said? Her breathing quickened as she struggled to think clearly. Her palms started to sweat. What else had Lotte drawn out of her, about Adam, about the past? Was it possible she'd told her about... about all *that*? Ros's insides chilled. *Surely not.* However drunk she was, that was one secret she'd never share, least of all with a stranger. *That* fear was buried too deep for words, something not even her closest friends knew.

So why did she suddenly feel so afraid?

5

ROS

Ros stood at the school gates, looking wistfully across the playground towards the long, low building. Moments earlier, it had, for the first time, swallowed up both her children, Sophie *and* Bella.

Bella had been unusually quiet over breakfast. Nervous, clearly, about her first day at big school. Ros had bitten her lip, feeling her eyes mist, as they had when Sophie had started at St Stephen's four years earlier.

All around her, parents, mostly mothers, were crouching low to say goodbye to their children, straightening collars and flattening messy hair. They sent each child off with a final kiss and stood for a moment, watching them go, walking or running across the playground to the teachers at the main doors, small ships setting sail into a new school year.

'Hi, Ros. Good summer?'

'Hi, Josie. Oh, my goodness, he's gorgeous!'

Josie, who had a daughter in the year below Sophie's, had given birth to a boy just after the school had broken up for the summer vacation, and Ros hadn't seen her since. Josie was carrying him now in a sling, his small body pressed against her milk-swollen chest. Tiny arms and legs encased in cotton stuck out limply. A shock of dark hair protruded from under a small hat.

Ros stroked his cheek with the tip of her finger. 'How old is he now?'

'Seven weeks.'

'Well done you! How's it going?'

Josie jiggled and swayed as she chatted. She had the rigid smile and glassy gaze of a woman going without sleep.

Ros felt something touch her leg. She looked down to find a small girl of about two glaring up at her, straining out from her buggy seat. Her small fist opened and closed in the air as her mum manoeuvred the heavily laden buggy a few inches further away from Ros and gave an apologetic smile.

'Sorry. She's in a bit of a mood. Aren't you, Matilda?'

The mum bent over her daughter and tried to distract her by tickling her neck, even as Matilda, furious about being constrained by the buggy straps, bucked and kicked and tried to fight herself free.

At the edge of the group, several childminders, younger than the mums, chatted quietly in a cluster, forming their own micro-culture. Ros recognised the tall one from last year but couldn't remember her name. She'd dyed her hair blue over the summer. It looked good. Funky. The kids must love it, even if the mums didn't.

Around her, chat sparked back and forth.

'Thought I was going to be late. We were just leaving the house when the phone rang.'

'Isn't that always the way!'

'Good vacation?'

'You look brown! Where did you go? Portugal? Lucky thing. We only got as far as the Lake District. Two weeks in a caravan in the rain. Never again.'

'Lovely weather today, though.'

It was. The summer was giving a final kiss goodbye. The sun had been warm enough for Bella and Sophie to enjoy a final week or two of cotton dresses before they had to succumb to warmer, fall clothes.

Ros's closest friend, Diana, came hurrying through the crowd and gave Ros a hug. 'How are you, lovely? You look amazing! Good summer?'

Ros beamed. 'Great, thanks. You?'

Diana chatted on about their vacation in Greece. Phil, her husband, loved water sports and always managed to find a family break where he could indulge his passion. This time, apparently, it had been water-skiing.

When they had been children, many years before, Diana had been in the year above Ros at St Stephen's. The gap had been enough to stop them getting to know each other well. They'd only become real friends when they'd met again at ante-natal classes, Ros pregnant with Sophie and Diana with her firstborn, Posy. They'd soon made the connection and realised that their husbands too, also both from Ilkley families, had known each other as teenagers. Ilkley was that sort of place.

'How's Max feeling about big school?'

Diana's second child was, like Bella, just starting in reception.

'Fine, thanks. Pretty excited. He thinks he's catching up with Posy at last.' Diana seemed distracted as she was speaking, looking around at the fellow mothers. 'You're coming for coffee, aren't you?'

Ros nodded. 'You need help rounding people up?'

Diana looked grateful. 'Please.'

There were a lot of new faces. Ros helped Diana identify the parents with children in reception and herd them away from the school, down the cobbled alley and around the corner to the local café, where Diana, one of the two reception year class reps, had booked a few tables.

It was one of the many parents' meetings that Ros knew would happen over the year. They bit into the working day but she reasoned that, however much her business needed her, her children needed her more. Besides, it was a close-knit community, and she never knew what work it might throw her way.

In the café, the parents flowed around the scrubbed wooden tables, several with young babies or toddlers in tow, while Ros helped Diana extract a complicated group coffee order – all skinny lattes and oat milk cappuccinos – and then head to the counter to relay it to the staff.

Once the servers had the order, Ros stood at the back of the group as Diana rapped her knuckles on the tabletop for quiet. She introduced herself and gave everyone a quick welcome, explaining to the new mums about joining the class WhatsApp group, how to contribute to joint presents for the teachers and about the end-of-term Christmas Fair. 'I hope this will be the first of many occasions to get to know each other,' she went on. 'Do take the chance to mingle over a cuppa and feel free to ask me if you have any questions.'

Ros politely turned to the woman on her left and introduced herself. As the woman, Beth, started to talk, Ros found her mind wandering – thinking whether the dad in the red shirt really had asked for camomile tea or if she'd misheard, about what she was going to feed the girls later and the volume of work she needed to tackle, now the girls were back in school.

Someone across the table leaned forward to get Beth's attention and Beth turned and greeted her. Diana had been swamped by a cluster of earnest new parents, all eager to say hello and ask for more information about the second-hand uniform sale, open mornings and the reading scheme.

Ros excused herself, scraped back her chair and headed to the counter to check on their drinks' order. They only had an hour before most parents would need to leave. She was just trying to catch the eye of the young waiter when she heard a clear, confident voice behind her. A very familiar voice.

'Excuse me, is this the right place for the St Stephen's school coffee morning?'

As the café owner started to answer, Ros spun round. Her jaw slackened. She blinked and stared, then blinked again at the neat, slim figure in heeled boots and a tailored navy mac.

Lotte, catching sight of her, broke into a smile. 'Well, hello there! Ros!'

'Lotte?' It was her. The vacation woman. It really was. But what was she doing there, in the middle of Ilkley? Ros opened her mouth to say something more but just gaped.

Lotte waved away the owner and stepped briskly towards her. She kissed her lightly on the cheek as if they were old friends. 'I know! Isn't it amazing? I can hardly believe it myself.'

Ros shook her head, befuddled. 'But how, I mean, what did you—?'

Lotte shrugged. 'It just stuck in my head. *Ilkley*. I thought if the people are half as lovely as Ros, maybe we should try our luck up north. We had to move somewhere new, anyway. Our lease was up.'

'So you've actually moved here?' Ros was struggling to get her head around the shock of seeing Lotte there, in the middle of the school parents.

'Yes! Don't look so horrified!' Lotte laughed. 'But, dear me, the fuss getting Caitlyn into school without, like, a million years' notice! Honestly! Bradford council! Even after I'd seen Mrs Shore and she'd told me they had places, I still had to beg.'

Ros shook her head, dazed. 'Caitlyn's at St Stephen's?'

Lotte nodded. 'I asked Mrs Shore to put Caitlyn in Miss Grey's class, so she could be with Bella. At least that way we sort of know someone!'

Ros tried to smile. But she felt her cheeks flush as she remembered their bizarre night out together in Majorca and how drunk she'd been. She looked around at the polite, earnest faces of the parents and thought about the press of that hot, muscular man's body against hers. And, worse, she'd confided in Lotte, shared such embarrassing things.

And how far had she gone? She still wasn't sure. Had she shared with this woman, in her drunken state, the secret no one there must ever know?

Lotte reached out and took her arm as if they were old chums. 'Now, you must introduce me round. Will you?'

Ros felt herself propelled back towards the long table where the waiter was doling out the first drinks. Faces looked up expectantly and quickly fastened on Lotte. Ros watched as Lotte, all poise and confidence, found herself a seat and settled in at once, engaging the people around her in conversation.

Beth smiled at Ros. 'Is she a friend of yours?'

'No. Yes. Well, not exactly.' Ros wasn't sure what to say. 'We met on vacation, that's all. Last month.'

Beth looked surprised. 'Fancy that!'

Lotte was too far away down the table for Ros to hear her conversation. She claimed her coffee and sat quietly, letting the chat wash over her and sipping at the chocolatey froth.

She couldn't believe it. Surely Lotte hadn't travelled all this way up the country and chosen Ilkley, just because of their chance meeting by the pool? It was bizarre. She didn't even remember talking much about Ilkley, beyond saying they lived there. Lotte hadn't seemed particularly interested. If she'd been thinking about re-locating to West Yorkshire, surely she'd have said so and asked a lot more questions? Practical questions about housing and services and facilities for kids?

Ros frowned to herself, trying to make sense of it. Had she told Lotte which school the girls attended? She didn't remember discussing it. St Stephen's wasn't the only primary school in Ilkley. Was it just coincidence that Lotte had enrolled Caitlyn in the same place? She shook her head, slowly, thinking.

It can't have been if she'd asked Mrs Shore to put Caitlyn in the same class as Bella.

She took a deep breath and forced herself to shrug it all off. The fact Lotte had turned up was certainly a surprise, but maybe it would be a blessing. Caitlyn and Bella might really hit it off. It was always good to make a new friend – that's what she told the girls. And, as for Caitlyn, it couldn't be easy, starting school in a new place.

Beth touched her arm. 'You OK, Rebecca?'

'It's Ros.' Ros forced a smile. 'Yes, I'm fine, thanks.'

Beth sounded concerned. 'It's just, well, you've gone a bit pale.'

'Have I? Just tired. First week back is always a bit mad, isn't it? Ros lifted her cup to her lips. After the sweetness of the milk, the coffee was bitter. She'd been caught off-guard, she told herself. That was all. She hadn't expected to see Lotte there, out of context. It was a shock.

She wondered what Lotte was saying to the other parents that was causing them to listen so raptly – and she felt herself grow hot. She hoped Lotte wasn't explaining how they'd met, telling them all about their louche, drunken night out. Surely she wouldn't do that? *Not here, where everyone knows everyone else*. What if Adam found out what she'd said about him? He'd feel so betrayed.

That wasn't all. Surely Lotte wouldn't tell people about the fact her business was struggling? Not here, where she was trying so hard to build trust, to build a client base. No one would be so mean. Would they?

And that was the least of it. What else did she know?

At that moment, Lotte turned her head and looked down the table, right at Ros.

Ros's cup slipped suddenly in her hand, sending a swell of hot coffee sloshing out, splashing across the surface of the table.

'Oh, no!' She blushed as Beth and another mum grabbed paper napkins and dabbed at the spill. 'I'm so sorry!'

Beth, busy mopping up, said cheerily: 'No harm done!'

When Ros glanced down the table again, Lotte was chatting away, still holding court.

Beth, following Ros's gaze, said: 'But how great that your friend's joining St Stephen's! She looks fun!'

'She is.' Ros managed a weak smile, remembering. 'Great fun!' She pushed back her chair and gathered up the sodden mess of napkins to take across the café and drop in the bin.

Beth was right. Lotte was sure to liven things up. Ros should welcome her, not question why she'd decided to move.

But as she headed back to the table, Ros found herself slowing her pace. She couldn't put her finger on why she felt so uneasy. Maybe she was just knocked off-balance because it was all so unexpected.

She forced a smile. She was being absurd. She had nothing to worry about. There was nothing sinister about Lotte turning up there.

Was there?

6

ROS

By pick-up time that afternoon, Ros had convinced herself that she'd been ridiculous to be so thrown by seeing Lotte again. *It was just a surprise, that's all.* She should make an effort to be more welcoming.

The afternoon light was mellow. Around her, childminders, grandparents and parents slowly arrived and took up their places at the gates. Ros sensed the pent-up energy of the children in the school building, held back for another minute or two but already taking their places in the starting gates, ready to bolt outside as soon as the bell sounded to signal the end of the school day.

Diana appeared down the alley and hurried over to join her. She nodded towards the classrooms. 'Only seems five minutes since we were in there.'

They smiled at each other, remembering. The school had been smaller in their day.

'Remember the grass fights?' Ros said.

They had been a regular event. Children of all ages used to gather up the lines of freshly cut grass, left behind by the mower, and make piles to jump in.

'Who was that girl – was it Heather? – who went crying to the teachers and got everyone into trouble?'

'No, it was something like Helen,' Ros said. Then she snapped her fingers: 'Helen Calder. She was in my year.'

'Helen, that's right.' Diana nodded. 'She made such a fuss.'

Ros smiled. 'Well, we did stuff grass down her front. She came out in a rash.'

'Short with long hair and big glasses.'

'She worked in the opticians on The Grove for a while.'

'That figures.' Diana laughed. 'She wasn't exactly outdoorsy.'

Ros said, 'Don't suppose they're allowed now. Grass fights.'

'Probably not,' Diana said, caustically. 'No nuts, no grass.'

Ros was about to reply when Lotte came striding up to them.

'Hello, ladies!' She beamed at them both, then turned to Diana. 'I'm Lotte, Caitlyn's mum. I didn't have the chance to thank you earlier for the coffee morning. Really helpful. And everyone was so friendly.'

Diana looked flattered. 'That's good to hear. Did you take my number? Well, do send me yours and I'll add you to the class WhatsApp group.'

Ros watched as Lotte put her head on one side, nodding earnestly while Diana chatted about how lovely Ilkley was. There was something for everyone, she explained, there were so many societies and events: the amateur operatic society, the theatre, a choral society, the golf and tennis clubs, the literature festival.

Ros realised she was clenching her hands at her sides, and she made a point of wiggling her fingers to relax them. Of course Diana was warming to Lotte. Lotte was charming and always so interested in what people had to say. Ros's mind drifted back again to their vacation and how engaging Lotte had been. You couldn't help but make friends with her. She was that kind of person.

'It sounds wonderful,' Lotte said. 'It's such a breath of fresh air after London. We're renting an apartment overlooking the Riverside Gardens. It's half the price we were paying in Hammersmith and twice as nice.'

Diana said: 'Near the Riverside? Where, exactly?'

Lotte blinked at her, slightly surprised. 'On Bridge Lane. Number 5. Just near the junction with Lister Street. Do you know it? It's a Victorian conversion. Very nicely done. We've got the top floor. '

Diana looked from one woman to the other. 'Gosh!'

For a moment, no one spoke.

'What?' Lotte asked.

'Well, you two must be neighbours,' Diana said. 'Or practically.'

'No!' Lotte looked at Ros, delighted. 'Really?'

Ros just nodded. She felt herself flush.

Diana answered for her: 'They're just around the corner, in Lister Street. One of the terraces.'

'Well!' Lotte smiled. 'Small world! Caitlyn will be thrilled.'

The high electronic note of the school bell sounded and Ros turned away from Lotte towards the building. As the main doors opened, small bodies burst out, fanning across the playground, yelling and shoving, even as a voice behind them shouted, 'QUIETLY, children! PLEASE!'

Ros made a show of straining to see her own two girls through the blur of fast-moving bodies. Her heart was pounding. Number 5. She knew it, of course. One of the Victorian houses overlooking the riverside park, recently converted into two apartments. Adam had kept an interested eye on the building work from their windows. Lotte wasn't just living in the same town. She was practically in their back yard.

Ros blew out her cheeks and tried to calm down. It was fine.

The girls might think it was fun to have someone from school so close.

She focused on looking out for them. Many of the children were wearing their coats just by the hood, stuck precariously on their heads; their arms stretched gloriously free of the sleeves, which flapped as they ran: blue, grey and black material streaming behind them in a flock of superhero capes.

Lotte said in Ros's ear: 'Well, that settles it. You must bring the girls round. No excuses!'

Ros didn't answer. No sign of the girls yet. She wondered how Bella's first day had gone.

'How about tomorrow, after school?' Lotte said.

'Actually, Wednesdays are a bit tricky,' Ros said over her shoulder. 'Sophie's got Brownies.'

'Thursday?'

'Swimming.'

The first children reached the gates and bowled into the open arms of stooping adults. Posy came running out, beaming at Diana, her plaits bouncing on her back. Her little brother, Max, tailed her, a stocky kid with a mop of curly hair.

Bella appeared soon afterwards, signalling enthusiastically at Ros, her hand moving emphatically back and forth as if she were cleaning an invisible window above her head.

'Hello, sweetheart.' Ros dropped a kiss on the top of her mess of hair as she arrived and gave her a quick hug. 'How was it?'

'Fine.' Bella's eyes found Ros's bag, looking for treats. 'I'm hungry.'

Ros fished out a box of raisins and handed it over. 'Any sign of Sophie?'

She soon appeared, dragging her heels as she crossed the playground.

Ros opened her arms and drew her into a quick hug. 'Hello, beautiful.'

'Goodness, they are busy bees.' Lotte, still at her side, wasn't taking no for an answer. 'Why don't you say which days you're free and I'll make it work?'

Ros hesitated. She admonished herself for being rude. It wasn't like her to be unfriendly. 'We could pencil in Friday and see how it goes?'

'Perfect.'

Sophie looked up. 'What's happening on Friday?'

'We might go round to Caitlyn's house for tea.'

Sophie looked puzzled. 'Who's Caitlyn?'

Ros smoothed her daughter's hair. 'She's just started in reception, in the same class as Bella. This is her mum.'

Sophie tipped her head to look at Lotte. She considered her for a moment, frowning. 'Isn't she the vacation lady?'

Ros took a deep breath. 'Well remembered. That's right. We met her in Majorca, didn't we? Well, she and her daughter have moved to Ilkley. Just round the corner from us. Isn't that funny?'

Bella, raisins now eaten, pitched herself into ragged handstands against the metal fence. Her loose cotton dress flew down to skirt her face and she flashed pink knickers and skinny legs.

'Come on, Bella. Let's go.' Ros was just reaching for the girls' hands, calling goodbye to Diana and Beth and a few other mums she knew, and turning to leave, when her eye was caught by a short, quiet girl who was progressing alone across the almost empty playground. Her hair was unravelling from the remains of a straggly plait. Her face was tilted down, her eyes on the ground.

Ros hesitated, watching her. There was something forlorn about the child. Beside her, Lotte stepped forward. 'Caitlyn!'

The girl didn't seem to have heard. She made no move to hurry her steps.

Ros whispered to Bella: 'She's in your class, isn't she?'

Bella glanced up, nodded, not much interested. 'What's for tea?'

Ros put her hands around her girls' shoulders and drew them away.

I shouldn't judge a four-year-old on first sight, she thought, as they set off down the path. *That's unkind.* Maybe the poor girl was just exhausted after her first day. All the same, it was hard to shake the sense that she had looked a little strange.

7

ROS

Ros and Adam were just finishing dinner when her phone buzzed. She stacked the dishwasher, then went to check it as Adam started to make them both coffee.

He'd had a tough day, by the sound of it. He was working extra hours as he tried to catch up with patients who'd missed appointments while he was away. It was one of the downsides of being an osteopath: all those bad necks and strained backs only worsened without treatment. The extra workload hadn't been helped by news that one of the receptionists had quit.

Ros went to read the new message. 'Honestly!'

Adam looked up, his face softened by the rising steam from the boiling kettle. 'What?'

Ros tutted as she re-read it. 'You know that woman I met in Majorca?'

Adam grinned. 'The party animal?'

'Don't remind me.' Ros pursed her lips, eyes still on her phone. 'Guess what? She's turned up here. In Ilkley.'

Adam looked puzzled. 'Here?'

'I know. It's weird, isn't it? She showed up out of the blue at the coffee thing for new parents this morning. Her daughter's in Bella's class.'

'Well, that's nice.' Adam sounded uncertain. 'Isn't it?' He stirred milk into their mugs and headed towards the lounge.

'And that's not all. Guess where she's living?'

Adam knew better than to answer. Ros hurried after him. 'Bridge Lane!' she said. 'Just round the corner!'

'Really?' Adam looked thoughtful. He liked to keep an eye on local property prices. 'A house?'

'That new conversion at number 5. She's got the top apartment. Renting.' Ros tried to push him back to the point. 'Don't you think that's weird, though?'

'Well, Ilkley's not that big a—'

'I think it's weird,' Ros cut in.

Adam frowned, settled into an armchair and reached for his coffee. He looked tired, his skin dull. He'd started to seem more relaxed by the end of their vacation and Ros had begun to hope that he was finally starting to adjust to his brother's death. Charles had been such a dominant force in his life, even if they had been estranged in recent years. She pursed her lips. She didn't want to think about that. It hurt too much.

She wished things were different. They should be reaching out to Alexandra, Charles's widow, to see how she was and show support. Their daughter, Cassandra, would sit her A-level exams next year. That couldn't be easy, so soon after losing her father, however exclusive her private school.

Ros sighed, thinking about all the unresolved bitterness in the family. She knew Adam would jump down her throat if she suggested contacting his brother's family, and probably remind her who was to blame for the bad blood between them. Ros wasn't even sure how Alexandra would react.

She thought back to that final, disastrous weekend they'd spent together, all those years ago. Pregnant with Sophie, she had felt so full of goodwill. She was the one who'd pushed

Adam to arrange the family get-together. How naïve she'd been. How stupid.

She remembered how, at dinner on the Saturday night, she'd suggested, gushingly, that Cassandra might come to stay with them in Ilkley in the summer vacation. She'd be ten by then, just the right age for an adventure without her parents, for walks and picnics at Bolton Abbey and, if the weather was warm, trips to the Ilkley lido. And, of course, she could help out with the new baby.

Charles and his wife had exchanged a covert stab of a look that had made it clear they would never agree to any such thing. And that was even before the trainwreck later in the evening, which had ended any hope of reconciliation. Alexandra's goodbye at the end of the weekend had been very final. Ros hadn't forgotten her icy politeness, verging on disdain.

Ros flushed. Adam had never forgiven her for the damage she'd done. After that, Charles and Alexandra had made it clear that they wanted no direct contact at all with Adam and his young family.

Every year since then, the only communication was the glossy Christmas card they received from Charles and Alexandra, with an impersonal, printed newsletter enclosed. The image on the front would show the three of them raising a glass to celebrate their latest achievement, or grouped, smiling, in front of some esoteric landmark on the other side of the world.

As the years passed, they had steadily aged, only Cassandra for the better. And no one could have imagined that the previous year's card would be the last to be signed by both Alexandra and Charles.

'Earth to Ros!'

She looked up to find Adam was watching her, his face expectant.

'So, you were saying – party girl's been in touch?' He looked amused. 'Let me guess, she wants to take you out for drinks again?'

Ros grimaced. 'Never again.' She pointed at her phone. 'She wants me to help her find a job.'

He blinked. 'That's good.'

Ros sat down, eyes on her phone. It was hard to read between the lines of such a short message. She shook her head and looked up at Adam again. 'And she's asked us round on Friday, after school. For tea.'

'What, with the girls? Great. Can't imagine she knows many people here.' Adam looked at her, reading his wife's face. 'Why, what do you think?'

Ros didn't know how to put into words the feeling in the pit of her stomach. The knot which told her that she was anxious without quite knowing why. It wasn't just the lingering embarrassment of their drunken night out and her uncertainty about what exactly had happened. While those were details she really didn't want splashed messily all over her calm, close world here, it was more than that. It was a sense of unease that she was sure Adam wouldn't understand, not least because she didn't understand it herself.

She took a deep breath. 'Seriously. Don't you think it's peculiar? I meet someone in Majorca and suddenly she shows up here, living practically on top of us, with her kid in the same school as ours?'

'Not necessarily.' Adam pulled a face. 'Maybe that's why she wanted to go for a drink when she met you, because she was thinking of moving north and wanted to ask you more about Ilkley. It's had a lot of publicity recently. She might have seen that piece in the Sunday papers about the top ten places for families. Ilkley was mentioned, wasn't it?'

Ros nodded. It hadn't just been mentioned, it had been awarded the number one spot in the country. She remembered all the comments it had generated on the Ilkley chat sites: a mixture of pride and wry concern about whether it might encourage hordes of relocating southerners.

'She didn't, though.'

'Didn't what?'

'She didn't ask me about Ilkley. I'd have remembered.'

Adam reached for the newspaper and folded it to the puzzles page. He liked to do the Sudoku in the evening, the numbers helping him unwind. 'Are you sure about that? I mean, you were pretty out of it, weren't you?' He waved his pen at her in self-defence. 'Just saying. Not criticising.'

Ros sat on the sofa and sipped at her coffee, her phone on the table. Her forehead creased as she worried. Maybe Adam was right. Maybe Lotte had already been casting about for somewhere new to live and meeting Ros and the family had inspired her. She bit her lip. It was perfectly plausible.

Adam put in a few numbers, then paused and looked across at her. 'Look, you don't have to make her your best friend. But she's a client. Find her a job, bank the fee and move on. Right?'

Ros nodded. 'You're right.'

Adam shook his head. His gaze was steady and suddenly sharp as he faced her down.

Ros hesitated, watching him. 'What?'

'Don't. Just don't do this. Don't start being paranoid again. There's no reason for it, OK?' His tone had hardened. 'Remember what happened last time?'

Ros felt herself flush. Her eyes slid guiltily away from his. Of course she remembered. How could she forget?

She sensed Adam staring at her for a few moments longer before his gaze finally dropped back to his newspaper. She sat very still for a little longer, tense, giving her heart rate time to slow and settle.

When she was calm again, she picked up her phone and typed a polite, business-like reply to Lotte. Yes, she'd be happy to help. She asked Lotte to email her a CV and details of the kind of position she was hoping to find.

All the time, she kept telling herself: *He's right. I'm being paranoid. The job stuff is business and, as for the girls, who knows? Maybe they'll really hit it off.*

A moment later, a reply pinged: *Thanks so much, lovely! I knew I could count on you!*

It was followed by a series of emojis: a love heart, a smiley and a face blowing a kiss.

Lovely? Ros didn't reply.

8

ROS

'So, what made you choose Ilkley?'

Ros perched on one of the two tall kitchen stools and leaned an elbow on the high counter. So far, Bella and Sophia seemed to be getting on alright with Caitlyn, playing together in the small lounge at the far end of the apartment, but Ros had left the kitchen door open, just in case. Lotte was making her a complicated coffee in a machine which looked as if it had been designed by NASA. She didn't answer for a moment. Either she was too focused on frothing milk or she was considering how to respond.

'No reason, really,' Lotte said at last. 'Chocolate?' She held up a metal sifter.

'Please.' Ros was determined not to let Lotte distract her. 'But why here? It's a big decision, to up sticks and travel halfway up the country.' She paused, watchful. 'Had you been here before?'

'Nope.' Lotte set down the coffees, pulled out the twin stool and settled beside Ros. She picked up her espresso shot and gave it a tentative sip. 'I was intrigued, I suppose, after you mentioned it. So I did a bit of research online and liked what I saw. The moors, the dales, good schools... it just seemed worth a try.'

'It is a lovely place.' Ros smiled. She'd always known how lucky she was to have grown up there. It was a caring, well-heeled community, with good primaries and the grammar school that was just up the hill from the town centre. The moorland that overlooked the town on either side of the steep Wharfe Valley was special. So was the lure of the Yorkshire Dales, with their picturesque stone-walled fields and grazing sheep and endless walks.

'I grew up in London. Well, south London. Kingston,' Lotte went on. She turned her shoulder to Ros and addressed the window. 'I want something different for Caitlyn. Somewhere more stable. With fresh air and real people. Somewhere she can put down roots.'

Ros shifted her weight to peer through the window too. They were so close, their shoulders almost touched. It was a great view. Beyond the road, the Riverside Gardens sloped gently towards the trees that edged the banks of the River Wharfe. Children ran and swung and spun in the fenced-in playground, watched over by mums and grandmas on benches. Dog walkers ambled along the paths, swinging leads and long plastic ball launchers.

'Thanks for sending over your CV,' Ros said. 'One thing – I wondered why you left advertising? You seemed to be doing so well.'

Lotte said airily. 'I got bored of playing the corporate game, I suppose. I wanted more variety.'

Ros considered this. By the look of it, Lotte had taken a massive pay cut, moving from being an account executive with a decent sized ad agency to becoming a personal assistant in a company manufacturing cardboard boxes. That must have been a tough drop in salary for a single mum. And for what? From then on, all she'd done had been semi-skilled office work in a range of different businesses.

'You're not tempted to get back into it? There are several agencies in Leeds. I could make enquiries, if you like.'

Lotte shook her head, sipped her espresso. 'No, thanks. I'm done with all that. I'd rather have something more local. A personal assistant job or receptionist would do me fine. Nothing too arduous.'

Ros hesitated. 'I'm sure I can fix you up with something like that but, well, frankly, it wouldn't pay very well. Rates here are much lower than in London.'

Lotte shrugged. 'That's OK.'

'Right.' Ros didn't push it. She was a client, not a friend. 'You didn't mention what hours you were looking for. Were you hoping for something to fit with the school day?'

'Not especially. Mrs Shore said they run a breakfast club and something after school. I can put Caitlyn into those.' Lotte tipped back her head and downed the rest of her espresso.

Ros thought about Bella. That would be a long day for a four-year-old. She'd never do that to her. Still, she wasn't a single parent. 'I'll put out some feelers,' she said. 'See what I can do.'

'Cool.' Lotte jumped down from her stool, put her cup in the dishwasher and switched on the pristine oven. 'Thanks.'

'Can I help with tea?'

'No, you're fine.' Lotte rummaged in the fridge and brought out a packet of sausages. 'What do you make of their teacher, Miss Grey? She looks terribly young. Is she any good?'

'She's new,' Ros said. 'Bella seems to like her.'

'I bet the dads do too.' Lotte looked around from the oven, her eyes mischievous. 'I mean, she's quite something, isn't she? That long straight hair, the big brown eyes. I bet they're all drooling. Fantasising about being put in detention.'

Ros made an attempt at a smile. She assumed that was supposed to be a joke.

'Speaking of dads, how's Adam?' Lotte reached into the freezer and shook some frozen oven fries onto a tray. 'What does he do again?'

'He's an osteopath.'

'Really?' Lotte looked at her. 'Here in Ilkley?' She rolled her shoulders. 'Do you think he'd see me?'

'What, for treatment?'

Lotte just said: 'Stiff neck. Too many years pounding a keyboard. Where does he work, exactly?'

Ros reeled off the name of the practice and described the location: over a dress shop in a row of shops at the back of the main parking lot.

'I'll give him a call.' Lotte turned back to the grill. 'Thanks.'

'No problem.'

Lotte tipped a tin of baked beans into a bowl, ready for the microwave, then clattered in a drawer and set three places at the kitchen table.

Ros climbed down from her stool. 'I'll go and check on the girls.'

She headed off down the long, narrow corridor that ran from one end of the apartment to the other. The owners of number 5 had done a great job with the conversion, with that sleek new kitchen and its picture windows. The other rooms were, well, compact was putting it kindly, but at least they had the high Victorian ceilings. Lotte had given Ros a quick tour when they'd first arrived. It hadn't taken long. The sunny kitchen at one end, a poky lounge at the other, a modern shower room and two bedrooms: small, but creatively furnished.

A crash of cascading plastic emerged from the lounge as she opened the door.

'Everything OK, girls?'

Sophie was slumped on a beanbag in one corner, her shoulders hunched, leafing through a book. She glowered at her mother.

Bella was sitting on the floor of the lounge, surrounded by mini plastic animals. She jumped up when she saw Ros and ran to her, hugging her around the knees, her face imploring. 'Can we go home now?'

Only Caitlyn, crouching by the wall over a mess of widely strewn building bricks, didn't look around.

Neither of Ros's girls had been enthusiastic about the play-date. Sophie had shaken her head and lifted one eyebrow with that disconcertingly scathing look she'd recently developed. Bella had looked horrified.

'I just thought you and Caitlyn could get to know each other a bit better,' Ros had lied. 'It must be hard for her, starting school in a new place, not knowing anyone.'

Bella had grimaced. 'I don't really like her.'

'Don't like her?' Ros softened her tone to conciliatory. 'Maybe we should give her a chance. After all, we've only just met her.'

Bella had shrugged, embarrassed. She was not a child who liked to find fault with other people, unlike her sister.

Now, Ros took in the messy hair, the dull look in Caitlyn's eyes, as she gathered together the bricks to rebuild whatever she'd just so aggressively demolished.

Ros kissed Bella on the top of her head. 'Caitlyn's mum's just getting tea ready,' she said, brightly. 'Sausage, fries and beans by the look of it!' She bent lower to Bella and whispered. 'We'll go home after tea, OK?'

Bella pulled away miserably and headed back to her spot on the carpet. She didn't look up as Ros turned to leave.

The kitchen swam with rising heat and the meaty smell of cooking sausages.

Lotte had pulled out the grill pan and was turning them with a fork. They spat and sizzled, already striped unevenly with brown.

Ros said: 'Anything I can do?'

'No, you're fine. Nearly ready.' Lotte pushed back the grill pan and turned to put the bowl of baked beans in the microwave.

Ros went back to her perch by the window. She thought about Caitlyn. One thing that had struck her when Lotte had shown her around the apartment was how little sign there was that a four-year-old lived there. She thought of Sophie and Bella's chaotic rooms, their beds piled with stuffed animals, the floors littered with half-finished colouring and felt-tipped pens, with scraps of modelling clay and origami paper. *There's nothing like that here.*

The microwave beeped and Lotte lifted down the bowl, stirred it, put it back inside and programmed another thirty seconds.

A short, sharp scream.

Lotte and Ros both froze; looked at each other. Neither spoke. They strained, listening. A fraction of a second later, a second high-pitched shriek.

Unmistakeable this time – they hadn't imagined it – from the lounge.

Lotte swore under her breath. Her oven gloves slipped from her hands and landed with a soft hush on the floor.

Ros reached the kitchen doorway first, then sprinted down the corridor, Lotte's feet pounding behind her.

Ros shoved open the lounge door. Her hand flew to her mouth. 'Bella!'

Bella's eyes were wide with shock. Blood trickled in a slow, meandering line down her pallid forehead.

'What happened?' Ros leapt forward, one hand on Bella's shoulder, steadying her, the other gently parting her hair. Blood, thin and bright, was spilling from a jagged gash at the top of her forehead, staining her skin.

Bella, trembling, started to cry in hard, heaving sobs. She tipped forward to push her face into Ros's chest. 'She hurt me!' Bella could barely form the words.

Ros said at once: 'Who did?'

'It wasn't my fault!' Caitlyn started to cry too. 'It wasn't, Mummy! It wasn't!'

Ros looked across at her. Caitlyn's face was red, her hands clawing at her cheeks. Ros wrapped her arms tighter around Bella, rocking her. Her own anger rose, sudden and savage. *I should never have brought them here*, she thought. *Never*.

Lotte rushed out and came back a moment later with a wad of kitchen towel. She pushed it into Ros's hand, and Ros held it firmly against the cut, stemming the blood.

'Maybe it's not as bad as it looks,' Lotte said. 'See? It's almost stopped bleeding.'

Ros didn't bother to answer that. She didn't trust herself to speak. She was seething. She lifted the paper towel, examined the wound and stemmed it again with a fresh, clean piece of towel.

Holding Bella tight, she said in a low voice. 'Tell me what happened.'

Bella was crying too hard to speak. She pointed at a heavy metal ruler that lay abandoned on the carpet by her side. One sharp corner was flecked with red.

Ros said: 'She threw it at you?'

Bella nodded vigorously, her chest heaving.

Caitlyn, sobbing, shook her head. Her terrified eyes were sunken in swollen lids. 'It wasn't me,' she wailed. She twisted and pointed a trembling finger at Sophie, who was sitting silently against the wall, her knees drawn up, her face white.

Caitlyn said: 'It was her.'

9

ROS

'I just don't know what's the matter with her.' Ros reached for her white wine and sipped it miserably.

Adam, beside her on the sofa, reached for her free hand and squeezed it. 'She just lost her temper. She's only eight.'

'About what, though? Bella said she hadn't done anything.'

Adam shrugged. 'You know what they're like. Maybe Bella was winding her up.'

'Even so.' Ros was brittle with tension. 'That's no excuse.'

Adam said, gently: 'I know. Sophie seemed as shocked as anyone when I tried to talk to her about it. Maybe she just threw it without thinking.'

'Bella might have lost an eye!' Ros swallowed hard. 'And this is the second time she's hurt Bella! I'm really worried. What's the matter with her? Sophie's always been intense, but she never used to flare up like this, did she?'

She only just managed to stop herself saying more. Sophie, clearly mortified each time she'd wet herself, had made Ros promise not to tell Adam about her accidents.

'I know but, well, they've had fun together, as well.' Adam

was always placating, trying to sound reasonable. 'Maybe it's just a phase. A growth spurt thing.'

They sat in silence for a moment, each with their own thoughts.

'She's seemed so on edge, though.' Ros stared at the red and blue swirls on the carpet, tracing them absently with her eyes as her brain whirled. 'Do you think it's about going back to school? That something's going on there that's worrying her?'

Adam shrugged. 'Work stress? They're starting to pile on the pressure, aren't they, now she's in year four? She seems to have a lot of homework. Far more than last year.'

'I've wondered that.' Ros frowned. 'Or maybe it's friends. She doesn't seem to have a best friend at the moment. She was big mates with Martha for a while and then they fell out, then the same happened with Ella. That's really upsetting at this age.'

'What did she say when you tried to talk to her?'

Ros sighed and took another mouthful of wine. It was already nine o'clock. She'd finally managed to settle a still-upset Bella; then, when she'd put her head around Sophie's door to say goodnight, Ros had found her hiding under the bed. It was something she used to do years ago, if she thought she was in trouble.

'She just clammed up,' Ros said. 'I haven't had a chance to talk to her new teacher yet but I could ask to see her, just to find out if she's noticed anything unusual about her behaviour in class.'

Adam looked uncertain. 'We don't want Sophie getting off to a bad start with her, though.'

'True.' Ros paused and considered. 'You think I should hold off, for now? I just think, if this carries on then the teacher ought to be aware, in case there's any bullying going on amongst the girls. Sophie's very sensitive.'

Adam reached for the wine bottle and freshened their

glasses. 'Why don't I take her out on Sunday, just the two of us? She loves walking and it looks as if it's going to stay dry. I've been meaning to try her on Beamsley Beacon. It's only about eight miles, round trip, she could do that. Take a picnic. Maybe if we're out in the fresh air all day, she'll relax and open up a bit.'

Ros nodded slowly. Maybe he was right. It might help if one of them spent proper time with her, one on one, away from everything. It was just hard to carve out that kind of time.

'And that way, Bella can have you to herself for a few hours,' he went on. 'She'd love that. A bit of quality Mummy time.'

'You're right. Good idea.'

Adam reached for the TV remote and, as he leaned back, paused to give her a light kiss. 'We'll figure it out,' he said. 'Don't worry.'

She tried to smile. 'Love you.'

'You too.'

As he started surfing the channels, Ros forced herself to her feet. She took her glass upstairs to keep her company as she logged on to her laptop. She liked to have a rummage around a few local chat sites in the evenings, keeping up her profile and making her presence known. Every now and then she slipped in a work question or two, either for anyone who was hiring or to a client looking for a local job. There were plenty of night owls online and if she pushed herself, she might manage a good hour or two before bed.

As she powered up the laptop, her mind was still on Sophie. She'd always been a sensitive child but these flashes of temper, this bullying behaviour, struck her as something new.

Ros opened up her emails first and ran her eye down the new ones, scanning.

It was hard to concentrate. She pushed down her worries about Sophie and, almost at once, the memory of Bella surfaced. Of her little girl's terrified eyes and the trickle of blood down her face.

She reached for her glass and took another gulp of wine. Her body tensed, reliving the surge of rage she'd felt as she'd held Bella tightly and rocked her.

She'd been gripped, in that moment, by such a powerful sense that her growing unease about Lotte had been right. That she wasn't being paranoid or uncharitable to think it was an impossible coincidence. That her instincts that she and her family were somehow under threat were sound.

She got to her feet, restless, and crossed to the window, holding her wine glass. *But it isn't as simple as that, is it?* Adam was right too. She had sometimes imagined things. He was right to remind her. She needed to be careful.

She looked out into the night. The room they shared as a study was over the kitchen, giving a view through the trees towards Bridge Lane and, beyond the row of houses there, the distant sweep of the park and the trees that edged the river.

It was dark. The only light was the low shimmer of street-lamps along Bridge Lane and, here and there, the leak of a warmer, yellowish glow from the backs of apartments and houses where curtains had not yet been closed.

Her eyes strayed to the back of Lotte's apartment at number 5. The windows were dark, silent eyes, watching her. She shuddered. How much had she told Lotte? Maybe that was all it was – her own guilt about saying too much?

She couldn't shake the sense that she'd said something about the past, shared the guilty secret she'd kept hidden for so long. Ros shook her head. It was no use tormenting herself. She simply couldn't remember. She pulled herself away from the window and settled back at her desk to work.

When she refreshed her emails, a new one popped into her inbox. It was from Lotte.

So sorry about this afternoon, it gushed. *Hope Bella's OK. It was great to see you. Caitlyn and I are really looking forward to getting you over here again very soon. It's wonderful to think we're real friends now, not just vacation pals! Which reminds me! I've been meaning to say, don't worry at all about our wild night out. Your secrets are safe with me!!!*

Ros froze, staring at the text on her screen. Her stomach fell away and her breathing became shallow as she struggled to swallow down a sudden, rising panic.

10

LOTTE

I took a break from web surfing around lunchtime so I could go for a run. The truth was, I needed to get out of that tiny apartment before I suffocated.

I pulled on my running shoes and a fleece and headed down into the watery sunshine. It was colder out than it looked. I hunched my shoulders and braced myself.

In the first week, I'd taken easy routes. There were muddy paths along the river, under the trees. They were pleasant enough but so many people kept getting in the way: mums or dads pushing pre-schoolers in buggies, and retired folk strolling with dogs.

Already, too many people were starting to recognise me. With Caitlyn in early and late clubs at school, I was avoiding most of the school gate crowd but, even so, it was harder to be invisible here than in London. The downstairs neighbours seemed determined to be friendly and the woman in the newsagents kept asking questions about where I'd last lived, reaching for me with busy, picking fingers.

I turned the corner into Lister Street. I slowed as I passed Ros and Adam's home, a squat two-storey house, slotted without distinction into the rising terrace. No sign of life, upstairs or down. I imagined Ros must work from a room at the back of the house, overlooking the garden: I'd seen the light on in there, late into the evening.

It didn't look as if either of them was much of a gardener. The bushes at the front were overgrown, and the short gravel path to the front door was peppered with weeds. I moved on, feeling a satisfying pull down my calves as the sidewalk sloped upwards. I jogged to The Grove, tree-lined and picture perfect, studded with tea shops, crossed it and headed steeply upwards, climbing towards the moor which sat there, overlooking the town.

By the time I reached the edge of the moor, I was out of breath and sweating. I slowed to a jog, let my hands swing freely and unzipped my fleece to let cold air flood in.

I avoided the paved path which sloped off left, giving access to the tarn, and cut straight ahead, climbing higher, heading towards the smudge of rocks, set about with wind-blown trees, in a cleft in the moorland.

The bracken swarmed around my legs, reaching for me as I pushed through. I was steeped in the smells of damp undergrowth and peaty earth. The ground underfoot was uneven, mud pock-marked with stones and roots and the hard, round pellets of sheep droppings.

A panting dog appeared and galloped down to sniff around my feet before rushing on. Moments later, a middle-aged man, following the dog and taking broad, rapid strides down the slope, nodded at me and smiled as he passed. I turned my head away.

When I reached the gully, I found a flat rock and, hot now, climbed onto it for a rest. I perched there, knees drawn up, and brushed bracken spores off my trousers. I sipped water and looked down at the map of the landscape below.

It was dramatic. The river cut its way deeply through the

valley, its path studded by trees. My eyes ranged across it, taking in the old, familiar landmarks. There was the tip of the spire of the church at the end of The Grove; the pattern of tightly packed lines of houses running back and forth; the flat shapes of the station, the glass panels in the roof glinting with light. On the far side of the river, the gentler, south-facing slopes of Middleton with its multi-million-pound mansions and, perched high above, the stone buildings of the old monastery.

My stomach ached and I leaned forward to protect it, sweating from more than the exercise. Anxiety, that was all. Something up here had triggered a memory. The thick, rank smell of the bracken all around? Or the sight of the purple blooming heather?

There were emotional tripwires everywhere. I hadn't expected that. It was all so long ago and so deeply buried inside me that I'd thought I was immune. I wasn't. Ever since I'd arrived, I'd been battling these sudden unexpected releases of fragments of memory. I felt ambushed by them, winded. I needed to battle them, to keep myself together, but it was hard.

The wind tugged hair from my ponytail and flung loose strands across my face. The clouds, batted along by the breeze, darkened the view as they passed over the sun, then dramatically threw it back into sunlight as they moved on again. I felt my breathing ease and settle as I drank it all in, then zipped up my fleece again and wrapped my arms round my body, suddenly chilled.

A memory rose, unbidden. My eyes watered and I wiped my cheeks. For a moment, I felt my mouth buckle. A sob rose in my throat. I bit down hard on my lower lip, stern with myself, tamping down the past. Not now. This was not the time. I owed her more than that.

I eased myself back onto my feet, muscles cold now, and started to stride back down the moorland. I moved slowly at first, then picked up the pace, bouncing from one stone, one muddy foothold, one tuft of wild grass to the next.

As I descended, I thought about Ros.

Already I was seeing another side to her. Here, back on her home turf, she was different from the friendly, rather self-conscious woman I'd encountered by the pool. She was sharper and tougher and more determined. I saw the fierceness with which she guarded her family. However passionate she was about building her business, and it was clear she was, she still broke off every afternoon to race to the school gates and stand there, arms open, as her girls came tumbling out to her.

I stopped, panting, warm again now, then tipped back my bottle and took another swig of water. I filled a cupped hand and splashed my face and neck. I thought about my own past and the grief there, the stories I kept secret. Stories that had brought me back here, to this small moorland town with its close-knit families.

I frowned to myself. It was too late to be sentimental now. I had to steel myself, to remember only in order to act.

I pulled out my phone. My hands trembled as I started to dial. Somehow, I had to close my mind to sympathy, to compassion. I must focus on what I'd come here to do, whatever pain it caused. Then leave. That was all.

I listened to the ringtone, waiting, waiting, hearing the soft puff of my breath in the mouthpiece as I readied myself to speak.

11

ROS

Ros sipped her coffee and checked again through the local websites and chats she used, dipping in and out to see if anything fresh had been posted since she'd last looked, late the night before.

Nothing. She couldn't shift the gnawing feeling that she was doing something wrong. She wasn't sure what. But whatever it was, she needed to figure it out soon and fix it. She couldn't let Adam keep shouldering the financial burden for both of them. It just wasn't fair. He'd looked so much better on vacation but already, he was looking tired again. His day out walking with Sophie on Sunday seemed to have done them both good and they'd been lucky with the weather. Ros nodded to herself. She'd enjoyed time on her own with Bella too, baking cupcakes.

She pulled her mind back to her work and bit her lip, scrolling down through the comments. There were no responses at all to the feelers she'd put out to local companies about jobs. She knew they must be out there. Either she wasn't reaching the right people, or they didn't want to use her. A lot were already signed up with one of the larger recruitment agencies in Bradford or Leeds.

She eased off the pain in her shoulders and drank some more coffee. She thought of the email she'd received that morning, saying their direct debit payment for gas and electricity was going up again. Everything was rising so steeply. Food, as well. Their Spanish vacation had almost cleaned them out. If things carried on like this, they'd struggle to pay the bills each month.

She sighed to herself. Adam was being brilliant about it, telling her not to worry. *It takes time to build a business*, he kept saying. *Your hard work and networking will pay off.*

She was starting to wonder, though. Maybe she ought to give up on this idea of her own business and go back to agency work. It would tie her down to office hours – and that would mean less time with the girls – but at least it would be a steady income.

She sent out a few speculative emails to local businesses she'd worked with before, asking if they had any upcoming vacancies and, if so, if they'd consider using her to help fill them. These fishing expeditions were generally low yield, but she needed to warm up her contacts. And, once in a while, she did reel something in from them.

She turned next to Lotte's CV and read through it again, making a few notes of words she could use to describe her to prospective employers. She was still intrigued about that sudden decision to leave advertising. It looked, from the roles Lotte had held before that, as if she'd been rising rapidly. Why take such a big pay cut and move from an interesting, responsible role to become an office assistant?

She thought back to Lotte's response when she'd asked her about it. She'd moved the conversation on pretty quickly. How had she dismissed it? She'd been 'bored of playing the corporate game'.

Ros shook her head. There was something off about it. She

couldn't quite put her finger on it. Then she frowned. Adam would tell her to stop overthinking, she knew he would. But she couldn't help it. It bothered her.

She found the number for the last ad agency Lotte had worked for, dialled the number for the switchboard and asked to speak to someone in HR.

The woman who answered the phone there became curt and dismissive before Ros had even reached the end of her sentence. 'I'm afraid I can't help you,' she said, cutting in. 'We're not at liberty to divulge information on past employees. If she's taken permission from a member of staff to include them as a referee for her application, you'd need to contact them directly.'

The woman seemed about to hang up.

Ros took a deep breath and forced herself to smile at the noticeboard on the far side of her desk. 'I do understand and I'm so sorry to be a nuisance. Unfortunately, the applicant didn't specify a referee. I just wondered if you could—'

'No, I'm afraid not.'

'May I finish my sentence?' Ros felt her jaw clench. 'I quite understand that you can't release personal information. Obviously. I just wondered if it might be possible to confirm the facts of her employment. I can give you the years she says she was employed by you, and her roles. Might that be possible, please?'

'I really don't—oh, just wait a minute.' Abruptly, the woman put Ros on hold.

Ros sat, drumming her fingers on her desk, listening to a tinny recording of classical music and trying not to let herself get mad.

Eventually, a new voice came on the line. 'Hello? Can I help?'

It sounded like an older woman. Her tone was softer. Ros wondered if the young woman who'd first spoken to her had been overheard and interrupted by a more senior colleague. She could just imagine the youngster fuming.

Ros put the smile back into her voice. 'I'd be so grateful if you could. May I explain?'

She ran through the details again and heard the tapping of fingers on a keyboard. She spelled out Lotte's family name: Humphries.

'No, I'm sorry, there's nothing in the system.' The woman at the other end of the line sounded distracted as she searched. 'What did you say her last role was?'

Ros gave the post and date again and waited. Her heart was pounding. Had she been right to be suspicious? Was Lotte's work history fictitious? Perhaps she hadn't expected any future employer to check this far back in her employment history.

'Ah, I know what it is!' The woman's tone had changed from puzzlement to one of relief. 'I bet she didn't change her name on the system when she got married. That must be her married name, yes?'

Ros hesitated. Married? 'Possibly. Humphries was the only name she gave.'

'And Lotte, short for Charlotte?'

'I assume so,' Ros said. 'She didn't say.'

'I get it now. Yes, that makes total sense.' The woman sounded brisk, as if a mystery had been solved and she could now get back to her work. 'She must be using her married name now. That's what threw me. They had that lovely little girl, didn't they? I remember going down to the main floor when she'd brought her in to see us. Sweet little thing. She probably carried on using her maiden name professionally, when she was with us. Most women do, if they're already established. Otherwise, it's like starting all over again.'

'So the dates and roles she gave us, they match, then?' Ros asked.

'Yes, absolutely. Well done you for checking. I'm always amazed how few employers do. Anything else I can help you with?'

'No, thank you. That's very kind.'

Ros rang off and stared into her cooling coffee. What had she expected? She'd been so sure, when the woman initially couldn't find any trace of her, that Lotte had spun her a web of lies. But she hadn't. It checked out.

She sat for a moment, staring at the noticeboard and the sticky notes plastered on it. *Except it doesn't quite check out, does it?* Lotte hadn't said anything about being married.

She strained to remember those first conversations they'd had over cocktails in Majorca. What had Lotte said about Caitlyn's father? Something about not even being sure exactly who he was, from what she could recall. She'd definitely come away with the impression that Caitlyn's father had run a mile before the baby was even born.

And yet, according to that woman, Lotte was married and living with her husband when baby Caitlyn came along.

She chewed the end of her pen, thinking.

Maybe the HR woman was right, and Lotte had carried on using her maiden name for a while in her professional life after she married. Then, perhaps more recently, as her jobs became less high-powered, adopted her married name. But if that was the case, why had she omitted mentioning a husband when she gave her potted life story to Ros?

Ros considered. Or maybe it *was* the CV which was falsified, as she'd first suspected. Maybe she'd just appropriated the career history of another woman with a similar first name, not expecting she'd ever be found out?

Ros frowned. She wasn't sure what to think. She pushed back her chair and paced around the room, ending up at the window. In the daylight, the back of Lotte's apartment at number 5 looked unremarkable. The curtains were open, showing the square lines of furniture near the lounge window. She could almost hear Adam's voice in her head: *Stop inventing*

secrets and lies which simply aren't there. Haven't you caused
enough trouble, doing that? Have you learned nothing?

She craned forward. She'd seen something, there in the window. A sudden flicker. She narrowed her eyes as she strained to see. It came again: a crease of reflected light bounced off something shiny, just above the bottom of the window.

Her pulse quickened. It was almost as if someone were crouching there, spying on her. She took an abrupt step back. Her legs trembled and she reached behind her for the chair to steady herself.

She shook herself and took a deep, slow breath. She was being ridiculous. There must be a simple explanation; it could be light flashing from a screen, or reflecting off a mirror or something, that was all.

It was just odd that she'd never noticed it before.

12

LOTTE

There was a time, not so long ago, when I thought I'd put it all behind me.

'You're strong, Lotte,' Jon used to say, his eyes full of love. 'You're a survivor. You don't know how special you are.'

Me? Special? Yeah, right.

For a long time, I pretended not to care. I blush now, thinking back, thinking how much time I squandered.

I'd treated him, in the beginning, the same way I'd always treated men. It was all I knew.

I'd thought it was cool to be aloof and scornful. It was cool to see someone a night or two and then ghost them. Keep them on their toes, keep them guessing. Relationships were all about power. If one person had it, the other person became vulnerable. Simple as that. No prizes for guessing which end of the seesaw I wanted to sit.

That whole ethos was perfectly reinforced at work. Advertising? That was another emotionless transaction. The strong player, devious if needed, always won the bid. Colleagues were friends for as long as an alliance suited them. Get in their way and you soon found out how shallow that friendship ran.

I was good at it: I'd grown up protecting myself from hurt. I wasn't liked at work. That was for wimps. But I was respected. I knew how to fight, and I knew how to win. Bigger and better contracts, larger opportunities, higher bonuses. I was formidable.

I even looked the part. I dyed my hair blue at that point and wore it sharp and spiky. I paraded myself in skimpy, tight-fitting clothes that showed off the muscle I worked hard to cultivate. It sent just the right message: *Don't mess with me.*

Jon was the first person who didn't seem to care about any of that. He wrong-footed me from the start, that first day he knocked on my front door one Saturday morning to explain that he was moving in across the hall and to apologise for the noise. That slow, deep voice. That big, disarming smile.

A few hours later, he knocked again and invited himself in for a cup of tea. He admitted later that his claim that he couldn't find his kettle was as feeble an excuse as it had sounded.

I had raked my fingers through my spiky blue hair self-importantly and told him, sorry, actually, I didn't have time, I was right up against it, at a critical moment in a bid for a major contract. He hadn't looked at all impressed, just shrugged and smiled and said: 'Next time, maybe?' in a puppy-dog hopeful sort of way. I'd shut the door in his face.

When I was disturbed by a third knock, an hour or so later, I opened the door angrily to find a takeaway pizza sitting on the mat, with a handwritten note stuck to the box: 'They sent two by mistake. Thought you mightn't have eaten. Your new neighbour, Jon.'

I'd rolled my eyes at the smiley face after his name. Of course they hadn't sent an extra one 'by mistake'. What a loser. I made a point of leaving it there to congeal and stink out the landing.

I didn't want another person in my space. I'd only just escaped the nightmare of apartment-sharing land and started earning enough to rent my own place. It was small and out in the sticks, but you expected that in London and I was just thrilled it was mine.

I'd made it pretty damn stylish too. I don't do clutter. It suffocates me. I certainly don't do girly. I'd endured years in rented properties with chintzy curtains and flowery carpets and I was sick to death of it. My place was sharp and functional, as minimalist as a hotel room. The colours a man might choose: grey and cream and an occasional accent in blood red.

Besides, I didn't spend much time there. I lived at work. After slogging all those years as a junior copywriter, I was finally starting to get noticed in the ad agency and, at twenty-seven, was promoted to creative director, running my own small team. I didn't mind putting the hours in. We all did. Well, the men did, especially. As they approached thirty, the women gradually started to fall away, just when it was most important to keep focused, to stay climbing the ladder.

It struck me as stupid. I'd watched these women work themselves senseless through the early years and then, just as they were starting to get somewhere, just when promotion was a real possibility, they wavered. As soon as management sensed they were putting their work second to their home lives, they were out of the game.

Why did they do it? They were crazy. They were selfish too. It wasn't just a car crash for them, as it affected all the rest of us: all the women who were struggling to be taken as seriously as the guys. It was such a cliché. It was totally letting the side down.

It damaged us every time a new card went around the office. For the men, it was all about progress at work: 'Congratulations on your new job!' For the women, it was: 'Congratulations on your engagement!' Then, if they were still around by then, that final death card: 'Congratulations on your happy news! You're going to be a wonderful mother!'

Wow! 'Congratulations on the fact you've just dropped a nuclear bomb on your career.'

Sure, there were a few exceptions. One or two high-powered women who popped out babies, lobbed them straight into nursery for twelve hours a day and pretended they were still just as committed as the men.

But despite all that effort, all their milk-stained shirt fronts and under-eye concealer, they still weren't free to jump on a plane to another country at zero notice for a face-to-face with a major international and they didn't have the stamina to enter-tain visiting clients till one in the morning. So no, thank you, I was perfectly happy paddling my own canoe.

And then Jon came knocking on my door and just refused to go away.

I was used to defending myself against blame and silent hatred, against anger and abuse. But against love? That was a new one.

He was devastating. Every time, his face lit with happiness when he caught sight of me. He seemed to see something wonderful inside me and wanted to cherish it, wanted to be with me.

It took him a long time to break down the barriers. I tried my best to hurt him. But every time I insulted him or drank too much and railed at him, he'd just frown and look sad, shake his head and say: 'I know you don't mean that, Lotte,' or 'That's not you. You know it isn't, deep down. You're better than that.'

Eventually, he won. I started looking inside for the extraordinary person he claimed to see. I made myself vulnera-ble. I stopped fighting. I let myself love him.

Do I regret it, looking back now? It isn't an easy question. He rescued me from myself, from the damage of the past. I even listened when he talked about forgiveness and insisted on inviting my bitter parents to the wedding.

The years we had together were the happiest of my life.

Those first years as a couple, then as a young family, with our new baby, Caitlyn. He adored her as much as he adored me.

I let him change me. I agreed not to go back to those all-consuming, fourteen-hour days. Jon was earning well enough as a solicitor and he encouraged me to find a less demanding job, with more family-friendly hours. So, after all I'd vowed, I quit advertising, just like the women before me, the ones I'd despised. *I can always go back to it*, I told myself, if I wanted to.

A lie, of course. There was no going back. There never is.

I was blinded by happiness, finally high on endorphins instead of on cocaine and booze.

But then he broke our lives apart and, despite everything he'd promised, everything he'd done, I found myself spiralling out of control, back into the past he'd tried so hard to help me escape.

13

ROS

Ros was in the kitchen, buttering bread for a sandwich and listening to the news headlines, when her phone rang. The screen said: *Number withheld.* It was probably one of the companies she'd made contact with that morning. She took a beat to breathe deeply and prepare her business voice before she answered.

It wasn't work, though. It was school.

The school secretary's voice was cool. She wasn't giving anything away.

'Come in now?' Ros battled to understand, trying to screen out the background noise of the radio. 'Why? What's happened?'

She set down the knife on the bread board. Her appetite fell away, to be replaced by queasiness. Thoughts flashed through her mind of Bella or Sophie cut and bleeding horribly or with a sickeningly broken arm. She blinked and tried to focus. No, it wasn't that. Not if they wanted her at school. That would be hospital, surely.

'Of course,' she heard herself saying. 'I'll come right in.'

She sent a quick text to Adam as she ran to grab her bag. He switched his phone off when he was seeing patients, but he'd check it eventually. And it wasn't a practical thing, this need to tell him. He couldn't do anything. It was just instinct. She just wanted him to know.

Ros had been told to use the school's official entrance, approaching the building from the main road and taking the front path through landscaped gardens. It was unnerving. She was more used to the informal approach around the back, through the playground.

She hurried through the double doors. The reception area was quiet. It smelled of boiled beans and cheap gravy. The muffled clamour and screams of the playground drifted through from the back of the school.

The secretary slid back the glass window to her cubicle. 'Mrs Crofter? Would you take a seat? I'll just check if Mrs Shore is available.'

The secretary was usually friendly but today her manner was formal. Ros sat down with a bump. She felt as wracked with nerves as if she were five years old again, sent to the office because she was in trouble. She wished she'd changed into smarter trousers.

A moment later, she was ushered into Mrs Shore's small, cluttered office.

'Thank you for coming in, Mrs Crofter.' Mrs Shore waved her to one of the low, upholstered chairs across from her desk and took a seat beside her. 'I'm afraid there's been a rather unfortunate incident.'

Ros's hands fumbled awkwardly in her lap. Her mouth was dry.

'It's Sophie.' Mrs Shore's eyes were intent on Ros's face. 'She became very distressed in class this morning and, well.' She paused. 'I'm afraid she attacked another pupil.'

'Attacked someone?' Ros felt herself flush with guilt and misery. For a moment, her mouth trembled and she thought she might cry. She breathed out hard as Mrs Shore continued.

'From what I understand,' Mrs Shore said, gently, 'Sophie had an accident in class. A toilet accident.' She paused, watching Ros's reaction. 'Of course, she was embarrassed and it seems that a boy in her class, Frederick Pearce, well, he said something about it. Teased her, in some way.'

Ros's jaw tightened. She knew Fred Pearce. He was an idiot. Sophie had never liked him. She could just imagine.

'Sophie punched him in the face. Hard. His mother's taken him to the hospital, to the minor injuries department. Let's hope it's nothing serious.'

Ros swallowed hard. 'I'm sorry to hear that.' Her mind was racing as she tried to process it all. She was mortified. What was the matter with Sophie? She never used to be a violent child, not until recently. She imagined too how humiliated Sophie must have felt when she realised she'd wet herself in front of everyone.

'What did he say?'

Mrs Shore raised a questioning eyebrow. 'Frederick?'

'Yes. What did he say to her about, about her accident?'

'I'm not sure of the exact words he used, Mrs Crofter, but I think we can both imagine the kind of remark a child of that age might make.'

Ros looked down at her twisting hands. She felt sickened by the whole episode. By the idea of her daughter feeling so desperate; by the thought of another child, however much she disliked him, being hurt. It must be her fault. Something she'd done or failed to do as Sophie's mother. 'I'm so sorry,' she mumbled.

Mrs Shore plucked a tissue from a box on the table beside them and handed it to Ros.

After a few moments, once Ros had composed herself again, Mrs Shore said: 'Is something worrying Sophie, Mrs Crofter?'

Ros looked up and searched for the right words. 'Sophie hasn't quite been herself this year. There've been one or two things. Quarrels with Bella that have gone a bit too far.' She thought of the trickle of blood down Bella's face. 'It's not like her.'

Mrs Shore nodded, thoughtful. 'I agree. I was surprised. That's why I wanted to have a chat with you.' She hesitated and leaned forward slightly. 'Is everything alright at home? Anything at all that would give her cause for concern? It's amazing what children pick up on.'

'Everything's fine.' Ros frowned. 'I wondered if it was school, actually. If there was some bullying going on. Girls can be awful at this age.'

Mrs Shore paused, as if she were considering. 'I can certainly have another chat with her teachers and see if they can shed any light. I can assure you that we take allegations of bullying very seriously at St Stephen's.' She hesitated again. 'I will be asking Sophie to spend playtime tomorrow morning in the classroom, making a card for Frederick and his family. It's a way of saying sorry. She must realise that, however much she may have felt provoked, assaulting another pupil is unacceptable. I'm sure you understand that.'

'Of course.' Ros nodded and blew her nose.

'In the meantime, if you and your husband could try to talk to Sophie...? Come and see me if you have any concerns or anything you think I should know.'

Ros sensed the interview was over. She got to her feet.

As she reached to open the door, Mrs Shore added: 'And it might be worth keeping some spare underwear in Sophie's school bag, just in case. I believe this is the second time this has happened recently. It may not be the last.'

. . .

As soon as she was clear of the school building, Ros fumbled for her phone and tried to call Adam. It went straight to voicemail and she left a short message, asking him to call her.

The traffic along the main road blurred as she hurried back towards home, blinking away tears.

She had been trying to comfort herself with the thought that she was overreacting, that Sophie had just hit a difficult phase and that it wasn't that unusual. But she remembered Mrs Shore's calm, searching look. The headteacher's eyes on her face as she studied her reaction. Clearly, Mrs Shore thought it was more than just normal development.

She thought of Fred and his mother at minor injuries. Sophie must have hit him very hard, with real aggression.

She pulled out her phone and stared at it, willing Adam to call her back. She needed him. *Right now.* She wanted someone else to feel the same way she did, to share her distress.

But there was nothing; she was completely alone.

14

ROS

When it got to two thirty, Ros couldn't sit still any longer.

She headed out of the house and down to the Riverside Gardens, her phone in her hand. She picked one of the narrow paths threading its way down past the children's playground towards the river. There was sunshine, but the wind blowing off the river was cold and she hunched her shoulders and pushed her hands into her pockets as she walked.

It was quiet. She looked across at a grandma who was pushing a toddler on one of the baby swings and singing to him. It didn't seem five minutes since the girls had been that age. She bit down on her lip. There had been times she and Adam had talked about having a third child, but she was thirty-nine now and it wasn't just her mind which told her she was finished; it was her body too. She wasn't sure she had the energy for another pregnancy, another birth and then another year or so of sleepless nights.

The line of trees along the river threw a moving pattern of shadows across the path. She was just getting into her stride when her phone rang. *Finally.*

'Are you OK?' Adam sounded breathless. 'I'm so sorry. I only just got your message. It's been wall to wall appointments.'

The sound of his voice, warm and concerned, made it impossible for Ros to speak for a moment. She stopped at the next bench, set back from the path amongst the trees, and sat down. She focused on the loose stones she was digging out of the dirt with the toe of her shoe as she told Adam what had happened.

'That's awful.' He sounded winded, as shocked as she was. 'Did Mrs Shore say what sparked it off? That doesn't sound like Sophie.'

Ros hesitated. She'd promised Sophie that she wouldn't tell Adam about her recent embarrassing bathroom accidents. She didn't want to break that promise. But she could also see why Adam would struggle to understand if she didn't give a proper explanation.

'She felt humiliated about,' she paused, 'about something. This boy made her feel worse, by the sound of it, by making fun of her.'

Adam didn't speak for a moment. He could tell she was withholding something from him, she was sure. Finally, he said: 'Did Mrs Shore have any insights into what's going on?'

She shook her head. 'I told her we were concerned that it might be bullying. She's going to talk to the teachers.'

'Good.' Adam sounded worried. 'It does sound like you're right. She was fine when we were out walking yesterday. Just like her old self.'

Ros nodded. Sophie had come home exhausted after her day climbing Beamsley Beacon with her father. She'd had a quick bath and fallen straight into bed. Ros could see the adventure had done them both good. Those two had always had a special bond.

'And she didn't say anything?' Ros was repeating herself, she knew. She'd asked Adam the same question over dinner last night. It just seemed even more urgent now to get answers. 'No clues at all about what's upsetting her?'

'I'd have told you.'

Adam sounded exhausted. She felt bad about bothering him at work – he was under a lot of strain, she knew that – but, selfishly, she felt better now they were sharing this.

Adam said: 'Who's the other kid? Fred, was it?'

'Fred Pearce.' She snorted. 'He's the youngest of about four brothers. He's always causing trouble. Remember that party last year with the bouncy castle? He was the one who kept barrelling into the girls. He knocked Sophie over twice, and she was livid. And he made Fiona Ashcroft cry.'

Adam sighed. 'Mrs Shore is right though, isn't she? However much Sophie might like to, she can't go round thumping people.' Suddenly his tone changed. Work was intruding, Ros could tell. A patient must be waiting. 'Look, I'm really sorry but I've got to go. Let's talk tonight. Love you.'

'You, too.'

She sat there for a moment after he'd rung off, thinking. She ought to get back to her desk. She needed to carry on chasing down leads and trying to make appointments to see people in some of the bigger local companies to pitch her services to them. She just didn't have the heart, not right then. She was too sick with worry.

She looked at her watch. It was less than an hour to school pick-up. She wondered how quickly news of Sophie's attack on Fred would spread and where the sympathies of the other mothers would lie. She groaned to herself. She hoped Diana wasn't late arriving at the gates this afternoon. She really needed to see a friendly face.

She was about to haul herself back to her feet when she saw a trim figure at the top of the park. A young woman, carrying something bulky in her arms, was hurrying down one of the sloping paths from Bridge Lane. Ros narrowed her eyes to see better. It was her. Lotte.

She was dressed in jeans and a loose sweatshirt, her hair pulled back into a low ponytail. She strode on with her head down, her eyes intent on the ground as she headed across the grass towards the far end of the park, where the riverside path disappeared under the road bridge above.

Ros couldn't take her eyes off her. There was something furtive about the way she was moving. As if she really didn't want to be seen.

Ros, slightly screened by the trees around her, sat very still and watched. Lotte drew closer, her pace never slackening. She didn't look around. As she came nearer, Ros saw that the package in her arms was a long bouquet of flowers. It was wrapped in cellophane and tied with a red bow. It looked expensive.

Lotte passed the flagpole and the stone war memorial at its base, then headed towards the corner of the park, where the path under the trees left the gardens and pushed into the darkness under the road bridge. A moment later, she disappeared from view.

Ros felt her pulse quicken. She didn't know why but she was suspicious, her senses alert. Lotte was up to something. She wanted to know what it was. She jumped to her feet and followed her. As Ros left the brightness of the open air and let the path lead her forwards under the bridge, she was hit by the mustiness of the old mossy stones and the mulch of rotting fall undergrowth. Overhead, traffic rumbled. Flickering light, bouncing off the surface of the moving water from the river below, threw undulating patterns across the underside of the bridge, cutting through the shadows there.

Ros blinked as her eyes adjusted. Her heart beat hard. She felt disadvantaged, as if unseen eyes were watching her. She emerged on the far side of the bridge where the path was edged by a stone wall and hemmed in by brambles. She paused, scanning ahead. There was no sign of Lotte.

She pushed on more cautiously, her muscles tense. She half expected Lotte to jump out and challenge her. She narrowed her eyes. The path ahead ran straight and empty. The only other people she could see were an older couple, strolling along arm in arm, a dog's lead swinging from the woman's free hand. How had Lotte managed to disappear?

Ros pressed on, puzzled. To her left, the grassy verge beyond the path gave way to a sheer drop down to the river. The other side was bounded by the wall.

After a few minutes' walking, the land on her right opened up into the broad expanse of the cemetery. She paused and stood, surveying the scene. The cemetery was an atmospheric mix of ages and styles. Many of the monuments – crooked stone crosses and rounded gravestones with weeping angels – were a century or two old, weathered now and greened with mildew.

Beyond them, gathered together to one side, modern headstones had been erected in neat rows. Many were low, angled slabs of polished granite, still fresh, their engraved names and dates easy to read. These departed souls were still mourned by the living. Shining stainless-steel containers were filled with flowers at various stages of decay, or by drooping silk posies.

And there, standing with her head bowed in front of a granite slab, was Lotte. Her shoulders were rounded as she hunched forward against the cold. Her head was lowered and there was an intensity in the way she held herself, as if she were lost in thought as she gazed down at the inscription on the gravestone – or offering a prayer. A tissue or handkerchief was balled in her hand and, as Ros watched, Lotte lifted it to her face to wipe her eyes. The bouquet she'd carried had been placed at the foot of the stone.

Ros took a step backwards and half-hid herself behind the edge of the boundary wall. She craned around it as far as she dared. What on earth was Lotte doing? This was the woman who'd said she'd never been to Ilkley before, that she knew nothing about the place. And there she was, clearly emotional, paying her respects at a grave. But whose?

Ros kept her eyes riveted on Lotte. She'd never seen her so still, so solemn. What was her connection to the person buried there that made this visit to the grave so intense? She needed to know.

'Afternoon!'

Ros jumped out of her skin. The couple that she'd seen strolling along the riverside path ahead of her had drawn level with her.

The woman gave her a wary look. 'Sorry, did we startle you?'

'Not at all.' Ros kept her own voice so low it was almost a whisper. She tried to smile but her lips were tense. 'Lovely day, isn't it?'

The couple passed her, then, a few steps further on, slowed their pace a fraction and the woman twisted to look back, frowning slightly as she checked on Ros who was still standing there, watching them.

Ros pulled away and strode quickly on. She mustn't risk Lotte looking up and catching her spying. How would she explain that away? Lotte must never know what she'd witnessed.

Her mind was churning. She didn't understand. Lotte had definitely told her that she'd never been to Ilkley before. Had Ros just exposed that as a blatant lie? She tried to calm herself, to stop her hands from trembling. She must be logical. She must be fair.

Maybe it was still possible that she hadn't been there before. It could just be a distant relative buried there. Ros shook her head. She didn't buy that. Everything she'd witnessed suggested that Lotte had been really upset. It wasn't a visit made out of curiosity about her family tree; clearly, Lotte had a genuine connection with this place. A connection that was important to her.

Ros breathed hard as she walked. She knew what Adam would say. He'd tell her that she was overthinking again. That she was seeing secrets and intrigue and danger where there was none. She should leave the poor woman alone. What did it matter to her, anyway? There was no point getting more involved in Lotte's life than she already was. Her personal life was none of Ros's business.

But Ros found that she didn't care what Adam would say. She needed to find out, to know more.

When she had the chance, she took a right turn and struck inland from the river, then looped round, heading back towards the far side of the cemetery. Her eyes scanned the stones and the spaces between them, looking for Lotte's lone figure. There was no sign of her.

Ros found a turn-off that led through the grass into the modern section of the graveyard. Without letting herself pause to reconsider, she took it.

The place was deserted. The only sounds leaking through from the outside world were the distant rumble of traffic and an occasional warning cry from a bird, hopping through the grass. Lotte was nowhere to be seen.

Ros darted further forward and made roughly for the area where Lotte had been standing so solemnly. She hurried up and down the rows, peering down at the headstones, glancing at the line of names and dates. Every now and then, she anxiously lifted her gaze to look around, wondering if she was being watched. She imagined Lotte's still figure, obscured by the darkness under the trees, quietly observing her.

There! Ahead, lying across the outline of a grave, she recognised Lotte's flowers. The vivid red bow stood out dramatically against a background of chipped bark. Ros quickened her pace, reached the grave and bent down to read the inscription on the polished slab at its head.

In loving memory of Rosemary Anna Foster, much loved wife and sister. Always in our hearts.

Further down, a second inscription had been added, six years later:

In loving memory of James Andrew Foster, beloved son and husband. Reunited in Heaven.

A married couple, then. Ros studied the dates. James had died more than twenty years ago, in his sixties. She pulled out her phone and took a few quick photographs.

Were they Lotte's parents? She puzzled it out. If Lotte was in her mid-thirties now, as Ros thought, she'd have been a teenager when they died. And – she counted back – they'd have been in their forties when she was born. It was a slight stretch, but perfectly possible that they were her mother and father.

She looked again at the inscription. *Much loved wife and sister. Beloved son and husband.* No mention that they were anyone's parents.

And their name. *Foster?* She frowned. She couldn't see what that name had to do with Lotte.

A sudden sound from behind her made her heart pound. She swung around. The low, sweeping branches of a tree swayed and shivered. She peered more closely, her body tense. Was someone hiding there, watching her? 'Hello?' Her voice sounded weak and insubstantial on the air. No reply. The foliage stilled.

She pushed her phone back into her pocket, suddenly aware how alone she felt there, how vulnerable. Her chest was tight. She wanted to get out of this creepy place, to get home.

She waited a moment longer, her body rigid, her eyes scanning for any sign of movement. The greenery was dense. If anyone was there, they were well hidden.

Nothing. She shook herself and started to walk quickly away, picking her way between the graves. She was being ridiculous. It had probably been just a gust of wind stirring the branches. She was anxious, that was all. She just wished she wasn't so easily frightened.

15

ROS

'Leave me alone!'

Ros reached the landing just as Sophie slammed her bedroom door. She paused and listened. The sound of angry crying erupted, tipping over now and then into shrieking.

Ros crossed the landing and tapped on Sophie's door.

Sophie paused for long enough to shout: 'Go away! Leave me alone! You don't care!'

Ros forced herself to take a deep breath. She put her hand on the handle, considering going in, then thought better of it. She said as steadily as she could through the door: 'I'm sorry you're upset, Sophie. I'm just trying to help. If you could just—'

'Go AWAY!' That time it reached a top-of-the-lungs screech.

Ros clenched her jaw, turned and headed back downstairs. She clattered dishes around, feeling the tremble in her hands and trying to take deep breaths to calm herself. Behind her, Bella was hunched over her colouring, unnaturally quiet and showing a studied interest in her work.

Finally, Bella, clearly sensing an opportunity to capitalise on her sister's distress, said: 'She's very mad, isn't she, Mummy? It scares me when she gets shouty.'

Ros kissed the top of her younger daughter's head and pointed to her drawing. 'That's good, Bella. Love that swirly blue and green!'

They were both only pretending to behave normally. They were both only too aware of the screaming still seeping down from upstairs, and upset by it. Ros saw the way Bella gripped her crayon, the way her eyes rose warily to search her mother's face for clues about how she was feeling.

Ros's own eyes darted often to the kitchen clock, counting down. Adam would be home soon. She couldn't wait. He'd do a better job with Sophie. He always seemed to know what to say to calm her down. All Ros had done, so far, in gently trying to talk to Sophie about what happened that day and what exactly Fred had said to make her so mad, had made matters worse and sparked the awful meltdown.

Later, Ros and Adam sat side by side on the sofa, eating their meal and staring at the television.

By the time they reached coffee, Ros couldn't stand it any longer. 'Can we talk?' She nodded at the screen.

Adam reached for the remote and switched off the news, then turned to her and waited.

'What did she say? When you went up?'

Adam paused. She sensed him considering different words and turns of phrase in his mind, taking care before he spoke. He was a fair-minded man. She loved that about him.

'She didn't say very much, really.' He hesitated again. 'I asked her why she was so upset. If it was because of what had happened at school. Then I tried to ask her about what Fred had said and that, you know, however annoying or hurtful it was, hitting was always wrong. The usual stuff.'

Ros blinked. He made it sound so easy. She was sure she hadn't said anything very different but look at the outburst she'd provoked. 'And?'

'I told her what you'd heard at the school gates, about Fred being OK. Nothing broken. She seemed relieved.' Adam reached across and put his warm hand on hers. 'I think she frightened herself, I really do. She seems overwhelmed by big emotions and she doesn't know how to handle them.' He shrugged. 'I don't know. I think it's probably a phase. I know it's awful but we just need to keep reinforcing the same message. That she needs to use her words if she's upset. Tell us or a teacher, if she needs to. And that she can't go around thumping people.'

Ros squeezed his hand in reply. 'I guess so.'

Adam nodded, reading her face. 'Let's keep trying and see, yes? I know how hard it is. I'm upset too. But I just think we might make matters worse if we make a big deal out of it, you know? She's clearly going through a rough patch, whatever the cause. She needs to know we're on her side.'

Ros gave a deep sigh.

Adam said: 'She's a great kid. We know that. Maybe we need to trust in that, you know?'

'You're right.' Ros leaned in and kissed him lightly on the lips. 'I guess, in the scheme of things... I just, well, it was so awful getting the call from school and dashing in. I've always been so proud of the girls.'

'Of course. Me, too. Sophie's just an intense kid. She really feels things. We need to help her manage that.'

Ros dropped her shoulders, trying to relax. Suddenly, she felt very weary. 'I might head up and do an hour's work,' she said, heaving herself to her feet. She wasn't sure she had the energy. All she really wanted to do was settle down with a cup of tea beside Adam and find a mindless TV programme to watch. But, on top of everything else, she needed to send out another batch of emails before she went to bed. She was still struggling to get appointments with local bosses, in the hope they might lead to contracts.

'Love you.' Adam reached again for the TV remote.

'You, too.'

As she reached the door, Ros remembered the strange incident with Lotte in the cemetery.

'Adam, do you remember a Mr and Mrs Foster in Ilkley? Rosemary and James. They'd have been a bit older than our parents.'

Adam wrenched his attention away from the television screen and looked over his shoulder at her, puzzled. 'Foster?'

'Foster. Just wondered if you'd come across them at the rugby club or somewhere. Friends of your parents, maybe. Doesn't ring a bell?'

He pulled a face and shook his head. 'No, sorry.' The channels started to flick again as he searched for something to watch.

Ros headed upstairs, thinking. She'd intended to check her work emails but she was too restless to do that just yet. Instead, she powered up her laptop and googled Rosemary and James Foster's names, along with *Ilkley*. At first, she didn't find much: there was photograph of a smiling teenage James Foster in Skipton, posing in football kit, but it had only been posted a few years earlier; then a link to the profile of a middle-aged businessman in Leeds with the same name. Clearly, neither of these were the James Foster she wanted – they weren't even close to the right age.

Ros frowned to herself. Maybe the couple she was trying to research were just too old for their milestone events to appear online. And it was unlikely that the *Ilkley Gazette* would have archived all its marriage and death notices, especially not ones that dated back years. She sat for a moment, her eyes on the screen, trying to think it through. Maybe they hadn't always used their full names. She refreshed her search, first trying

Jimmy or *Jim Foster*. Nothing appeared of interest. Then she typed in *Rose Foster* and *Ilkley* and pressed enter.

The top result struck her at once. She clicked to open it.

It was an old-fashioned, printed announcement from the *Telegraph & Argus*. It looked like an original cutting that had been photographed, then posted online.

Ros's breath stuck in her throat as she read it.

A heartfelt thank you to all our friends in Ilkley for flowers, cards and prayers. Your kindness brings such comfort at this time of tragedy.

James and Rose Foster.

Ros blinked. It was dated nearly thirty years ago.

She closed the item and scrolled on, desperately searching for anything else that might shed light on what that meant. There was nothing more. That was the only reference.

Ros went back to the original announcement, opened it again and sat at her desk, staring in frustration at the sparse message on her screen. Her heart raced as she willed it to reveal its secrets to her.

'Tragedy' surely wasn't a word someone would use lightly. That suggested more, far more, than a normal bereavement.

She shook her head. Whatever terrible event had befallen them, it had something to do with Lotte. And while she couldn't know that for sure – Adam would never believe her – she *felt* it. The hairs prickled on the back of her neck.

But what had 'it' been?

16

LOTTE

As a young child, I used to think about a life as a straight line. I imagined it starting when I was born and stretching away to the horizon, limitless.

I soon changed my mind. Too early in life, I learned how finite that line was and also that a life, my life anyway, was not so much straight as a series of loops.

I was at work when they came. It was a perfectly normal day. Thursday. Early spring. Bright with promise.

I'd thought that morning, as I'd wrestled Caitlyn into her woolly jumper and a warm, padded anorak that was ready for the wash, that we should all go out at the weekend and buy some summer clothes for her. A light denim jacket, maybe. T-shirts. Shorts. Jon was generous about kitting Caitlyn out. He was so proud of her, besotted from the moment she was born.

I was in the back room, scanning documents into the computer system for my boss, when I heard my name. I tuned in at once, of course, wondering who it was and what they were saying about me. It was an unfamiliar voice.

Sylvia, the office manager, appeared in the doorway. It was the look on her face that alerted me. There was a whole story written there. She was sad, pitiful, anxious and wary of me, all in that moment.

Behind, I glimpsed two figures in dark blue uniforms, peering past her for a glimpse of me.

I sat down on a pile of cardboard flatpacks with a bump. The strangest thoughts ran through my mind.

Whatever she's going to tell me, I'm going to remember this for the rest of my life. Along with: *Not here, in this scrubby back room. Why should this dingy place be scorched into my memory?*

Then a sudden sickness. Something rose in my throat, and I knew I couldn't speak for fear of throwing up.

Sylvia stood there, blinking, watching.

I thought: *It's Caitlyn. We knew this was going to happen. We knew.*

Jon and I had been talking, just a few days earlier, about a nursery in the papers that was being investigated after a toddler choked to death on an uncut grape. How could something so mundane be so catastrophic? We'd been horrified on the parents' behalf, but, more acutely, frightened on our own. Caitlyn had just started at nursery. What if the same thing happened to her?

'I don't know how you'd get over that,' Jon had said.

I was sure that he too was imagining our daughter laid out on a slab, limp and pale. These tragedies happened so easily. A carefully nurtured life could end in a matter of seconds.

'It won't happen to us,' I said.

He hadn't said anything else, but I'd sensed what he was thinking. Those poor, desperate parents in Norfolk had probably thought exactly the same and yet it had happened.

Now, shaking my head, I managed to say: 'Caitlyn?'

Sylvia's eyes widened a fraction. Was she judging me in that moment, thinking I cared more about my daughter than my husband? I've wondered since. Maybe if I had been called on to make a bargain with God, I'd have given up Caitlyn to save Jon. I know what that makes me but it's true.

Sylvia shook her head and stood to one side to let me struggle to my feet and make my way out into the bright main office to face the police officers. When she showed us all into the best conference room, the one with the view, I knew it was really bad.

It wasn't Jon's fault, apparently. A van crashed through a red light, right into him. I knew that junction. I could just imagine it. Metal pieces from his mangled bike scattering and skidding across the surface of the road. Spreading bloodstains on the asphalt.

He didn't suffer. That's what they kept telling me.

I found that hard to believe.

I imagined there were women who evolved into tragic and dignified widows, honouring their dear husband's memory by polishing their framed wedding photographs with pride and devoting themselves into pouring love into their children, the way he would have wanted.

I wasn't that sort of woman.

First, I gave up work. I needed the freedom to fall apart. Also, I discovered, after meetings with Jon's accountant, that I could afford not to work, at least for a while. After years of grafting to earn enough to cover the bills, I was suddenly well off. Jon's life insurance paid off the mortgage and left me with a modest income. That was the one kind thing Jon had done in making me a bride, only to make me a widow: he'd planned ahead to make sure he kept us safe.

Our new existence without Jon stuttered on. I tried to keep life for Caitlyn as normal as possible, dropping her off each day to nursery. Since the loss of her father, she'd become a quiet child. The staff there described her as rather withdrawn. She was better off with them, with stories and games, sand and water play and the noisy chaos of other children. I was sure of that. We were both grieving, each in our own way. We both needed our space.

As much as I loved her, our time together was strained. Just the sight of her hurt, she reminded me so much of him. Those were Jon's eyes, looking back at me. Jon's thoughtful look on her little face. At the weekends, I took her to the park and tickled her when I pushed her on the swings and waited with open arms and an inane grin at the bottom of the slide for her to whoosh down to me. I tried so hard.

Too hard.

Everywhere, there were fathers playing with their children and, now and then, just out of sight, I almost saw Jon. Watching us. Smiling. Striding towards us. Sometimes, I sensed that she felt him too. Until we turned to look and the spell was broken and we realised it wasn't him after all, just a stranger.

I tried to show how much I loved her but it was hard. I was numb. Sometimes, I felt too numb to love anyone or anything ever again.

Then, worst of all, I started to see myself as the person my parents had always painted me: a selfish, irresponsible child who'd destroyed the person they most loved. A cursed figure who was destined to damage those who cared for her. Those she loved. Maybe that's also why I needed to send Caitlyn off to nursery each day. Maybe, in my own way, I was trying to protect her from me, better than I'd protected her father.

I started to drink. At first, it was just in the evenings, once Caitlyn had fallen asleep. Then I started having a glass or two at lunchtime, to help me nap. Then, finally, a glass of chilled white wine or two as soon as I'd dropped Caitlyn off at nursery and made it home. *Hair of the dog*, I told myself. *Just a little something to kickstart the day.*

I graduated from wine to spirits. They numbed the pain

faster, more efficiently. I welcomed the hangovers. The torture of an exploding head and the misery of vomiting bile – that was a way of punishing myself, the way I deserved to be punished.

I stopped answering my phone or the front door. The few friends we'd made locally stopped knocking. I was an embarrassment.

My parents were the only people who seemed unsurprised by Jon's death. It was as if they'd expected it. After all, they didn't believe there was any such thing as an accident, not really. Jon had condemned himself by loving the wrong person. That was what they thought, I was sure. He'd died because he'd believed in me, and he'd been wrong.

Fatally wrong.

That whole summer passed in a blur. When I look back now, I have so few photographs of Caitlyn from that lost time. I must have clapped when she said her first word, cheered when she learned to throw a ball.I just remember so little of it.

17

LOTTE

As the days started to shorten again, after that lost summer of alcohol and grief, I began to brood.

I spent my days going through the boxes that were stowed away in the attic and under the stairs. I worked steadily and miserably through Jon's belongings, sitting cross-legged on the lounge floor, a glass of whisky to hand. Before I destroyed them, I read the bundle of letters he'd kept from childhood and his file of glowing school reports. I ran his toy cars up and down the carpet and held in my palm the building bricks he must have loved as a boy. I flicked through photographs of him as a child, with a ready grin and guileless, open face.

It confirmed everything he'd always told me. That he'd had a happy childhood, had been doted on by loving parents. He'd taken it for granted. As if happiness were a default, a normal state of affairs. No wonder he'd had such an easy capacity to love.

Behind his boxes, pushed back into the darkness, I found another box. A much smaller one. My own.

I opened it warily. Not even Jon had seen the items inside. I rummaged through the yellowing newspaper clippings and lifted out the photograph I'd stolen years ago from the jumble inside my parents' sideboard.

It was a dog-eared colour picture of me with my sister when we were young.

I hunched over it, numbed by whisky, and stroked a finger over the celluloid faces. We were children from the distant, vanished land of the past. We looked as normal and as happy as Jon had done at the same age. I barely recognised myself. The girl looking boldly out at me was still innocent. At six, I still thought I had the right to a wonderful life. I dreamed, by turns, of being an astronaut or a vet, a train driver or a pop star. Anything I wanted.

I couldn't remember exactly when or where it was taken. The sun was shining, and we were standing in a clearing in a wood, dappled by slanting light filtering through the surrounding trees. We were wearing shorts and T-shirts, our feet in sandals. I remembered those sandals, and the white bars the straps drew by the end of summer across my tanned feet.

In the picture, I was pushing forwards slightly, as if I wanted to run towards the camera. I had an unselfconscious smile, proud of the new gaps in my teeth. My hair, cut into a bob, was messy and my cheeks were grubby.

My younger sister clutched my hand, pulling on it. She looked about four years old. She stood slightly behind me, hanging back shyly. Her long hair fell in two long plaits, finished off with clip-on ribbons. Her eyes were large and trusting but also uncertain – as if she had some intuition, even then, of the horror that lay ahead.

I blinked, gazing at her, then angrily wiped away the tear that splashed down across the sunlit trees.

That night, I dreamed of her. It was the same dream that used to haunt me, before I met Jon. She was reaching for me through the water, crying; her eyes, big brown pools in the churning foam, fixed on mine. I strained, felt the brush of our outstretched fingertips but, try as I might, I couldn't reach her. I could never reach her.

I woke, sweating, my breath hard, and clicked on the light. *It was a dream. It wasn't real.* I squinted in the brightness, gradually taking in the solid outlines of the bedroom: the wardrobe, the chair draped with the next day's clothes, the half-open door to the landing.

The emptiness at my side where Jon had once lain.

I padded across the landing to Caitlyn's room. Her hair was spread across the pillow as if it were in water. Her eyelashes, impossibly long, fluttered as she slept. Her stuffed toys lay around her, better guardians through the darkness than I could ever be. I didn't bend to kiss her, I just watched her sleep, calmed by the steady rhythm of her breathing and the soft rise and fall of her tiny chest.

The next morning, I dropped Caitlyn off at nursery and drove home as fast as I could. My head pounded but instead of feeding my hangover the first drink of the day, I swallowed back aspirin and drank off two large glasses of water.

I forced myself to stride purposefully through the house, gathering together the half-filled bottles hidden here and there – behind sofa cushions and pillows, under my bed and at the back of cupboards and wardrobes. I was engulfed in fumes as I stood resolutely at the sink, my hands moving briskly as if they were independent of my fuggy brain. They twisted off one metal cap after another, then poured the contents down the drain. The sink flashed amber, then brown, then again amber as it gurgled and disappeared.

I pulled my dirty hair into a ponytail, dug out dusty trainers from their place in the hall and set out for a run, pushing myself as hard as I dared. I came back with a carrier bag of fresh fruit and salads and started to chop myself a healthy breakfast.

Once I'd showered, my clean hair flopping around my cheeks, I powered up my laptop and set to work. For the first time since Jon's death, I had a sense of purpose. In the night, feeling my sweet, kind sister straining towards me, begging me for help, I'd remembered what I truly was.

Jon had been a diversion. He'd tried to change me, with all his talk about love and trust. He'd softened me into putty. Now I had to find my real self again, to strip all that cotton wool away and reveal again the hard, steel core that had sustained me through my fragmented childhood. The core that had helped me break away from the parents who could hardly bear to look at me. The core that had served me so well in my career.

I did have a reason for existing. It seemed obvious to me now, as I opened up website after website and started to search.

I wasn't like Jon. I never had been. My life was never meant to be about love.

It was about revenge.

18

ROS

'What do you make of Lotte?' Ros reached for her frothy coffee, her eyes on Diana's face, waiting to see how she'd respond. This was the first post-drop-off coffee they'd managed together so far, just the two of them. It was good to catch up.

'Actually, I wanted to talk to you about Lotte. She's asked us round for a playdate. On Thursday, after school.' Diana looked embarrassed. 'You don't mind, do you? I mean, I know you two are friends.'

'We're not really friends.' Ros shrugged. 'We just met on vacation, that's all.' But she was struck by her feeling of unease. About her suspicions about whether Lotte had told her the truth about why she'd moved there, about Caitlyn's father and whether she'd been married. 'I'm not even sure I trust her.'

'Oh.' Diana looked taken aback. 'Why not?'

Ros hesitated. 'We had a bit of a wild night out together. Just the two of us. When we met on vacation.'

'Really?' Diana's eyes widened. 'How wild?'

Ros sighed. 'I can't remember. I don't even know how I got to bed afterwards.'

'Blimey.' Diana looked impressed. 'That *is* wild.'

Ros frowned. 'Anyway, I think I might have, you know, overshared.'

'About what?'

Ros hesitated, backtracking. She'd known Diana a long time. She trusted her implicitly. Even so, this was a secret even she must never know.

'That's just it,' she stalled. 'I don't know exactly.'

'That sounds very mysterious.' Diana, thoughtful, reached for her coffee and took a sip. After a pause, she said, 'What are we talking here? This doesn't involve an indiscretion, does it? Some sort of, how shall I put it, vacation romance?'

Ros couldn't look her in the eye. It was all so awkward but, if she had to admit something, that was the lesser evil. She gave a quick nod, remembering the blond guy with his muscular body and firm, hot hands. 'Not romance,' she muttered. 'You know I wouldn't do that to Adam. But I was out of my tree so, I don't know. Yes, an indiscretion, maybe.'

'Ros!' Diana stared.

Ros kept her eyes on her coffee cup. She felt suddenly sick. Diana looked so shocked. If this was her friend's reaction to the possibility of, well, maybe a drunken kiss or two, Ros couldn't imagine what she'd think if she knew Ros's worst secret.

A couple of other school mums smiled and nodded as they passed them, on their way towards a table at the back, coffees in hand. Ros gave them a quick, strained smile but didn't say hello.

Diana said quietly: 'I'm guessing Adam doesn't know about this?' She seemed to take Ros's silence as an answer, then added: 'No wonder you were so taken aback when she showed up in Ilkley. Ouch.'

'Ouch is right.'

Diana frowned. 'OK, you're stressed about what she might know. I get that. But are you really sure you can't trust her? She hasn't said a word about it, so far, has she? Certainly not around me. Why would she be so mean?'

Ros, miserable, didn't respond. She couldn't explain how she felt about Lotte. It would sound paranoid, she knew it would.

Diana went on, 'And, you know what? Even if she did, you'd just deny it. Straight up. People know you. They like you. It would be your word against hers.'

Ros shrugged. 'Unless she's got evidence.'

'Evidence?' Diana sat up straighter.

Ros looked around at the other mums. 'Keep your voice down.'

Diana leaned in closer. 'What sort of evidence?'

'I don't know. I don't know how far it went. Just some drunken dancing, I think. I mean, that's all I remember. Maybe a kiss?'

Diana's eyes widened. 'You really don't know?'

'Stop it. I feel bad enough already.'

Diana took a deep breath. 'OK, worst-case scenario, she might have a blurry photo or two. A smooch or something. That's worst-case, right?'

'I guess so.'

'So, forget about it. Honestly, Ros, I'm sure she's moved on. Maybe you should too.'

Ros squirmed. 'She sent me an odd email.'

'Odd?'

'*Your secret's safe with me.* Something like that.' Ros watched Diana closely, but her friend's face was carefully neutral. 'Don't you think that's a bit passive-aggressive? I mean, why would she say that? It feels like a threat.'

Diana hid behind her coffee cup for a moment. Finally, she said carefully: 'Don't you think you might be over-thinking this? I mean, I can see you're feeling a bit guilty.' She grinned. 'Don't deny it, lovely. It's written all over you. But maybe it means exactly what it says. You don't need to worry.'

Ros shook her head. She wasn't convinced. 'And what about her daughter? Don't you think she's a bit, I don't know, strange?'

'No, not really.' Diana hesitated. 'She struck me as shy, but you'd expect that, wouldn't you? New place, new school. It's a lot to handle. She's only four. She'll come out of her shell once she makes some friends.'

Ros pulled a face. 'That's another thing. Why's Lotte being so pushy? She practically forced me to take the girls round last Friday and it was a disaster.' She gave her friend a quick summary of the nightmare playdate, ending with Sophie's attack on Bella.

Diana blew out her cheeks. 'How awful. I'm sorry. That doesn't sound like Sophie.'

'I know.' Ros hesitated, reluctant to say too much more. 'Actually, there've been a few things recently. Angry outbursts.'

They sat in silence for a few moments, and then Diana said slowly: 'Posy said something after school the other day.' She was feeling her way, her eyes on Ros's face. 'I hope you don't mind. I mean, I'm sorry, I can imagine it's a sensitive...' She trailed off.

'Was it about Sophie and Fred?'

Diana nodded sheepishly.

Ros broke eye contact and started to stir the dregs of the chocolate powder into the milk froth for a moment. 'Is it all over school?'

'I don't think so. Look, I'd have told you if it was.' Diana paused. 'But is Sophie OK?'

Ros shrugged. 'Adam thinks it's just a phase. A development thing. I hope he's right.'

'I'm sure it's something like that. If there's anything I can do...'

Ros didn't answer. She didn't trust herself to speak.

Diana moved on. 'Anyway, are you sure you don't mind if I take the kids round to Lotte's? It feels rude to back out but I don't want... I didn't know how you felt about...' She left the thought hanging. 'And then, I guess, well, I'd need to invite them back.'

Ros slurped the rest of her coffee and set down her spoon. 'I tell you what,' she said, 'why don't we do it together? I owe Lotte a playdate. I could invite you all over and get it out of the way. Sophie and Bella won't be as cross about Caitlyn coming round if Posy and Max are there too.'

Diana nodded. 'Great. I could bring dessert, if you like—? Something for the kids and something more upmarket for the three of us?'

'Perfect!' Ros felt her anxiety ease a little. She still wasn't reassured about Lotte, but she always felt better for seeing Diana. 'Let's do that. Maybe this Friday? I'll say it's an invitation from both of us.' Her thoughts ran on. 'Do you think Phil could get back in time to join us for a beer before you leave?'

'I'll ask him.'

'Adam would love that. He needs to chill out. He's working too hard.'

'He's amazing.' Diana ran a hand over her shoulder. 'Did he tell you I'd been in to see him? My shoulder's playing up again. Too much tennis. But honestly, a few sessions with him and I'll be good as new.'

A fresh gaggle of school gate mums came clattering into the café and waved across at Ros and Diana before they headed to the counter.

Ros bent in closer and lowered her voice. 'One more thing about Lotte,' she said. 'She's asked me to find her a job.'

'Has she?' Diana raised her eyebrows. 'What sort of job?'

'Back office, admin, that sort of thing. Not that there's much around.'

Diana picked up on that at once. 'Business still slow?'

Ros sighed. 'August's been dead. I'm hoping it'll pick up now.'

Diana grinned. 'Well, if anyone can make it happen, it's

you. Phil thinks you're going to make a fortune, once you get off the ground. I think he wants to take out shares in you.'

Ros shrugged, pleased but embarrassed. 'I don't know about that. Making enough to pay a few bills would do me.' She considered her friend thoughtfully. 'What about you, Di?'

'What about me?'

'Have you thought about going back to work? They're both in school now. You could, you know.'

'Maybe.' Diana stared intently into her coffee cup as if she were reading the future in the grounds.

Ros knew Diana had worked in the charity sector before she'd had Posy, but she'd never talked much about her role; she'd just given the impression it had been rewarding but long hours and poorly paid. By contrast, Phil was an insurance broker in Leeds and seemed, at least according to Diana, to be paid a lot for doing very little.

'I could help you put a fresh CV together if you like. Start putting out a few feelers. You never know what might come up.'

Diana didn't answer. Her eyes stayed fixed on the inside of her cup. Her face was stiff with tension.

Ros said gently: 'Are you OK?'

'Absolutely fine!' Diana's tone was brittle. She made a show of checking her watch, then pushed back her chair and jumped to her feet, making it clear the conversation was over. 'Hey, we should go!'

Ros jumped up too, hastily pulling on her coat and gathering together her things. It had been a long time since she'd seen Diana so rattled. Clearly, she'd unknowingly hit a raw nerve.

And it was just as clear that, whatever crisis Diana was having about her work life, it was a secret she was determined not to share, even with her closest friend.

19

LOTTE

Adam's osteopathic practice was tucked away at the back of the main parking lot, in the centre of the town. It was a small outfit. There were only two names on the board at the foot of the stairs, alongside an absurdly overpriced dress shop.

Adam Crofter, Osteopath

Samuel James, Physiotherapist

I was buzzed in and climbed the narrow stairs to the first floor.

It was a poky area, barely big enough for the reception desk on one side and the two-seater settee on the other. The young woman behind the desk checked her computer for my appointment and gave me a form to fill in, attached to a clipboard.

I took a seat on the settee and worked my way through the tedious list of questions about my medical history. The place smelt of sawdust and recently brewed coffee. A magazine rack, bolted to the wall, held a few battered copies of *Hello!* magazine and *Yorkshire Life*. A blackboard and easel stood by reception with a chalked advertisement for an online seminar on tackling back pain, ten pounds per person.

I handed back the form and settled down to wait. My

stomach fluttered with nerves. My hands, when I looked down at them, were kneading each other. I glanced at the receptionist but, if she'd noticed I looked anxious, she was ignoring it.

I set my hands, palms down, at my sides and took a few deep breaths. *Easy*, I told myself. *You can do this.* If he says anything, I'll just tell him I'm always a bit stressed, seeing someone new. He won't guess the real reason.

A stout man with greying hair emerged from the consulting room and hovered at the reception desk to pay. He fumbled in his wallet for a card to tap on the machine, which whirred and spat out a receipt.

He was in the middle of negotiating the time of his next appointment when the consulting room door opened again and there was Adam, a tight smile on his lips, calling my name with a hint of a question in his voice, then nodding to me to come inside.

As I moved past him into the small room, I made a point of raising a hand to rub at my neck, massaging it as if it felt stiff.

A moment later, he shut the door behind him and walked towards me. We were alone.

20

ROS

A few evenings later, Adam was all smiles when he walked in through the front door. 'Guess what!'

Ros, in the middle of brushing out the tangles in Bella's hair, paused and looked up. 'What?'

Bella jumped up and ran across to him, her hair flying. 'You met an alien, Daddy! Did you?'

He gave her a hug and kissed the top of her head. 'Well, not exactly that, Bella-boo. But that would be cool, wouldn't it?'

Ros smiled at the two of them. 'You've won the lottery?'

Adam raised his eyebrows at her over Bella's head. 'Just as unlikely, I'm afraid. No, not that. Shall I put you out of your misery?'

'I think you'd better.' Ros brandished the hairbrush at Bella. 'Come on, you. Let's finish the job.'

Adam said: 'We've got a new receptionist.' He raised a hand. 'Don't worry, you'll still get your finder's fee! I told her she had to go through all the proper channels.'

Ros stared. 'How come? A walk-in?'

Adam grinned. 'Not exactly.' He was enjoying the surprise,

she could tell. 'It's someone who came to see me for treatment. Someone not a million miles—'

Ros burst out: 'Diana! It's her, isn't it? Adam, she'll be great! I was just telling—'

Adam looked confused. 'Diana?'

'Isn't it?' Ros's mind was whirring as she tried to recalculate.

'It's Lotte!' Adam pointed vaguely towards the riverside. 'Your vacation buddy. Our new neighbour.'

Ros's insides froze. She felt her face tighten.

'Ow, Mummy!' Bella squirmed away, her hands clamped down on her head. 'You're hurting.'

'What?' Adam stood there in the living room, his hands splayed in a gesture of helplessness. 'I told you, you'll still get the commission.'

Ros took a step backwards and sat down heavily. 'Not her. Please, Adam.'

Adam tutted, his mood of playful excitement soured. 'For heaven's sake! I thought you'd be pleased. You're friends, aren't you? Isn't she coming round on Friday, with Phil and Diana? What's the matter with you?' He turned on his heel and headed out of the room. His bag dropped against the hall wall with a thud, then his feet pounded up the stairs.

Ros sat very still. She was gripped by a sudden fear, a leaden sense of inevitability.

Bella reached out and touched her arm. 'You OK, Mummy?'

Sophie, reading at the far end of the room, lifted her head from her book. 'What? What is it?'

Ros woodenly lifted her arm and Bella at once snuggled under it, pressing against her side. She sensed Sophie's eyes on her face but she couldn't answer, not yet. Her stomach was weighted by foreboding, as if something menacing was closing in on her family and she was powerless to stop it.

Of course, Lotte had gone behind Ros's back. Of course,

when she'd gone to see Adam for treatment, she must have heard about the vacancy and jumped on it at once. Now it had happened, it made perfect sense.

She just hadn't seen it coming.

Once the girls were settled in bed that evening, Ros and Adam sat in the sitting room in silence. Ros picked at her food, feeling too sick to eat. Adam unfolded the newspaper and buried himself in the news.

Adam wasn't a man who raised his voice or threw tantrums. He was rarely mad and, if he was, he retreated into hostile silence.

Ros had her own theory about why. He was a bottler, she'd decided long ago, when she'd first been introduced to Adam's domineering big brother and equally loud father, because he'd grown up feeling belittled by them both. In a childhood world like that, it was generally better to keep quiet than risk conflict.

Finally, when it was almost time for bed, Ros took a deep breath and turned to him. 'I'm sorry,' she said. 'About Lotte. But I just don't trust her.'

He didn't answer. His jaw was set.

'Put her on the shortlist, if you really have to,' she went on. 'But don't rush into anything. OK?'

Adam lowered his paper and turned to her at last. 'What's the big deal, Ros, really?' His tone was cold. 'Last time you mentioned her name, you said you and Diana were having her round here for tea with her kid. Remember? I've said no to a patient on Friday afternoon so I can get home in time to see Phil for a beer. Ring any bells?'

Ros stared at him. 'Of course. I know. But that's not because I like her.'

'Right.' His tone had turned dangerously sarcastic. 'You're

asking her round because you *don't* like her. Got it. That makes total sense.'

'Just listen, will you?' Ros tried to stay calm. 'It's true. I have asked her round. Di and I both owe her a playdate and I thought this was a way of getting it over with, that's all. Hopefully it's a one-off.'

Adam looked exasperated. 'Fine. And this is business. I'm not asking her to be our new best friend. It's Belinda's last day on Friday. We need someone else, fast. Lotte is easy to talk to, well-organised, mature. And she's actually enthusiastic, which is more than I can say for anyone else we've seen. The minute she heard we were looking for someone, she was all over it.' He sucked in his breath. 'I just don't understand you sometimes. I thought you'd be pleased for me. I really did.'

Ros swallowed hard. 'Just give me a bit more time to find someone else, will you? I'm sure there are—'

'No.' He shook his head. 'We haven't got time. Sam likes her too and if we hadn't snapped her up, someone else would have. I'll still make sure you get your fee, don't worry.'

Ros stared at him. It wasn't about the fee. 'You've actually offered her the job?'

He nodded curtly. 'She's starting on Monday. I'm sorry you've taken a dislike to her but there you are. You're not the one who'll be working with her.'

He lifted his paper again, signalling that the conversation was over.

Ros hesitated. She didn't want a row. She hated arguing. But she felt compelled to keep trying. She needed to do everything she could to block this from happening. 'Adam, listen.' She tried to keep her voice calm. 'I just think she's up to something. Moving here out of the blue like that. Choosing somewhere just round the corner. Putting her daughter into the same class as Bella. It's creepy.'

'Not all that again.' He was losing patience. 'For heaven's sake, Ros.'

She lifted a hand. 'Just listen a minute. I can't explain it, not properly, but she's trouble. I can just feel it. I think she's a liar, for one thing.'

'Really?' He crumpled the newspaper into untidy folds and swivelled to face her. 'Alright, go on. Tell me. What's she lied about, exactly?'

Blood thumped in Ros's ears. 'She told me she wasn't sure who Caitlyn's father was. But I spoke to someone in a company she used to work for. They said she was married.'

Adam raised his eyebrows in disbelief. 'That's it?'

Ros felt her confidence drain. 'And she said she'd never been here before but I saw her, I *saw* her, putting flowers on a grave in Ilkley cemetery. The grave of a couple called the Fosters.'

'So what?'

'So,' she faltered in the face of his mounting anger, 'so she must have known them, mustn't she?'

Adam flung down his paper. 'Can you hear yourself? Can you? You've been checking up on this woman, spying on her? Trying to stop her getting a job? And for what? You know what I think it is? You're guilty. You had a boozy night out with her on vacation and frankly made a fool of yourself and now you're frightened. She's pitched up in your cosy little world and instead of welcoming her, you're scared to death she'll tell everyone and embarrass the hell out of you. That's it, isn't it?'

Ros shrank away from him. 'That's not fair.'

'No, it's not.' Adam got to his feet and towered over her. 'It's not fair on her and it's not fair on me, either.' His eyes bulged. 'Have you forgotten, really? Don't you remember what harm your paranoia can do?'

Ros, cowering beneath him, went rigid. She couldn't speak. She could scarcely breathe.

He pointed a stubby finger in her face. 'Stop it. You hear me? Right now.'

Adam stormed out of the room.

Ros was still awake hours later when Adam finally came to join her in bed.

He turned his back on her, one arm round his pillow, one shoulder hunched.

She inched across the mattress towards him, threaded an arm around his chest and touched her lips tentatively to the soft, warm skin between his shoulder blades.

He didn't respond.

Ros rolled away and lay stiffly in the darkness. Slowly, Adam's breaths lengthened and his body slackened into sleep. A distant electronic beeping cut into the silence as, outside, a car reversed into a parking space. A few moments later, its door slammed and the night settled back into quietness.

Ros wondered if Lotte was awake. She imagined her lying in her pristine bedroom, just around the corner at number 5, suffocatingly close. Ros clenched her jaw. Did Lotte know that she was already causing problems, raking up past bitterness between Ros and her husband? Maybe she had made a terrible mistake in the past. Maybe she had caused irreparable harm by being paranoid, as Adam had angrily told her.

But that didn't necessarily mean she was wrong this time, about Lotte. Maybe this time she wasn't imagining a danger. Maybe it really was there.

She turned away from Adam, onto her side, facing out towards the ghostly outline of the fitted wardrobes, the bedroom door.

After a while, she pulled back the duvet and slid out of bed, padding through to check on Sophie and Bella. They were both fast asleep, hair splayed, skin soft with sleep.

Ros stroked back Bella's trailing fringe and bend down to plant a gentle kiss on her forehead. She breathed in the scent of her little girl's body, of soap and shampoo.

Lotte wanted something, Ros was sure. But whatever that woman was up to, Ros was determined to keep her family safe. *I'll protect my girls,* she thought. A sudden physical memory came again, of the intense rage that had flashed in her the day she'd run through Lotte's apartment to find Bella injured, her face dripping with blood, and caught her up in her arms.

I'll protect my girls, she thought again, fierce now. *However far I have to go.*

21

LOTTE

The hardest part of my research had been the first stage: establishing their full names.

I'd spent hours online, googling property details for their home, then setting up a fake profile on chat sites and posing as someone who'd previously lived in the area and wanted to get back in touch with some childhood friends. *Can anyone help?* In my posts, I said I couldn't quite remember their family name, only the older boy's first name and where they'd lived. I gave a rough description of them and an estimate of how old they'd be now.

It didn't take long before someone, who claimed to have known the family, came up with a suggestion. My hands trembled as I typed the older boy's name into the search engine. Within seconds, there he was. He looked around mid-forties now. His hair was cropped close and flecked with grey at the temples. His face had become full and fleshy. But I knew him. The look in his eyes. The shape of his face. I was certain it was him.

I sat for some time, staring into those eyes, remembering. My lips twitched convulsively with a mixture of grief and rage as the horror of those days came flooding back. For a moment, I thought, *I can't do this. I can't be in the same room as him. It's too much.* I pushed back my chair and paced vigorously up and down the room, trying to calm myself, fists clenched at my sides.

By the time I sat at the laptop again, I'd composed myself. I was strong. I *could* do this. They'd already escaped once. The thought of their living out the rest of their lives scot-free was too much to bear.

I searched out some online gardening sites, found what I was looking for and put in an order for the plants I wanted.

Then, I started to search out every detail about him I could. His professional profile showed me how his career had progressed and where he now worked as a senior manager, based in his company's headquarters in the city. He seemed to confine himself to work-related sites.

I was disappointed not to find any details about his personal life. I'd simply have to put the work in myself.

I started the following Monday. Once I'd dropped Caitlyn at nursery, I called the company where he worked, gave a false name and asked to be put through to him. I'd hung up as soon as the receptionist tried to connect me and I'd heard his extension start to ring.

I just wanted to check he was really there. Talking would come later.

I dug out my advertising industry clothes, one of the tight, tailored dresses offset by high-heeled shoes, the old-me look that Jon had described as my battle armour. I added a generous mask of make-up and took the train, then tube, into central London.

There was a back-to-school feeling in the bustle on the streets. An army of professionals, relaxed and tanned after the summer break, were pouring themselves back into work wardrobes, polishing their shoes and heading back to their offices. I bought a copy of the *Financial Times*, chose an Italian deli almost opposite the entrance to the building where I now knew he worked and settled myself in a window table with an espresso and a brioche, the paper folded to the crossword, to watch and wait.

Several hours passed. Still no sign of him. My heart started to flutter. Maybe the receptionist had been wrong and he was travelling. Maybe he'd called in sick or was working from home. I picked up my newspaper and moved a few doors down to a sandwich chain. I lingered there with a bottle of water, wondering how long to give it before I headed home.

At lunchtime, a man emerged from the revolving doors in a smart woollen suit and tie and stood at the kerb to hail a black taxi. I sat up and stared. He was wider and more jowly than the studio shots he'd posted online – they must have been taken several years ago. But although his body had softened and thickened, and it had been nearly thirty years, I knew him at once. I knew the contours of his face, the small, arrogant eyes, even the way he held himself, was much the same as when he'd been a boy.

He disappeared for just over two hours. I wrote the times neatly in a notebook. When he came back, also by London cab, his cheeks seemed flushed.

I hung around the street, hopping from café to café, for the rest of the afternoon, but he didn't reappear and by five-thirty, I left and headed back to collect Caitlyn from nursery.

That evening, once Caitlyn had fallen asleep, I took a trowel and the bag of fresh peat I'd bought and carefully planted the plants I'd ordered online in several colourful pots. I set them in shallow trays along the kitchen windowsill where I could tend them and, as time passed, watch them bud and flower.

Gradually, in the days that followed, I built up a picture of his movements. Early starts and late finishes. Sometimes, I arranged for the babysitter to collect Caitlyn from nursery and put her to bed so that I had more time to wait, time to see him emerge at six thirty or seven in the evening, at the end of his working day.

Most evenings, he hurried straight to the tube station. I tailed him, invisible in the crowd, as he reached Waterloo, then hurried across the concourse to take an overground train out to the suburbs, a copy of his newspaper tucked under his arm.

I watched and waited, ready for my chance, for the moment that would change everything.

22

LOTTE

Finally, one Thursday night, the man headed not to the station but to Covent Garden. I watched him scurry along the sidewalk. He seemed agitated; excited, perhaps, flattening down his hair with his palm and checking himself fleetingly in shop windows as he passed.

He ducked down a side street, away from the tourist crowd, and pushed open the door to a discreet Italian restaurant. I paced slowly past, trying to see inside. The interior was dim, the tables candlelit and intimate. I took a deep breath and followed.

I told the maître d' I was meeting someone there and, after making a show of struggling to find me a table because I didn't have a booking, he finally relented and led me through to the back.

I spotted him at once, sitting in a cosy corner with his back to the wall, his eyes flicking to the entrance as if he were expecting someone. His wife, perhaps. Or a mistress.

I chose an empty table as close to his as I could and slid into my seat in the semi-darkness, ordered a glass of wine, then sat quietly, nibbling on breadsticks and sipping at the rich red wine in its goldfish-bowl glass.

I was closer to him than I'd been for so many years, so close I thought I could smell his aftershave.

I was wrong about his dining companion. After a few moments, an older man, late fifties perhaps, was ushered across to his table. He rose to his feet and made a performance of greeting his guest, shaking hands and fussing as he sat. A business contact, then. He was titillated not by a woman but by the prospect of some business deal. I shrugged to myself. Either way, I could use it to my advantage.

I ordered soon after they did, apologising with a show of embarrassment to the waiter about the fact my date was starting to look like a no-show and choosing a mid-range pasta dish for myself. As I'd hoped, the waiter took pity on me. Perhaps he thought I'd been humiliated enough. He cleared away the second setting and served me attentively from then on.

I stole glances across at the man every chance I could. He wasn't handsome, but he had a certain monied style, I had to admit that. At that time of day, he had a peppering of stubble and his contemporary take on the pin-striped suit fell in just the right folds around his body. Made to measure, probably. Certainly expensive.

I stole a look at his shoes under the table. You can tell a lot about someone by their shoes. Very nice. Black leather with a decent shine. He caught me looking and for a moment our eyes met. I gave him a shy half-smile, flirting, then acted coy and turned my attention abruptly back to my wine.

Now and then, I checked my phone, trying to give my best impression of a young woman struggling to make the best of a disappointing evening.

Now and then, I slowly uncrossed my legs, then languorously re-crossed them, letting the slit in my dress fall open.

I knew he was watching.

Next time I glanced across, he was looking past his dinner

companion, right at me. He glanced quickly away. As he lifted his glass to his mouth, something flashed in the candlelight. The gold band of a wedding ring.

For a moment, it seemed a setback, then I recovered and smiled to myself. Perhaps that too was for the best.

It was much the same for the rest of the evening. He and his companion chatted, leaned back in their chairs and laughed as the wine flowed. It was clear that he was in charge of their meeting. He was the one who reached forward to top up their glasses when they needed refreshing, who motioned over the waiter once they'd finished their steaks and ordered desserts, then coffee and brandy.

I acted my heart out, flirting with the waiter, sighing disconsolately into my wine glass, eating delicately. Again and again, I glanced across at him, gradually prolonging eye contact, steadily appearing more bold.

Once I'd had coffee, I twisted around in my seat and gestured to the waiter that I was ready to pay.

As the waiter retrieved the paperwork and totted up my bill, I saw the man set down his napkin and scrape back his chair.

I rose quickly to my feet too and intercepted him in the shadows at the back of the restaurant, near the doors to the restrooms. 'Hello.'

He looked surprised, then smiled. 'Hello.' His teeth were white and even.

I ran a hand through my hair, trying to give him the impression I was a little drunk. 'I've been watching you,' I said.

He inclined his head. 'I know.'

'Really?' I lowered my eyes and blinked hard, all faked confusion.

'I've been watching you too.' He lowered his voice, leaning a little closer.

'Oh!' I lifted a hand and touched his shoulder, pretending to pick a speck of something from it. 'You know what I was thinking?'

He raised an eyebrow. 'I hardly dare guess. Why don't you tell me?'

I giggled. 'You sure you want to know?'

He nodded, his eyes roaming across my dress, my body.

I pressed closer to him and whispered: 'I was thinking, *I'd really like to get to know that man.* There! Are you terribly shocked?'

He gave me a knowing look. 'Not shocked. Flattered.'

'Good.' I swallowed hard and pretended to sway slightly, reached for the wall to steady myself. 'How about a nightcap then?' I glanced back at his table. His business associate was busy with his phone. 'We'd have to ditch your mate.'

'Easily done.' He nodded, thoughtful. 'There's a bar next door. We could meet there. In, say, ten minutes?'

I nodded, trying hard to look nervous but thrilled. I pointed to his ring. 'She won't mind?'

'Don't worry.' He gave me a cool look. 'She won't know.'

We could agree about that much at least.

23

LOTTE

I hung back in the dark doorway of the bar next door and watched him as he clapped his business associate on the shoulder and said hearty goodbyes.

He dallied on the street for a little longer after he'd gone, making sure his companion had disappeared from sight, swallowed up by the London night. Then he turned to me and smiled.

The bar was a Covent Garden secret for those in the know, advertised at street level only by a faded painted sign on a shabby door. He led the way down narrow, steep steps that descended into musty wine cellars. The walls of the vaults had been stripped back to reveal ancient brickwork, forming a series of low arches and columns. Piped music hummed in the background. The air carried the dank, dead smell of a crypt.

I blinked, trying to acclimatise in the gloom. It was impossible to see how many people were down there. The beer barrel seats and tables sank back into a succession of rounded hollows, making the cramped groups of drinkers almost invisible, one to another.

It struck me at once as seedy, almost decadent. Certainly, it was the perfect place for an illicit tryst. It was also clear from the way he guided me across the stone flagged floor, sticky with spilt beer, and handed me into a tiny round alcove, that he was a regular there. Whoever his wife was, I pitied her.

He disappeared to get drinks and I sat there, suddenly tense. I'd been so pleased with myself, riding high on the adrenalin of the chase. Now I felt uncertain. It had been too easy. Was I the one who had fallen into a trap? Had he recognised me, seen in my adult face the glimmer of the girl I'd once been, just as I'd seen the boy in his? I shuddered.

He reappeared, his sweaty face glistening where it caught faint, glancing light. He set down a bottle of red wine and two glasses and eased himself in beside me. His leg pressed, hot and hard, against mine.

'So,' he said, pouring us both generous measures and handing me a glass, 'here's to new beginnings.' He took a sip, then leaned in closer. The whites of his eyes gleamed. 'You looked rather sad and lonely, eating dinner all alone. I'm guessing someone stood you up?'

I nodded, trying to look dejected at the memory. 'You guessed right,' I lied. 'And that's the last time. He doesn't deserve me.'

'I'm sure he doesn't.' His breath was scented with wine as he kissed my cheek, then arched backwards and placed a second, sloppier kiss on my neck. A meaty hand planted itself on my thigh. 'Still, his loss, my gain.'

I felt myself stiffen, still wondering if he suspected who I really was.

I forced myself to cover his hand with mine, squeezing his sweaty fingers as if I were excited by his touch, rather than repulsed.

His eyes glistened with anticipation. This time, reading

him, I found it easy to return his smile. He hadn't the slightest idea that we'd met before. He had no sense of what I was planning for him.

'Oh, no,' I whispered. 'Trust me. The pleasure will be all mine.'

24

LOTTE

After that first mauling in the wine bar, I made sure that the next time we met, it was at lunchtime in a busy public place.

We strolled together along the South Bank, making small talk as we passed the busy restaurants, their diners spilling out onto the sidewalk terraces to catch one of the final sunny days of the year.

I made him pause and wait when we reached a second-hand-books stall. I rummaged through the wooden racks and tables and pretended to be engrossed, aware of his eyes on the nape of my neck, my breasts, his body twisting to check out my bottom.

It made my skin crawl, but I forced myself to smile up at him and shyly suggested that we tried to get something to eat at the café nearby.

I moved quickly to grab an outdoor table. No more dark corners. I didn't trust him.

As we ate our bowls of pasta and salad and sipped at glasses of red wine, we told each other more about ourselves. Or pretended to. I told him my name was Ellie. He told me his was Tony. They were both lies, of course. He lied easily and fluently. About where he'd grown up, where he'd been to school, even where he worked. I'd already confirmed that he was married but he didn't refer again to his wife or family. I'm sure he would have lied about that too if it had suited him. I sensed that he considered the spectre of a wife in the background to be useful, a safeguard to make sure I never misunderstood his intentions as anything other than dishonourable.

He was a serial adulterer, that soon became was clear. He knew all the tricks. He mentioned his club in Piccadilly, suggesting we might have lunch there another time. I smiled as if I were impressed. I'd heard of the place and was all too aware that it was standard practice for its members to arrange discreet access to a bedroom there for a few hours during the day.

I'd already bought with cash a cheap, pay-as-you-go mobile from a dodgy shop in Shepherd's Bush and made sure that was the only number I gave him. He had something similar. The more I watched him, the more I realised how practised he was at deceiving his wife.

The sense of secrecy, the game, seemed to amuse Tony. At the end of our lunch, he lunged for me, his mouth moist. I closed my eyes and tried not to think about Jon and how sad this soulless encounter would make him, if he knew. Instead, I fixed my mind on the leafy plants on my kitchen windowsill, already starting to flower, opening their delicate purple petals.

The tension grew as he paid. He seized my hand and drew me against the riverside wall, turning me to face outwards, towards the churning waters of the Thames. He pressed himself against me, pinning me there, and put his mouth on my neck. 'I want us to do more than eat and talk,' he whispered into my ear. 'Much more.'

I shivered, then took a deep breath and twisted round to face him, trapped in the prison of his arms. 'Me, too,' I said.

He seemed to mistake my flushed face and fast pulse for signs of passion, rather than nausea.

'Can I tell you what I'd really like?' I hesitated, trying to look shy. I lowered my voice to a whisper. 'There's something I've always wanted to do. A sort of' – I glanced up at him through my eyelashes – 'a sort of fantasy.'

His eyes glistened at once. 'You can tell me.'

'You won't be shocked?'

His smile broadened with anticipation. 'Don't worry. I'm very broad-minded.'

'Well,' I put a hand on his chest, holding him further away, 'you're sure you won't laugh at me?'

He pulled his face straight. 'Of course not.'

'OK.' I took a deep breath. 'So, this is what I like to imagine. There's an important businessman, rather like you—'

'Glad to hear it!'

'And he's booked a hotel room for himself – somewhere anonymous, you know. The kind of place where no one would notice who's coming and going.'

He considered. 'OK. So what happens?'

'Well, he lets himself into the room and takes off his clothes. Maybe he's thinking of taking a shower.'

'And?' He licked his lips.

'And there's a soft knock at the door and this perfect stranger's standing there. Me. I've just got the wrong room, you see. But then I see him and, well, I can't help myself. I decide to go on in.'

He laughed. 'I can see where this is going.'

'But they have to take their time, you know. Because they're strangers. That's the whole point. He's desperate for her—'

'Well, I would be!'

'But she needs winning round. She's never done anything like this before. See? Softly, softly. She's got some wine and they drink it together and talk and she's shy so she makes him wait until he's so damn hot for her, he can hardly bear it—'

'And then he pounces on her!' He laid one of his large, hot

hands on my breast, then squeezed it. 'That's your fantasy, eh? Well, my dear, maybe we'd better see if we can make it come true.'

'Really?' I blinked. 'You'd do that for me?'

'Oh, yes. My pleasure.'

'Mine too.' I gave him a naughty wink. 'But here's the thing. You have to do exactly as I say. Otherwise, it won't work.'

'You want to be in the driving seat?' He chuckled. 'I can live with that.'

I smiled and gave him a chaste kiss on the cheek before wriggling free. 'I'll text you when and where,' I said, then strode off, leaving him gazing after me.

I was telling the truth. It was my fantasy.

I just hadn't told him about the ending yet.

25

LOTTE

The following day, I texted him the name of a hotel.

I'd already scoped it out: a cheap, high-rise building with few staff. I told him to book a room in his name and text me the number.

When the time came, I made my preparations at home with care.

Then I took the tube to the hotel, a light scarf wrapped round the lower part of my face. No one gave me so much as a glance. I waited outside the grey building until I was sure the small lobby was empty, then entered, crept straight across to the stairwell and hurried up the stairs, making sure no one saw me. It was just after one. The corridor was empty.

I crept along it, tense, listening for footsteps. Nothing. I reached the door of his room and tapped on it.

He stood there, stark naked, his small eyes gleaming.

I played my part as well as I could, feigning astonishment: 'Oh, I'm so sorry! I must have the wrong room!' Then I tried to look coy, as if I'd only just caught sight of him in the flesh and added: 'But perhaps I'd better come in? If you don't mind, that is.'

I pulled two glasses from my bag and set them on the table, then drew out the bottle I'd brought, opened it and poured him some wine. It was full-bodied red; rich enough, I hoped, to disguise any bitterness.

All the time, I fed him some silly, girlish banter about how nervous I felt, how unexpected all this was and how handsome he looked.

I handed him the full glass. 'Please,' I said, 'you start with this. I just need a moment. You see, I've never done this before. I mean, not with a perfect stranger.'

He drank off the wine hungrily in several gulps, impatient, then lay back on the bed, his eyes never leaving mine.

'I'm almost ready,' I said, softly. 'But first, I need to go into the bathroom. Don't move, will you? I need to change into something special.'

He nodded, leering, eager to be surprised.

Once inside, I took a towel from my bag and used it to mask the click as I quietly locked the bathroom door. Then I crouched on the floor, my knees raised, the tiles cold and hard under my flesh. I pressed my fingers hard in my ears, trying to block out any sound that might come from the room.

My stomach heaved.

What if it doesn't work?

I imagined him blundering to the bathroom door and managing to wrench it open, furious and accusing. He could kill me if he tried. What if he cried for help? What if he screamed in pain? I couldn't bear to hear a sound. All I could hear was the hard thump of the blood in my head.

I sat there, hunched and frightened, and counted down the minutes. Five, ten, then twenty, thirty. I imagined him writhing on the sheets, vomiting, perhaps, or soiling himself. There was no phone in the room but maybe he'd reach his mobile and call for help. Maybe he'd manage to crawl to the door and be seen?

I waited until almost an hour had passed, then lifted my

hands from my head and dared to listen again. It was silent. I eased myself up from the floor, my body cold and cramped, and listened. Nothing. Slowly, fearfully, I eased open the door and peered out through the crack across the room.

My body was shaking, stiff with adrenalin. Maybe I'd failed and he was still alive. Maybe he'd realised all along who I was and known what I was planning.

I crept, step by step, into the bedroom.

He was lying back on the bed, his body twisted to one side, his contorted mouth open, his eyes glassy, gazing sightlessly towards the damp-stained ceiling. The empty glass lay on the floor at his side.

I whispered: 'Tony?'

Was he the one acting now? Or could the aconite really have worked, just as I'd hoped? I took a step closer. Every muscle twitched in my body. I imagined him suddenly jumping up from the bed, grabbing me by the throat, strangling me, saying *I know what you tried to do*.

Nothing. His chest glistened with sweat. His bare thighs were slumped lifelessly to one side. His chest was still and silent.

I didn't touch him. I couldn't. I poured the rest of the wine down the bathroom sink and let the water run for a while to clear all traces of it. Then I picked up both glasses and stowed them, with the wine bottle, back in my bag. I used my towel to clean off all the surfaces I might have touched: the bathroom door handle, the edge of the table, the side of the bath; then stuffed that back in my bag too. I found his burner phone, the only one with any trace of his messages to me, and pocketed it. I'd smash that into pieces later and scatter the bits in the river.

Before I left, I bent low beside him and put my mouth near his ear. 'You know who I really am?' I whispered.

He couldn't hear me. I knew that for certain now. He'd

already gone, already crossed the threshold from life into death. But it was something I needed to say, just the same.

'I'm little Charlotte,' I hissed. 'Remember me? Emma's sister.'

I needed him to know. I needed him to understand why he'd died. I wanted him to hear the truth, at last.

'This is just the start. Now, I'm going after HIM.'

26

LOTTE

I'd expected to feel triumphant once it was done.

I didn't.

The nearest I came to feeling anything was a dull spike of panic, mingled with fear.

Back at home, I swept up the stray particles of soil from the kitchen floor where, just hours earlier, I'd snipped the roots from my carefully cultivated pot plants and crushed them to a fine powder with a pestle and mortar, before adding them to the wine. The plants, repotted and watered, regarded me calmly from the sunny windowsill.

I scoured my fingernails, making sure they were clean, then made myself a coffee and sat in silence in the kitchen, thinking. I didn't think I'd made any mistakes. I didn't think there was anything to link him to me. I'd been careful.

But I was more guilty, more anxious, than I'd thought possible.

That evening and the following one, I put Caitlyn to bed and then waited alone in the darkness, listening for heavy footsteps and a knock at the door, for a stern-faced detective ready to accuse and interrogate me.

They never came. As the days passed and became weeks, the choking anxiety started slowly to ease its grip. I googled his name often and eventually found a short death notice.

Died suddenly from natural causes. That's all it said about the way he'd died. The aconite had worked its magic perfectly. His massive heart attack must have looked utterly convincing. It must just have seemed like the price a podgy middle-aged man could expect to pay for a diet of work stress, too much steak and alcohol, and too little exercise.

I've got away with it.

I wanted to celebrate but, inside, all I felt was numb.

I thought of his white, twisted body on the sheets. In my determination to kill him, I'd given him a hefty dose and he'd died more quickly that I'd expected. I found myself wanting the chance to do it again but, this time, to make him suffer. I wanted to look him in the eye as he was dying and see remorse there, or, if he was incapable of that, at least to see some real under-standing of who I was and why his life was being cut short.

I'd succeeded in ending his life, but I hadn't ruined it; the way the two of them had ruined mine. It wasn't enough.

I found too, as I brooded about what had happened, that I needed to know more about him. I wondered about his wife and how much she knew about his philandering. Clearly, his liaison with me hadn't been his first flirtation with adultery. I imagined angry scenes as she confronted him, screaming that she was leaving him, that she'd ruin him. It was the kind of reckoning he'd deserved.

But that hadn't happened. Instead, he'd died without those sordid secrets being spilled.

Beloved husband, father and brother, the death notice had said.

The words made me feel physically sick. Even in death, he'd escaped me. The world had been left with no idea of the monster he was.

I thought I'd feel powerful, liberated by what I'd done. Instead, all I felt was cheated and dissatisfied.

I fell easily back into drinking. I gazed often at the battered photograph of me with my sister, at the dappled light falling through the trees and striping her shy face.

I'd failed her again.

Next time, I promised her. *Next time, I'll get it right.*

27

ROS

The more Ros thought about it, the less she wanted that woman in her house.

Maybe she should just call the whole thing off.

'You can't do that!' Diana looked horrified when Ros broached the subject as they walked away from the gates after drop-off the next day. 'Why?'

She looked thoughtful when Ros explained about the job.

'And Adam's going ahead with it, is he?'

Ros nodded. 'He won't listen. I've told him I don't trust her. He thinks I'm being ridiculous.'

Diana didn't answer for a moment. They slowed their pace as they set off down the cobbled alleyway. 'Maybe he thinks it's him you don't trust?'

Ros paused, glanced sideways at her. 'Him?'

Diana shrugged. 'You've got to admit, she's pretty hot. She's in great shape. She's single. And she's young. Younger than you and me.'

'Not much younger.' Ros felt stung. 'How old do you think she is?'

Diana shrugged. 'Mid-thirties?' Diana had turned forty

earlier in the year and it clearly still bothered her. She was always dropping hints about Ros's own 'big birthday' coming up next year.

Ros shook her head. 'Anyway, that's ridiculous. Adam knows me better than that.'

They reached the end of the alley and stood on the corner, before they went their separate ways.

'You know what?' Diana looked thoughtful. 'It really is too late to cancel now. No, listen.' She raised her hand to stop Ros from interrupting. 'If you do, it'll be obvious why. Adam'll be furious. Right? He'll think you're being rude, for one thing, and he'll assume you're punishing him. You'd be denying him the chance to catch up with Phil too which, I can tell you for nothing, Phil's really looking forward to. And I bet Adam is as well.'

Ros hesitated. 'Maybe you, Phil and the kids could come over on your own?'

Diana pulled a face. 'Right. When she's living round the corner. What if she sees us? Then whatever feeble excuse you've made will be revealed for what it is, an out and out lie. No, you need to do this, Ros. However you feel about her, just be the bigger person. You don't ever have to ask her again, if you don't want to. See? And who knows, maybe you'll actually enjoy it.'

'You think so?'

'I do.' Diana put a hand on her shoulder and squeezed it. 'I'll be there. I've told you, I quite like her. And her daughter.'

Ros sighed. 'I'd rather not.'

'I know. But you've got to. Pull out now and you'll make matters worse.' Diana took a step away, preparing to leave. 'You can do this, girlfriend. Stand firm.'

At the other end of the spectrum, Sophie and Bella had kicked up a fuss when Ros told them the plans.

'Bella, I know you're not exactly best friends with Caitlyn,' she started, as she brought their sandwiches through to them. Sophie had done her homework and Bella had done her reading practice, sounding out a few simple words with Ros, and the girls were settling down to watch CBeebies on the iPad. 'But we ought to make an effort. It must be hard, being new. They don't know anyone here.'

Two faces looked up at their mother at once.

Sophie's eyes were sharp. 'We are NOT having them to tea,' she said, sticking out her chin. 'NO, Mummy.'

Ros sighed. 'That's not very kind, Sophie.'

Sophie rolled her eyes.

Bella picked up her cream cheese and ham sandwich with both hands and considered it. 'Do we have to?'

Ros said, firmly: 'I think we should. She invited us to her house.'

'Yes, and it was AWFUL,' Sophie said at once.

Ros pursed her lips. 'It wasn't that bad—' she began.

'It WAS!' Sophie glared.

Bella took a nibble of the bread and swallowed. 'If she comes, can we have pizza?'

'Sure.' Ros sensed progress. 'And ice-cream?'

Bella beamed. 'Ice-cream!'

Ros focused on Sophie. 'I've asked Posy, as well. So you've got someone your own age.' She turned back to Bella, coaxing. 'And Max. You like Max, don't you?'

Bella shrugged.

Sophie reached for the iPad and opened the app, then scrolled through to the programme they'd agreed to watch together and chose an episode. 'There's no point arguing, is there?' Sophie said over her shoulder. 'I mean, you've already invited them, haven't you?'

'That's not fair, Sophie.' Ros frowned. 'And not very polite.' Even if it was true.

Bella said: 'If we're nice, can we have chocolate ice-cream with bits in?'

'Maybe.' Ros hesitated. 'If you're really nice.'

She stood for a moment, looking at the two dark heads pressed close together, large and small, already lost to their programme. Her heart throbbed in her chest.

Sophie gave a sudden snort of laughter. A moment later, Bella started giggling. She still had a little girl's laugh, high-pitched and heart-achingly innocent.

28

ROS

On Friday, the three mothers, Ros, Diana and Lotte, walked the children home together after school.

Posy and Sophie paired up at once and ran ahead as a whispering, giggling twosome, skipping up and down doorsteps along the street and playing hopscotch down the flags. Max and Bella hung by their mothers' sides, holding hands. Caitlyn trailed along on her own, her shoulders slumped, her eyes lowered to the sidewalk.

'So, tell me, how are you doing?' Diana was all smiles, chatting to Lotte as if she were an old friend. 'How are you settling in?'

The conversation stayed light, sustained by Diana's eager questions. Ros kept silent. She noted that Lotte made no mention of her new job. Perhaps she wasn't sure if Diana already knew. Perhaps she realised it might be a sensitive subject.

Once they arrived home, Ros shooed the children into the sitting room where she'd set out some baskets of the girls' toys, then joined the other women in the kitchen. Diana had already put the kettle on for tea.

Ros made them drinks and set out the fancy biscuits Diana had bought: chocolate shortbreads for the adults and iced gingerbread figures for the kids. She turned her back to the others to focus on cooking, estimating what quantities she'd need for five children.

Diana led Lotte over to the kitchen window and spent a few minutes confirming which building formed the back of Lotte's apartment. They breezily identified her lounge window which, Ros knew too well, stared straight back at them.

'I love the view from the front, over the park and the river,' Lotte was saying. 'Such a change from the grimy rooftops we looked out at in London.'

Ros stole a quick glance at the two of them as she unwrapped the pizzas. Lotte was gesturing theatrically with her hands as she chatted to Diana about how much she loved the moors, saying everyone was so friendly here, so warm. Ros frowned to herself as she arranged the pizzas on the top shelf of the oven. There was something about it all that just didn't ring true.

Once the pizzas were in, Ros popped through to the lounge to check on the children.

'Everything OK, guys?'

Posy and Sophie were being kind, she could see, patiently indulging the younger ones. They were helping Max and Bella build houses out of Lego, complete with windows, doors and garden. Ros watched Sophie bend forward over the box of bricks, scrabbling through them as she searched for a particular piece Max wanted. Sophie could be so big-hearted at times. It made the angry outbursts all the more baffling.

Ros's eyes fell finally on Caitlyn. She was sitting separately, to one side. A few dolls were scattered on the carpet in front of her, but she didn't seem to be playing with them. Her body was still and wary and she was silently observing the others. The look on her face was vague, as if her mind was divided: part present in the room and part elsewhere.

'We're here if you need us,' Ros said to the room.

None of them so much as looked up as she left and headed back to the kitchen.

'And how's Caitlyn settling in?' Diana was asking Lotte. 'It's a big change for her, isn't it? New part of the country, starting school.'

'OK, I think. You're right. It is a big change.' Lotte slipped down from her stool. 'Do you mind if I—?' She gestured vaguely down the hall.

Ros nodded. 'Of course! It's just through there, on the right.'

Lotte disappeared. A moment later, Ros heard her padding up the stairs, then the creak of footsteps overhead, crossing the landing. She frowned to herself, busy clearing the kitchen table. It sounded as if Lotte had gone upstairs, instead of using the downstairs toilet.

Diana nodded meaningfully at the doorway and lowered her voice. 'You doing OK?'

'Fine.' Ros managed a smile. 'Glad you're here.'

'She's good company,' Diana said.

Ros checked on the pizzas. The pungent smell of melting cheese wafted through the kitchen.

'What time's Adam coming home?'

Ros checked the clock. It was almost half past four. 'In about an hour—?'

Diana nodded. 'Phil should be here around then too. As long as they don't cancel his train again.' She rolled her eyes. 'I've been meaning to ask you, how're you getting on with wooing local businesses? Did you get any response to your emails?'

'Some.' Ros tried to sound upbeat, but was still dismayed by how few companies had replied. She didn't understand it. Many of them were companies she'd worked with in the past and she thought they'd established a good rapport. Several of those who had replied had given her a polite but chilly brush-off. 'I'm seeing White's next Friday. At their head office in Guiseley.'

'The garden centre people?'

Ros nodded. 'They're opening a new store in Shipley in the spring, according to their website. That'll be a fair few jobs.'

Diana gave her a thumbs-up. 'See! Perfect timing. Get in at the ground floor.'

'Fingers crossed.' Ros didn't say anything more. She didn't want to jinx it. She knew she was already pinning too much hope on the meeting. She really needed a break and there was little sign of one anywhere else. 'I was meaning to ask you, actually.' She reached into the cupboard for plates. 'Any chance you could have the girls for an hour or two after school? Just if I'm caught in traffic and late back.'

'Friday?' Diana considered. 'Sure.'

'Thanks. I'll owe you.' Ros checked again on the pizzas. 'Right. Nearly there.'

Diana jumped up. 'Want me to set the table?'

'I'll do that.' Ros was already opening a drawer and counting out cutlery. 'Would you go and check on the kids for me? They can carry on playing for another five or ten minutes, then it'll be time to come through and eat.'

'No problem.'

A moment after Diana set off down the hallway, Lotte reappeared. Ros heard the soft click of the kitchen door being closed and turned quickly from the oven.

Lotte was gazing right at her, her look intense. Ros felt a jolt of panic. With the door shut, she felt suddenly trapped.

'You OK?' Ros blinked. She felt blindsided in her own kitchen.

Lotte didn't answer. She came across and placed her hands firmly on the counter as if she were taking strength from it, then started to speak, softly and quickly, as if she knew they didn't have much time but needed to have her say.

'Look, I know it's awkward, but I can't stop thinking about it.'

'About what?' Ros turned back to the oven, pretending to busy herself with the pizzas.

'You know.' Lotte took a deep breath. 'Look, I get it. I know you're trying to avoid me. You're scared, aren't you? About what you told me in Spain?' She hesitated. 'I bet not even Diana knows, does she?'

Ros felt herself flush. 'I don't know what—'

'Oh, come on.' Lotte sounded impatient. 'You wish you'd never told me. Right? But it's a bit late for that. The fact is you did.'

Ros tried to laugh but the sound came out as shrill and unnatural. 'I don't know what I said that night. I doubt I made any sense at all, I was so drunk. Whatever you think I might have—'

'Well, I'll refresh your memory, if you like. Remind you what you thought you heard through that open window. Shall I?'

There was a steeliness about Lotte that took Ros by surprise. A hardness that made her shut up and listen. Lotte was making a point: she remembered exactly what Ros had told her and there was no point denying it.

'I was wrong, though.' Ros squirmed, hot with embarrassment. 'I was half-asleep. I really—'

Ros felt Lotte's eyes boring into her. The memory of it all came back to her, sharp and painful. It was that disastrous weekend, the one she'd suggested because she'd felt so happy, pregnant with Sophie. She'd longed for Adam and his brother to be reconciled, to be close again, as brothers should be.

She hadn't meant to listen. She couldn't help overhearing. Charles had such a loud voice, and it had been hot that evening. She'd been lying awake on top of the bedcover with the window open, in the hope of some air. The men were right beneath the bedroom window, alone on the patio with their after-dinner whiskies. It wasn't fair of Adam to accuse her of spying.

She closed her eyes and the angry exchange she'd thought she'd heard came back to her. In all these years, it had never really left her.

Now, Lotte jumped in, interrupting her thoughts. 'They said you were paranoid, didn't they? That you were imagining things.'

Ros couldn't look Lotte in the eye, couldn't speak.

She *had* told Lotte then, just as she'd feared. She'd told her everything.

'They made you think you were the one to blame,' Lotte ran on, relentlessly. 'That you'd caused a fresh rift between them, with your suspicions and accusations and paranoia. You told me that that's why you feel so guilty, now Charles has died. You think Adam's grief is so much worse because they were estranged. And that that was your fault.'

Ros said miserably: 'It *was* my fault. If I'd only shut the window and gone to sleep, like I said I was going to, instead of going down there and interfering... I wasn't getting much sleep, you see. I was too sick, with the pregnancy. A hormonal mess, that's what Adam called me.'

'But what if you weren't being paranoid?' Lotte pressed closer to Ros, making her want to move away. 'Don't you remember what I said, when you told me in Spain? What if you really did hear those things? What if it were all true?'

Ros shook her head frantically. 'But it's not. I trust Adam. You don't know him the way I do. He was right. They both were. I was dreaming, imagining things. They were just arguing about nothing, about football. They said so.'

The kitchen door flew open. 'You two alright in here?'

Diana, standing there, stared from one to the other. 'Am I interrupting something?'

Ros, released, jumped into action. 'Not at all.' She reached for the plates, keeping her face hidden from them both. 'I just closed the door while I was cooking, that's all. I didn't want to set off the smoke alarm.'

Lotte moved across the kitchen to the window and stood with her back to them.

Diana, clearly not convinced, persisted. 'Ros? You're sure you're OK?'

'Totally!' Ros, pulling the pizzas out of the oven, started to burble. 'Tea's ready. I was just going to call. Would you bring the kids in, please? That would be great.'

For a moment, both Diana and Lotte seemed frozen where they stood. Ros, her hands clumsy, sent a knife skidding across the counter and swore under her breath. She looked up and said again to Diana, her voice sharp now: 'Please? If you could get the kids in?'

Diana raised an eyebrow, then shrugged and set off down the hallway, calling to the children that tea was ready.

Left briefly alone again, Lotte turned back to look across at Ros. She didn't speak but the intensity of her gaze was chilling. It was a hard, knowing look, as if something significant has passed between them which couldn't now be undone. As if they both knew that a line had just been crossed and, now that they were on the other side of it, there was no going back.

29

ROS

From then on, Ros could hardly speak.

Diana came to the rescue. As the children ate, she filled the strained silence in the kitchen by keeping up a flow of inane chat, pretending to be unaware of the atmosphere. Almost immediately afterwards, Lotte announced that she and Caitlyn had to leave. Diana was the one who hunted out their coats and said cheerful goodbyes.

Diana ushered the remaining children into the lounge and put on a film for them while Ros set about clearing up the kitchen.

By the time Phil and Adam had joined them, standing with beers and chatting companionably together by the window, Ros felt as if her heart rate was finally starting to settle back to something near normal.

The large glass of white wine, which she'd already almost finished, also helped.

Her head was bursting. *You just need to get through the next hour or so,* she told herself. Act as normally as she could with Diana and Phil, then get the girls to bed. After that, she'd make some excuse to Adam and go upstairs where she could be alone and think.

'What was all that about?' Diana, topping up both their glasses again, kept her voice low.

'What?'

Diana gave her an incredulous look. 'Whatever was going down between you and Lotte. You looked as if you were about to have a heart attack when I walked in on you both.'

Ros shook her head, averting her eyes. 'Nothing.' She took a swig of wine, thinking fast. 'I just don't trust her, that's all.'

'But what did she say? Come on, you can tell me.'

Ros managed a strained smile. 'Nothing, honestly. She's just, you know, a bit much. In-your-face. I don't need that. I've got enough going on, right now.'

'I'm sorry.' Diana nodded. 'You are doing great, though. I hope you know that.'

They fell silent, Ros focusing on her wine, aware of Diana's eyes on her.

Phil's voice cut through the quiet. 'Thought about you last week,' he was saying to Adam. 'It was Charlie's birthday, wasn't it?'

Ros looked across at once. She saw Adam's forehead crease.

'Yeah, the twenty-first. He'd have been forty-five. No age, is it?'

'You're telling me.' Phil looked gloomily at his feet. 'Makes you think. Doesn't seem five minutes since we were all lads, hanging around outside The Fleece, trying to get one of the dads to buy us a pint.'

Adam nodded, forced a grin. 'And they never did, rotten lot. Remember George Dartford promising he'd see us right and then coming out with a bag of cheese and onion potato chips? Charlie was so insulted, I don't think he ever forgave him.'

They both laughed, tipping back their bottles and drinking off some beer.

Phil looked around, caught Ros's eye and said cheerily: 'How's business, Missus Entrepreneur?' He winked at Adam. 'Smart move, mate. You'll be rolling in it once she gets that business off the ground. Honestly, running a new start-up and still collecting the kids. I wish my wife had it in her.'

Ros saw Diana's expression stiffen as her friend twisted away, heading across to the kitchen counter to help herself to another tortilla chip. 'I'm sure she has,' Ros said, embarrassed. 'In fact, I bet she'd do a better job than I'm doing at the moment.'

She was about to say more but Adam gave her a warning glare over Phil's shoulder. He hated her to sound negative about the business, even with friends. Image was everything.

Ros held her tongue. Diana returned and handed around the bowl of chips. Ros didn't know whether to say something to her about Phil's crass comment. She couldn't find the words.

Instead, the two of them stood awkwardly, side by side, as the men turned back to each other and picked up the thread of their earlier conversation. They'd known each other a long time. Most of their chat was about old mates from school, people on the periphery of their lives, many of whom even Ros didn't know.

After a while, Phil asked: 'How's your mum and dad doing?'

Adam shrugged. 'Not too bad. Struggling a bit since, you know, since the funeral.'

Diana leaned into Ros and whispered: 'It really shook Phil, you know. The news about Charles. He still talks about it. I suppose Charles was the first one in their crowd to...' she hesitated, checking Ros's expression before adding delicately, 'to pass.'

'I know.' Ros swallowed hard. She thought about Lotte and the hard look on her face as she'd stood too close, pinning Ros to the wall with her voice.

Ros couldn't keep pretending to herself that she hadn't told

Lotte everything. Her fears had been true. But why had Lotte cornered her like that? Why had she said all that about Ros not being to blame after all, that evening? About what she'd imagined she'd heard being true?

What was she up to?

'Anyway,' Diana said, sipping again at her wine, 'it's a reminder to all of us to live every day, isn't it? Live every day as if it might be your last.'

Ros looked again at her husband, his head bent slightly towards his old friend, the toe of his shoe gently scuffing the tiled floor as he listened to Phil.

That's it, though, she thought. That was exactly how she was living right then – just not in the way Diana meant. In fact, it was how she'd been living ever since Lotte had moved into number 5, Ros realised.

As if catastrophe might be just around the corner and coming right for them.

30

ROS

All weekend, the relationship between Adam and Ros was strained.

Adam still seemed mad about Ros's reaction to his decision to hire Lotte. Ros was preoccupied, shaken now that she knew for certain that she had indeed disclosed their secret to Lotte. She was anxious about what Lotte might do next.

On Saturday, Ros struggled to behave normally with the girls, walking them to and from various sport and art classes, practising reading with Bella and helping Sophie in the struggle to learn her weekly spellings for the coming test.

In the evening, when she went up to the study to log on and put in some time on social media, she found Adam had printed off paperwork about Lotte's job and emailed her to show he'd transfer the finder's fee for Lotte, as promised, from the practice account to hers. Clearly, he didn't want to discuss it any further and she didn't mention it either, just filed it away in her accounts.

On Sunday, Adam disappeared to the golf club to play a round with his friends there, taking advantage of one of the last crisp, chill days before the fall rains came.

Sophie curled up with a book in the sitting room while Ros baked chocolate chip muffins with Bella. In the final stages – once the mixture was in the oven and it was time to lick the bowls – Sophie set her book aside and appeared in the kitchen to help.

She and Bella agreed on a wooden spoon each, then loudly negotiated a fair line down the centre of the mixing bowl, dividing into equal and opposite territories. They kneeled up on the kitchen chairs, just as they had since they were toddlers, each poking an index finger around to wipe clean their own half.

At the sink, Ros paused and watched them. The mixture always went everywhere with those two. Soon, the skin around their lips, their cheeks, the tips of their noses, was smeared with cocoa-coloured splodges and, when the bowl was empty, they fell instead to giggling at each other.

'Honestly, look at the pair of you!' Ros found herself smiling too, then, with a sudden swoop, gathered the girls to her in a fierce hug as her mouth wobbled and she realised she was in danger of tipping over into tears.

When Monday came around, knowing it was Lotte's first day of work, Ros tried to bury herself in work.

She *knew* it took time to establish a business. She *knew* times were hard just then, especially for the small and medium enterprises she was targeting as clients. It was understandable that not many were in a position to hire new staff.

Even so, she just didn't understand why so few of the companies she was approaching were replying to her or, even if they did, turning down her attempt to make an appointment to go in to see them.

Dismally, she checked over the income she'd had from the business in the last quarter. She'd deliberately kept her overheads as low as possible but, even so, the income didn't cover them. The stark reality of the numbers frightened her. If she carried on operating at a loss like this, she didn't see how she could justify carrying on beyond the end of the financial year.

Now and then, her thoughts strayed to Lotte. She imagined her behind the reception desk in Adam's practice, smiling and confident, taking charge of the place. Ros shook her head. Why had she gone after that job? When Ros thought about the power Lotte wielded over them, about how much she knew, it physically sickened her.

That evening, Adam didn't say a word about Lotte when he came home. Ros was too proud to ask.

Ros's first feedback came from Diana on Wednesday morning, when the two of them coincided at drop-off. Once they'd kissed their children and sent them, arms wheeling, across the playground to start their day, they fell into step as they walked away.

'So,' Diana said quietly, 'how's Lotte doing? What's the verdict from Adam?'

Ros said miserably: 'Hasn't said a word.'

'Really?' Diana raised an eyebrow, looking Ros over. 'Is he still mad at you?'

Ros shrugged. 'Apparently.'

Diana tutted. 'Don't worry. It'll blow over. Always does.' She paused and Ros felt her friend searching for the right words. 'She is good, you know. Maybe he's right.'

Ros pursed her lips. She didn't want to know.

Diana went on: 'I went in to see Adam yesterday afternoon for my shoulder.' She pulled her arm back as if she were preparing to launch herself into an imaginary tennis serve. 'Much better, by the way. Anyway, Lotte was there. She's super-efficient. That last one was always getting her times muddled. Drove me mad.'

They reached the end of the alleyway.

Ros didn't pause to talk any further, just said abruptly, 'Gotta dash. Great to see you.'

Diana looked surprised. 'Sure. You, too.' She reached out and patted Ros on the arm as she turned to leave. 'You take care of yourself, alright?'

31

ROS

Ros knew as soon as Adam walked through the door that evening, that something was wrong.

It wasn't the fact he was so unusually late – with not so much as a text to warn her. It wasn't the fact he didn't answer when she came to the kitchen doorway and shouted a cheery 'Hi, there!' down the hall.

It was the heaviness of the weight on his shoulders as he wearily closed the front door behind him and hung up his coat. Usually, he was an active man who carried himself well. Now, he stooped under some unknown sorrow, prematurely aged.

Ros saw his elderly father in him. That was what made her breath catch in her throat.

She went back into the kitchen to stir the spaghetti sauce. Her stomach clenched and chilled. She had a sudden need to call out to him, to tell him to stay where he was, not to come a step nearer. Whatever it was, part of her didn't want to know. She sensed, even then, that their lives were about to change.

She realised too, in that same instant, how much she loved their life together, with all its flaws and imperfections. Despite the fact she was worried sick about Sophie and her violent outbursts. Despite the utter exhaustion of running on their hamster wheel, of keeping it all together. Despite the lingering, unspoken resentment about Charles, which had clawed at their marriage for so many years. She had never loved their life together so intensely as now, when she felt in danger of losing it.

Adam's tread was slow and heavy along the hall. She stood there, doggedly stirring the sauce as if it was a spell that could protect them, sickened by the rich smells of tomatoes and onions and peppers.

He stood there on the threshold, this broken man, unable to look her in the eye.

She took a deep breath. 'What's wrong?'

He shook his head. For a moment, he looked as if he were frowning. Then his mouth gave way and he started to cry.

Shocked, Ros switched off the gas and went to him, put her arms around his shoulders, drew him down to her and pulled his head against her neck. He smelled of the car and of the world outside. His breath smelled stale, of beer.

'What?' she said again. 'What's happened? Adam, tell me.'

He started to sob, wetting the shoulder of her blouse. He didn't cry easily, like Sophie or Bella. They gushed tears. His crying was dry and jagged and hard. She stood there, holding him upright, murmuring to him and slowly stroking his hair as if he were a boy again.

Finally, she led him through into the living room. She pulled him down beside her on the sofa, the two of them sitting side by side. Thank goodness he was late home. Thank goodness the children were already settled up in their bedrooms, Sophie reading and Bella asleep.

She pulled a tissue from her pocket, crumpled but clean, and forced him to sit up, away from her, while she mopped off his red face.

'Please.' She took his hot hands in hers and pressed them.

She prepared herself for the news, bracing her body to bear it, as if it were a punch. 'What is it?'

He shook his head, blew out his cheeks, kept his eyes on the carpet, unable to look at her.

Her heart pounded. She thought wild thoughts: *My god, this is it. He's leaving me. He's gay. He's got terminal cancer. He's...*

'Just tell me. For god's sake.' It came out more aggressively than either of them expected but she needed this to end. She could only take so much.

'She's gone to the police.'

'Who has?' Something slotted into place even as she asked. She knew exactly who.

'Lotte. She's made an allegation against me.'

'An allegation?' Her insides roiled, even as she struggled to understand.

'She says I tried to' – he faltered, seemed about to break down again into tears, then swallowed hard and pulled himself back from the edge – 'force myself on her.'

'What?'

The clock interrupted, chiming eight o'clock. Some cog inside Ros's brain steadily counted them off. Eight, yes. She was grateful to it. There was still some order in their world, after all.

'She didn't come in today. I didn't think much of it. She was perfectly normal yesterday. I thought she must be ill or running late or something. Sam and I both did. It was a nuisance – no one to answer the phones or see people in – but we managed, between us, you know.'

Ros sat quietly, cradling his hands, waiting.

'At lunchtime, Sam tried to give her a call to check in with her, but she wasn't picking up. We thought maybe food poisoning or a migraine, something acute. We were worried. Then about five, just before I saw my last patient, Sam came in to see me and said he'd got a call from the police.'

'Why?'

He struggled to stay calm. 'They said they wanted to speak to him, away from the practice. He didn't know why, at that point.'

Ros shook her head. It was nonsense, all of it. It made no sense.

'He said he'd give me a call when he came out, just to let me know what was going on. I was thinking maybe it was to do with finances – you know. That Sam had made some screw-up with the accounting.'

'So did he call you?'

'He came back to the office to warn me. I don't think he's even supposed to talk to me, but he did.'

'Of course he did.' The two of them had been partners for years. 'What did he say?'

'That she'd gone to the police. She'd told them I assaulted her, touched her—' He stumbled, reddened: he was always embarrassed about anything to do with sex, he didn't like to talk about it, even with Ros. He was the most unlikely predator she could imagine. Which made it all the more absurd. 'She said I groped her. That I tried to pull her clothes off, to force her to...'

He couldn't say any more. He didn't really need to. She got the picture.

'That's ridiculous.' Ros shook her head. Her fear was turning rapidly to anger. She knew Adam. He was a total gentleman. He'd never do such a thing. 'Go and see them. Tell them it's nonsense.'

Adam seemed to be shrinking into himself. She squeezed his hands more tightly.

'I know,' he whispered. 'I know it is. But—'

'But what?'

'What if they don't believe me?' He looked anguished. 'It's her word against mine. You know what it's like now, all this #MeToo stuff.' He lifted a hand quickly. 'I support it. You know

I do. That's how it should be. But people assume the worst. They'll say, "No smoke without fire. Why would she go to the police if nothing happened?"'

Ros frowned. 'Isn't there any way you can prove you're telling the truth?'

'How?' He shook his head. 'She says it all happened in my treatment room. No one else was in. It was late on Tuesday, apparently. Sam had stepped out to get a coffee.'

She nodded, slowly. 'So there aren't any cameras in there?'

'No. Privacy issues.' He hesitated. 'I don't know what to do. Sam says he'll stand by me. But I'm not sure that's enough. Anyway, that's why I'm so late.' He raised his eyes to her sheepishly. 'I'm so sorry.'

'You've nothing to be sorry about.'

They sat for a while in silence, clinging to each other's hands. Finally, Ros said: 'Did Sam say anything else?'

Adam took a shaky breath. 'He thinks I should get a lawyer.'

'A lawyer?'

'Just to cover myself.'

'Oh.' It was real. A lawyer? *What will that cost?*

'He said maybe I should take some gardening leave. You know, lie low until it's all over.'

'Lie low?' She was indignant on Adam's behalf. 'Why should you?'

Adam started to shake. 'Once it gets out, well, what if people don't believe me? It's a small town. Half my clients are women. I'm finished.'

'Don't say that. You've done nothing wrong. We'll fight this, Adam. We will. We'll win.' Ros thought about the way they'd been the last few days, cool and brittle with each other, slow to make peace. It all seemed so petty. She felt sick. Her instincts had been right. *If only he'd listened. If only he hadn't taken that woman on.*

She thought about Lotte, the way she behaved at times, as if she were acting a part. Had she performed for the police? Trembling lips, watery eyes, as if she were traumatised but bravely trying to keep herself together. *Lies, all lies.*

'I tried to warn you about her, Adam.'

Adam blinked at her. His eyes were red.

Ros remembered, piecing it all together. 'She asked me about your practice, when I was at her place with the girls. She can't have known about the job then. But she said she'd go in to see you, get treatment for her neck. She must have been fishing, even then. I guess she heard about the vacancy when she was at the practice.'

Adam's expression shifted, hardened. 'No, Ros. Please. Don't start that again.'

She shook her head. 'But what if it's true? What if that's why she came here in the first place, to target us? Can't you see?'

'That's crazy.' Adam threw up his hands. 'Just stop it, for God's sake!'

He stormed out of the room, leaving Ros sitting alone in the silence.

32

ROS

Ros stood in front of the freshly painted front door of number 5, looking at the two buzzers:

Apartment 1

Apartment 2

Blood hammered in her ears. She tried to take a deep breath but the effort made her chest ache. It had seemed so easy, so obvious when she'd grabbed her coat and headed out of the house and just around the corner. Now, standing there, she felt suddenly lost.

She thought about Adam and the burden he'd carried as he came home, weighed down by the knowledge of the news he had to share. She imagined his shock when his mate, Sam, sat him down, hours earlier, put a beer in his hand and told him what had happened with the police. He'd risked a lot, doing that.

She saw again the panic and fear in Adam's face as he struggled to tell her what had happened. He didn't deserve this. He was a decent, kind person. He worked hard, he always had. He was devoted to his girls. He was devoted to her.

She thought about the day they'd married. He'd been so

sweet, almost bashful. He'd turned to look at her as she walked up the aisle on her dad's arm. She'd been slimmer then, and prettier. She'd felt so proud of herself in that amazing dress, the one that had cost her a small fortune but that, once she saw it, with its full satin skirts and tiny pearls, she knew she just had to have. She'd seen his eyes widen. His face was too tense to smile but he'd mouthed: *Wow!* As if he could see how amazing she was, not just in that dress but in herself, as if he was dazed by the fact the two of them had somehow made the strange journey from meeting to dating to coming to this church to marry, in front of all these people who made up the fabric of their lives.

She'd taken those vows seriously, every one, and she knew he had too. Things might not be perfect. She'd admit that. They weren't newlyweds anymore. They didn't have the energy. They didn't go out together often enough, as a couple. Babysitters were so expensive. Most nights, she went to bed and fell asleep before he joined her there. She couldn't help it. She was just too tired.

But even so, he'd never try to take advantage of another woman, never in a million years. Never. He was her husband. She knew him.

She lifted her finger and pressed the buzzer for Apartment 2.

Lotte was standing at the door of the apartment, waiting, as Ros came up the stairs.

She said, 'You heard then?'

Ros said, 'What do you think?'

Lotte held the door open and Ros strode in, headed for the kitchen. Caitlyn would be asleep in her room at the other end of the apartment. The place was silent.

Lotte leaned back against the kitchen counter and folded her arms across her chest. 'I take it you've got something to say?'

Ros thought: *If we were men, I'd punch you.* Suddenly she wondered if this was how Sophie had been feeling these past few months. But she wasn't a man and she'd never hit anyone in her life. Although she was taut with fury, it was all packed hard inside her and she didn't know how to go about being violent, even if she'd wanted to let it out.

'Why did you say that? About Adam. You know it isn't true.'

Lotte raised an eyebrow. 'How do you know it isn't?'

'Because I know my husband.' Ros glared at Lotte's tight-lipped face. 'And I can see what sort of person you are.'

'Pardon?'

Ros took a stuttering breath. 'All that stuff you said when we met on vacation. Our so-called casual chats. Asking me so shyly if I'd come out for a drink for you because you were all alone. You played me.'

Lotte glared at Ros. Her face was closed, as if she were in the witness box, facing a hostile barrister. 'I don't know what you're talking about.'

Ros nodded. 'Yes, you do.' She paused, her eyes searching for the smallest flicker of reaction in Lotte's face. 'You planned this, didn't you? How far back does it go?' Her mind was whirling. 'How did you do it, exactly?'

She thought of the online chats she'd taken part in during the spring, chats on Ilkley group sites. Everyone had been sharing tips about where to go in the summer, comparing notes on decent packages out of Leeds Bradford airport and recommending some of the most family-friendly vacations overseas. She narrowed her eyes. 'Was that you?'

'What?'

Ros strained to remember more from all those months ago. She'd looked at the Majorca vacation in the first place because another mum on the chat had raved about it. It seemed just what they wanted. It hadn't been a username she'd recognised; just one of the local army of friendly mums who put information out there. Now, glaring at Lotte, she said, 'Was that you, on the Ilkley chat? Pushing the link to that vacation under my nose?'

Lotte pulled a face. 'Don't be ridiculous.'

Ros shook her head. What was it about this woman? Why did she find it so hard to believe her?

'Did you set me up?' She was talking softly, almost to herself, scrabbling to understand. 'Right from the start? Did you?' She hesitated. 'But why?'

The silence lay heavy between them. Outside, somewhere below them, on the road running along the edge of the Riverside Gardens, a lad hollered at a mate. Rowdy. Pumped up for a Friday night.

'I don't know what you're talking about.' Lotte slowly shook her head. 'You need to leave.'

Ros focused on the sleek, vinyl floor. She needed to think fast. She was missing too many pieces of the puzzle to understand what this woman was doing but she couldn't shake the fear, deep in her gut, that, for whatever reason, she was out to destroy them.

Ros steadied herself and tried to keep her voice calm and steady. 'What is it you want?'

Lotte hesitated. 'Justice. That's all.'

'Justice?' Ros thought about Adam, his head sunk in his hands. 'We both know you've made this up. It never happened, did it? He didn't lay a finger on you. So why are you saying he did?'

Lotte glared at her. 'You don't get it, do you? You heard him with his own brother, heard them accuse each other of something so heinous they were both frightened it would put them in jail. And when they turned on you and said you'd imagined it, you actually believed them. You let them guilt-trip you.' She shook her head at Ros in mock disbelief. 'But part of you, deep down, has always been suspicious, hasn't it?

At some level, you knew they'd done something unspeakable. You just didn't want to deal with it. Far easier to close the door on it and swallow his lie that you were just being paranoid. Right?'

'That's got nothing to do with you.' Ros heard her voice rise. 'It was years ago! I was hormonal and half-asleep, that's all. That's got nothing to do with this... this *absurd* allegation you've made.'

'Hasn't it?' Lotte gave her a long, steady look. 'What if you're wrong about him? What if you always have been? Then what?'

Ros shook her head. 'I'm not.'

'Really?' Lotte's mouth was trembling. 'What makes you so sure? What if *he*'s the liar, not me?'

'He's my husband. I know him. He'd never, in a million years—'

Lotte pushed herself up from the counter and stood upright. 'You should go.'

Ros didn't move. 'Think what's going to happen if you pursue this. Think about Caitlyn! Everyone knows us here. They know Adam. They'll know who's lying.'

'Are you threatening me?' Lotte's eyes hardened. 'If you don't go, right now, I'm going to call the police. They've very protective of victims of sexual abuse. And quite right too.' She crossed to the kitchen doorway and stood there, waiting.

Ros sighed. 'You're making a big mistake.' At the door to the apartment, she paused. 'It's not too late. You can still put this right. Before it gets any worse.'

'You're wrong.' Lotte's eyes narrowed. 'It's far too late.' She closed the door abruptly.

Ros stood alone at the top of the stairs. Her fists tightened at her sides. Her nails made angry half-moons in her palms. She wanted to scream. She wanted to batter the door with her hands. She wanted to smash something.

Instead, Ros stood very still, listening to the anger coursing through her body, stiffening her shoulders, her arms. *No*, she thought. *Not that. That would make me no better than she is.*

She fought down the memory of Adam and Charles, dark shadows on the patio, rising to their feet and turning to her as she appeared at the door. She forced herself to focus instead on that other Adam, the gentle man looking down the aisle at her, wide-eyed, all those years ago, mouthing: *Wow!* She thought about Sophie clambering onto her lap – filling it now – nestling there, and about Bella tugging at the duvet in the night if she'd woken, afraid, and climbing in to press her slight, bony body into Ros's warm, fleshy curves.

She let out a long breath and turned to grope her way woodenly down the stairs, feeling a path through the darkness.

33

ROS

Ros felt sick as she approached the school gates the following afternoon.

The fathers, mothers and childminders were gathering. Groups stood along the metal mesh fence in twos and threes, bodies half-turned to each other, half towards the school building, chatting.

Ros wondered how many of them had heard about Adam, about the ridiculous allegations against him. It would only take an indiscreet comment from Sam or his wife, and the news would spread in a gossipy fire-flash.

She couldn't predict how people would react. Most of them were acquaintances, rather than real friends. They staffed stalls together at the school's Christmas and summer fairs, they shared coffee at parents' evenings and stood, balancing drinks and nibbles, at Parent Teacher Association socials, making small talk: *How was your vacation, did you go anywhere nice?* and: *How's your child settling into year three?* Some of them had brought their children to the house for playdates and parties.

But what did they really think of her, of Adam? She didn't know, but she suspected she'd soon find out.

She closed the distance, her eyes flicking uncertainly from one face to the next.

Was it her imagination or did those women, the ones with children in year two, glance across at her, then look quickly away as she passed? She forced herself to keep walking, not to look back over her shoulder and see if they were gazing after her.

There was Josie, jiggling her newborn in his sling in an endless, hot-brick dance. Josie caught her eye and smiled. Was it a sympathetic smile or a normal, friendly one? On another day, she'd have stopped and asked how she was doing, if the baby was sleeping any better. Not today. She didn't want to talk to anyone. She just wanted to collect the girls, go home and shut the door on the world.

Diana lifted a hand and waved her across with a smile. If she had heard, she was pretending she hadn't. Perhaps that was better.

Another reception-class mother reached Diana, smiling, just before Ros did. Ros hadn't learned her name yet but she and Diana already seemed to have hit it off.

Ros stood silently, letting the chat wash over her, trying not to catch anyone else's eye. Her heart thumped. She'd felt wretched all day, sitting at her desk, trying to focus on pitches and emails and struggling to concentrate. All she could see was Adam's crumpled face.

He'd stayed in bed until lunchtime. It had frightened her. He never slept in. When he'd finally got up, she'd traced his movement by sound. The tread across the landing, the pounding of water as he showered, the low hum of his electric razor. Then the front door had slammed shut. He hadn't been back.

She'd spent the afternoon worrying. She knew Adam was innocent but she had no idea how long it would take him to clear his name. An investigation might take months. In the meantime, they were tainted. What would he do with himself if he couldn't work? It would kill him.

She thought about the girls too. She imagined the taunts they might face from other children as word spread. She shook her head, miserably. She wasn't sure she could bear it.

And what about money? How were they going to manage if Adam didn't work? It would be down to her. If she didn't break through soon and make money with the business, she'd just have to give up on it and get a job with an agency.

All because of one woman's lies.

The school bell sounded. Ros, her stomach still leaden, focused on the opening doors and the tumbling stream of children.

At her side, Diana said: 'So it's tomorrow, isn't it, your big meeting? When I need to collect the girls.'

Tomorrow? Ros started, lost for a moment. 'Friday. That's right. Thanks, Di. You're sure it's OK?'

She spotted Bella in the unfurling stream of children, racing towards her, schoolbag bouncing. She felt something inside her melt for a second and raised a hand to wave.

'Of course!' Diana was waving too now. Max was hurtling towards her across the playground like a heat-seeking missile. 'Anything for you, Missus Entrepreneur!' Crouching now, Diana was bracing herself as Max reached them and crashed into his mother's arms for a hug.

'Hello, lovely boy!' Diana, unruffled, was all smiles.

Ros bent down to receive Bella, wrapped her arms tightly around her. She planted a kiss on the top of her daughter's head and swallowed hard. *This is what matters.* Protecting her daughters, keeping them safe in the midst of this madness. She glanced up to see Sophie approaching, her face older than her little sister's and already more wary. *I can't lose them*, Ros thought.

34

ROS

They arrived home to find a pile of boxes in the hall.

'Look, Mummy!' Bella ran to them at once, curious. 'What is it?'

Sophie hovered behind her. 'Is it a delivery? For us?'

'It's something for Daddy, I should think.' Ros shooed the girls into the lounge and went through to the kitchen to microwave the spaghetti carbonara she'd defrosted the night before, frowning to herself.

The girls sat at the table, legs swinging. Bella was perched on her booster seat but she was still barely high enough to see inside her bowl. Ros put a handful of freshly cut apple slices by each plate, added a piece of chocolate, then told them to behave themselves and headed upstairs to see if Adam was back.

He was sitting at his desk in their shared study, hunched over his laptop. He was wearing jeans and an old T-shirt, his hair tousled.

'Adam?' She stood beside him and ran a hand across his

warm back. He twisted around, clearly with effort, lifted his head and showed her a swollen, tearful face. 'You alright?'

He shrugged. 'Not really.'

She didn't need to ask why. 'What's with the boxes downstairs?'

'Sam brought them round.'

She had to lean in closer to catch what he was mumbling. 'Why?'

'From the office. It's my stuff.'

She shook her head. 'But you'll be back there soon. Soon as this is all cleared up.'

He didn't answer. A sigh rippled through his body.

'Don't let it get to you.' She lifted her hand and stroked his hair. She trusted this man with her life, with her children's lives. It was too cruel. 'We'll get through this, OK? We'll get through it together.'

Footsteps came thundering up the stairs, accompanied by noisy crying. She jumped up and headed for the landing, closing the study door behind her. She didn't want the girls to see their father like that. 'What's going on?'

Bella ploughed into her and clung to her legs.

'Honestly, I can't leave you two for five minutes! Now, come downstairs and tell me what's happened.'

She took Bella's sticky hand and led her down.

Ros had just settled Bella into bed and was hurrying Sophie into the bathroom when the front doorbell rang.

The woman on the doorstep looked about thirty. Her dark brown hair was pinned up in a sloppy bun, stray strands spilling out of a black net. 'Mrs Crofter? Detective Wright. Is your husband home?'

Ros felt a flutter of panic. For a second, she wanted to say that Adam wasn't home and, no, she couldn't come in and wait.

She swallowed and stared. The woman was stocky and wearing a dark blue trouser suit and lace-up shoes. She was holding up some sort of silver badge in a wallet.

Ros peered at it. She had no idea what a proper police badge looked like. She sensed a movement on the path and looked past the woman to a lanky young man in uniform. He was standing discreetly at the bottom of the steps, watching her.

She heard herself say: 'I was just putting the children to bed.'

The detective looked stern. 'We've come to see your husband. Adam Crofter?'

Ros moved back reluctantly and let the two of them follow her through the hall and into the lounge. Their police car was parked right outside the house. The neighbours would be whispering. She imagined their fingers, spreading the news on local chats. Her stomach contracted.

'He's upstairs. I'll just get him.' She hesitated at the lounge door and looked back at the two of them, standing awkwardly on the rug. They seemed to fill the room. 'Have a seat.' She was damned if she was going to offer them tea.

Upstairs, Adam didn't seem surprised. He splashed cold water on his face, raked his hands through his thinning hair and headed downstairs.

Ros checked that Sophie had washed and cleaned her teeth, then ushered her across the landing into her bedroom. 'You can read for a bit,' she said. 'Alright, lovely? Light out at eight, please.'

Sophie climbed into bed. 'What's going on, Mum?'

'Nothing.' Ros put her arms around Sophie's thin shoulders and kissed her. 'You've got your book?'

Sophie frowned. 'But who's downstairs? I heard someone.'

'Just someone to see Daddy, that's all. Goodnight, beautiful.'

Downstairs, the detective and the uniformed officer were

sitting in armchairs, both angled towards Adam on the sofa. All three of them were sitting stiffly, their backs unnaturally straight. The young lad had taken off his peaked cap and had a small notebook open on his lap. It was a formal scene, which looked out of place in their lounge.

Ros crossed the room and planted herself next to Adam, close enough that their thighs touched. She wanted him to feel her there, to know he was not alone.

'What have they said?' she said to Adam.

He hung his head and didn't answer.

'Mrs Crofter, I'm afraid we're investigating some serious allegations against your husband.'

Ros glared at her. 'They're lies.'

The detective's eyes widened a fraction. 'You're aware of them?'

Ros bit her lip. 'I just know my husband, that's all. He'd never break the law. He's not like that.'

The detective said calmly, 'Then he has no cause for concern.' She turned back to Adam: 'So, if you'd like to get your coat, Mr Crofter—?'

Ros put her hand protectively on Adam's knee. 'What? You're *arresting* him?'

'He is not under arrest, at this point, no.' The detective was already shifting to the edge of her seat, ready to get up. 'We're inviting him to come with us for a voluntary interview.'

Ros turned to Adam. 'You don't need to go then, do you? If it's voluntary?'

The detective cut in: 'It would be in your husband's interests to help with the investigation, Mrs Crofter.'

Ros, frustrated, said: 'What about me? Can I give a statement in his defence?'

'If you have something to say, Mrs Crofter, that is material to the case.' The detective gave her a sharp look. 'But I must warn you—'

The young police officer looked wary, as if he sensed trouble.

'It is material!' Ros felt her heart racing. 'I know the woman behind this! It's Lotte Humphries, isn't it? She's been stalking us.'

The young police officer's eyes widened.

Adam said, 'Ros!' Mad and exasperated.

Ros ploughed on. 'We met on vacation in Majorca. I think now she may have engineered it. I'd been chatting online, you see, about where we ought to take the kids. Then the next thing we knew, she'd followed us here, to Ilkley. She's renting a place right round the corner. She's even put her daughter in the same class as one of our girls! Then she heard about the chance to work for Adam and grabbed it with both hands.'

The detective frowned. 'Why would she do that?'

Ros hesitated. She sensed how improbable it all sounded but it was true. 'I don't know.'

The detective looked sceptical. 'Stalking is a serious offence, Mrs Crofter. Did you report these concerns?'

Ros shook her head. 'Not really. I mean, I talked to my husband about it, obviously.'

The silence hung between them, thick and dark. The detective's eyes were on Ros's face. Ros could almost see the cogs turning.

Finally, the detective said: 'Let me be clear, Mrs Crofter. You're suggesting that the alleged victim deliberately lured your family to a particular resort in Majorca with the express purpose of befriending you.'

Ros said: 'I know it sounds...'

The detective raised her hand and continued. 'Afterwards, the alleged victim relocated to Ilkley with her daughter, enrolled her in the same school as your children and took a job at your husband's place of work.' She paused. 'And she did all this in order to make a false allegation to the police of sexual assault.'

'Well,' said Ros, 'yes.'

The detective let out a heavy breath. 'I see,' she said.

There was a silence. Beside her, Adam bowed his head over clenched hands.

'I know how it sounds.' Ros looked from one disbelieving face to the other. 'But it's the only sensible explanation, isn't it? Don't you see?'

'Not really, Mrs Crofter, no. I'm afraid I don't see.' The detective gave her a steely look.

'She wants to destroy us. I don't know why.' Ros heard her voice rising. 'But she's set a trap. And you're walking right into it.'

The detective and the constable exchanged a quick look. As one, they rose to their feet. 'Mr Crofter?'

'But you don't seem to—' Ros blurted out.

Adam said, sharply: 'Stop it, Ros. You're not helping.'

Ros pressed her lips together, stunned. Tears started in her eyes. Her thoughts tumbled and spun as she struggled to think.

Adam, getting heavily to his feet and pushing his wallet into his back pocket, seemed vague and lost. He was in no position to defend himself. He needed her.

Ros looked at the thin-lipped detective, the young constable and at Adam's pinched, ashen face as he turned to follow them out.

She wanted to scream. She was the only one who realised how devious, how dangerous, this woman was, and none of them believed her.

35

ROS

It was nearly eleven when Adam came back.

Ros hurried into the shadowy hall as soon as she heard his key in the lock. 'Are you alright?'

He seemed stooped, as if the last few hours had prematurely aged him.

'What happened?'

He hung up his coat and gazed at her with empty eyes.

She took his arm. 'Oh, Adam.'

He went through to the kitchen to the cupboard at the back and poured himself a whisky. The edge of the bottle drummed the rim of the glass as his hand shook.

'Do you want anything to eat?'

He shook his head, heading with his glass to the lounge. Ros followed and, when he lowered himself heavily onto the sofa, she sat close beside him.

'What happened?' she asked again. She waited while he took a gulp of whisky and swallowed hard.

'They sat me in this room and told me exactly what she'd said, you know, what she's accused me of doing.'

'And?'

He shrugged. 'It's what Sam said. She says I asked her to go into the consulting room with me and, well, assaulted her.'

Ros shook her head. 'She's no evidence though, has she? It's your word against hers, right?'

'I suppose so.' Adam's body seemed to have sagged into itself. 'They said they'd interviewed Sam. Sounds like he stuck up for me. But you'd expect that, wouldn't you? I'm not sure how much it helps. I mean, he wasn't there to see what happened.'

'No, but it must still count for something.' Ros tried to sound confident. 'What happens now?'

Adam shrugged. He looked utterly defeated. 'They're investigating.'

'How long will that take?'

'I don't know.'

'So do we need to find a lawyer?' Ros tried hard to run through the school parents she knew and think whether any of them practised law. There was so much she didn't understand. 'And you can stay at home? Are you on bail?'

'I haven't actually been arrested.' He was starting to sound impatient. 'It's something else. RU-something. Released while they carry on looking into it, basically. They read me a list of things I can't do. I can't leave the country or contact the victim or go to her home.'

'Victim! You're the victim.' Ros thought about her own visit to Lotte. If the police knew about that, maybe she'd be done for harassment. 'So, what happens next?'

'Stop it!' Adam slammed down his glass. The crash made her jump. 'Stop asking so many questions! How the hell do I know? All you've done is make it worse!' He got to his feet and lumbered out of the room.

Ros heard his tread on the stairs and the slam of the door behind him as he shut himself away from her in the spare bedroom.

36

LOTTE

Friday morning, once I'd dropped Caitlyn off at school, I went online and started trawling the internet for some mention of Adam and the allegations I'd made. Not a word. Nothing in the local news. Nothing on the chat sites. Not yet.

It wasn't exactly an open and shut case, I knew that. It was his word against mine. Who was the liar? The respected osteopath, family man and pillar of the community? Or the newly arrived single mother? It was risky.

On the other hand, once there was reason to doubt Adam, what woman wouldn't take her safety seriously? I wouldn't shut myself alone in a consulting room with a man who'd been accused of sexual assault, even if he did protest he was innocent. Would they?

I sat back in my chair and drummed my fingers on the edge of the desk. I'd expected things to move more quickly than this, but the detective had made it clear, when I'd asked, that details would only be divulged to the media if the suspect was formally charged. That, it seemed, could take months, if it happened at all.

I pursed my lips. I wasn't a patient person and, besides, I

didn't have that long. I'd have to take a risk and push the process along myself.

I opened up a blank document and started to type.

Afterwards, when I read it through, the words made my heart race. I was pleased with myself. I didn't want it to sound malicious. I wanted it to have the credibility of a real news report, with a semblance of balance. The sight of the allegations laid out in black and white made it all the more real.

Local Osteopath Denies Rape Claims

Police are investigating allegations against an Ilkley man, Adam Crofter, after a woman accused him of attempted rape. The victim, a woman in her thirties, who hasn't been named, attended Mr Crofter's osteopathic practice in Disraeli Row, in the centre of Ilkley. She was allegedly assaulted by Mr Crofter when they were alone in his consulting room.

Mr Crofter's business associate, physiotherapist Samuel James, who works out of the same premises, said he was shocked by the claims. He said he'd worked alongside Mr Crofter for more than ten years and had always considered him to be 'a trusted professional'. Mr Crofter, a well-known local practitioner, has denied wrongdoing. Police say the investigation is continuing.

I set up a new email account under a false name, then copied across the email addresses I'd earlier downloaded in the office: the bulk of Adam's client directory. It took only minutes to set up a blind copy mass mailing. I cut and pasted the article, then took a deep breath and pressed send.

It wouldn't take long for news to spread. Once it had, gossip about my role in all this, as the alleged victim, would spread too. I had no illusions about staying anonymous in a town as small as this.

I rose to my feet and paused in front of the window that looked onto the Riverside Gardens below. The good folk of Ilkley were out in force, enjoying the late fall sunshine. Mothers were pushing pre-schoolers on the swings, takeaway coffees in their free hands, or crouching at the bottom of the slide to catch them in their arms. Older figures, retired perhaps, strolled down the paths towards the riverbank and under the trees.

I wondered how they'd all react once they knew I was the one making the allegations; whether they'd close ranks and protect one of their own, a local boy, from an outsider. It was always a risk. I was a bit high for a brick through the window, but it wouldn't be hard for them to shout abuse at me in the street, to smash unattended eggs in my shopping cart, to put hate mail through the mailbox.

I looked out at the rushing River Wharfe and the grand houses of Middleton climbing steeply on the far side.

I was stirring up a nest of vipers. I knew that. But I'd waited many long years for this. I couldn't back off now. It was time.

37

School

On Friday afternoon, whispers began rippling through the school, disturbing the calm.

Mrs Shore was one of the first to sense that something had happened. She popped in to see the office ladies after lunch. They always knew more than everyone else.

The two of them paused, hands on keyboards, as soon as she asked, then twisted to face her and started to fill her in.

'Apparently, it's Caitlyn Humphries' mother,' said one.

'You know.' Her colleague nodded meaningfully. 'The one who's always late picking up from after-school club.'

'What about her?' Mrs Shore frowned.

'Someone's made an allegation against Mr Crofter.'

'He's Sophie and Bella's father.'

The office ladies' hands left their keyboards altogether. They leaned towards the headteacher and lowered their voices.

'Ros Crofter's husband.'

The office ladies tutted.

'Poor Ros.'

'Poor kids.'

'What sort of allegation?' Mrs Shore asked.

The office ladies rolled their eyes.

'Very unpleasant.'

They lowered their voices yet further. 'Sexual assault.'

'Serious sexual assault. He tried to rape her.'

'How awful.' Mrs Shore was struggling to take it all in. 'Where did it happen?'

'Where he works. She got a job there. He's one of those bad back people.'

'Chiropractor?'

'No, the other one.'

'Osteopath?'

'I think so.'

'That's right.' Mrs Shore's sister had been there for her bad back. 'He's got that place in the parking lot.'

'Exactly.'

'That's the one.'

The school switchboard lit up and there was a short pause while one of the office ladies took a message, then turned back to carry on.

'My brother-in-law went to see him for his hip. He said he was very good.'

'Well, maybe he is. With men.'

The office ladies exchanged meaningful glances.

'No smoke without fire.'

'Is it an official complaint, then?' Mrs Shore asked.

'Yes!'

'She's got the police involved?'

'They're investigating him and everything.'

'Someone sent an email about it, apparently. Anonymous.'

'Anonymous?'

The office ladies nodded solemnly. Then one said, importantly: 'My sister-in-law got one. She's a patient there. She forwarded it to me this morning.' Then she added quickly: 'To my personal account. I checked my phone at lunch.' She looked at Mrs Shore. 'You want a quick look?'

She glanced around as if to check the coast was clear, then she reached into her top drawer, pulled out her phone and brought up the email.

'You can't write things like that.' Mrs Shore blinked as she read it. 'That's libel.'

'Well, it might be, but that doesn't mean it isn't true.'

'We shouldn't let it go any further.'

'Of course not.'

The office ladies exchanged furtive glances, thinking how many times they'd already forwarded it to friends.

Mrs Shore looked distressed. 'How awful,' she said again.

She carried on thinking about it as she headed back to her office. She wasn't sure how she felt about it. She'd been the victim of wandering male hands herself when she was a younger woman – it was almost accepted as par for the course in those days. Women just warned each other in whispers to *Take care with So-and-so*; and, if you found yourself alone in a room with So-and-so, you made sure you kept the door open.

No one dared complain. You'd either lose your job or be labelled a troublemaker. Besides, it was your word against his, most of the time, and his carried more weight.

She was glad people made more fuss nowadays. She didn't think the young women teaching at St Stephen's would put up with nonsense from any man. They were very vocal about their rights. That had to be a good thing.

On the other hand, she was very unsure about Caitlyn's mother. She'd come across as pushy when she'd swept into school at the start of term, pressing to see her and then making such a fuss about the admissions process. She'd been lucky to get her daughter a place anywhere, after leaving it so late.

And she knew the Crofter family. They'd always seemed delightful.

Of course, there'd been that awkward business about the older girl, Sophie, hitting Frederick Pearce, but Ros Crofter was an exemplary parent, always supportive and quick to volunteer for school events.

It was a horrid business. It was hard to know who to blame. But there was no doubt in her mind that, now, the battlelines had been drawn.

38

ROS

On Friday, Adam stayed shut away in the spare bedroom until it was almost lunchtime.

Ros had tiptoed in and out of their bedroom, listening for sounds of him as she dressed. On the way back downstairs, she'd paused at the spare room door. No sound.

She'd squeezed the handle and eased open the door a crack. The room was thick with shadow, the air fetid. 'Adam?' She whispered, frightened of waking him. 'You awake?'

If Adam heard her, he gave no sign of life. She closed the door on him and hurried downstairs to get the children ready for school.

Ros spent the morning chasing up emails she'd sent more than a week ago to past contacts. Once again, almost no one had answered. She frowned, trying to shake the feeling that had settled on her, like a fine, chilling mist, that something really wasn't right. She didn't believe her own excuses – that the companies were only just getting straight again after the summer break. That many had a hiring freeze but would get back to her when they were ready again. None of that explained why she was being met by a wall of silence or an occasional formal brush-off from people who'd been friendly in the past.

As soon as she heard Adam head heavily towards the family bathroom, she hurried downstairs and made him a sandwich, covering it with an upturned cereal bowl so it wouldn't dry out.

She'd been wondering during the morning whether to call Diana and cancel the arrangement they'd made, for Sophie and Bella to go home with her from school so that Ros could go to her meeting, on the grounds that Adam could collect them instead. Now, seeing what a state he seemed to be in, she decided to leave things be. Besides, she told herself, the girls were looking forward to tea at Posy and Max's. She didn't want to disappoint them.

She changed into her work wardrobe – a smart blue trouser suit and kitten heels – checked her make-up and headed out. She sent Adam a message telling him where she'd gone.

She'd visited White's headquarters before, when she'd worked for an agency in Leeds and they'd launched a recruitment drive for their Keighley store. Now, just by luck, she'd heard about the expansion into Shipley. If she could persuade them to use her, it might mean a lot of business.

She thought about Adam, shuffling around miserably at home, and the extra money they'd need to find for bills until he could work again.

It seemed a long time since she'd had the chance to pitch in-person to a potential client. Her body was strained with nerves. On the way, she tried to steady her breathing and push down her sense of panic. *I can do this*, she told herself. *I'm good at this*. She ran through her spiel in her head, but it was hard. She needed to sound strong and confident but she was struggling to feel it.

. . .

Stella White was the niece of the man who'd started the original garden centre store in the 1960s which, in more recent years, had spawned a modest but expanding chain. She was a down-to-earth, straightforward woman in her late forties who'd shown herself to have a shrewd head on her shoulders. The recent expansion was, Ros was sure, down to her ambition to grow the business.

Ros remembered her from the Keighley recruitment drive. Stella White had made a point of sitting in on the interviews of all the shortlisted candidates, from buyers to maintenance and till staff, and had made it clear, with some penetrating questions, that she understood the way their business worked at every level.

Now, as Ros was shown into her office, trying to swallow down her nerves, Ms White came out briskly from behind a desk piled with papers and crushed Ros's hand in her own.

'Good to see you.' She gestured Ros to a chair, then heaved a voluminous bag of compost off a second chair, dumping it on the floor, so she could sit with her. She called past Ros to the closing door: 'Tea, please, Heather!' then turned back to her, all smiles. 'You'll have a cup, won't you? We're sampling a new range of cupcakes for the store. Love to know what you think.'

They had tea, then Ms White sat quietly, her eyes on Ros's face as Ros delivered her pitch.

When Ros finally finished, Ms White didn't at once speak. She pushed the plate of cakes absent-mindedly towards her, offering her another, her expression appraising.

'You did a good job for us last time,' she said at last. 'That's why I decided to see you today. I'm a busy woman. I don't see everyone.'

Ros nodded. Her jaw was unnaturally stiff with tension. 'Well, yes, I really appreciate your time, Ms White. I can assure you that if—'

'Yes, yes,' Ms White interrupted, flapping a hand as if swat-

ting away Ros's flannel. 'I hear what you're saying about costs.
The agencies are good but expensive. I'd prefer one-to-one. And
I make a point of supporting local business talent, especially
women. It's not easy, setting up on your own, trying to break
into a tough market, the way you're doing. Not easy at all.'

Ros waited, holding her breath. She knew better than to
interrupt, but she sensed that something else was coming, some
reason why the business might not be coming her way after all.

'Can I be blunt?' Ms White looked at her knowingly and
leaned forward in her chair as if she were about to confide a
truth. 'I'm not a judgemental person. Each to his own. Or her
own. And, frankly, what you do in your own time is up to you,
as long as it's legal.'

Ros frowned, trying to understand. She could sense disapproval in the older woman's eyes, but she had no idea what she
was talking about. She waited.

'But now especially, when you're a start-up and trying to
grow a business, reputation matters and, well, image matters to
people too. Whether it's potential clients or potential employees. You might want to think about it, that's all – about what sort
of message you're putting out there.'

Ros shook her head. She was beginning to wonder if this
was all a misunderstanding. Maybe Ms White had mixed her
up with someone else.

The confusion must have shown on her face.

'Maybe set up a separate social media account?' Ms White
said. 'Keep one for the business and use the second one for,
well, for your private life. Sort that out and, yes, maybe I would
be interested in talking more.'

Before Ros could summon a question, Ms White got to her
feet, shook Ros's hand and headed back to her cluttered desk
and the work waiting there.

. . .

Ros drove home in a daze. She liked Ms White. She appreciated the fact she'd taken time to see her and that she'd been frank. It sounded as if she did have a chance of picking up business when White's launched its recruitment round for the new Shipley store in the New Year.

But what was it about Ros's corporate image that she wanted her to change? Ros had no idea.

Was it too dull? It was true that her company website wasn't the most dynamic in the world, but recruitment wasn't exactly a cutting-edge industry. A friend of a friend had designed and built the site for her.

Ros wasn't very diligent about updating it, and she had to think back. She didn't think she'd posted any updates since the start of the school summer vacation. If she had something to say, she usually posted on a chat site or went onto social media. The whole point of the website was that it was pretty self-sufficient. It didn't need much maintenance. That was the way they'd set it up.

It was just a shop window. If someone liked what they saw and wanted to get in touch with her, all they had to do was submit details on the contact form and it fed directly into her email.

She thought again about her interview with Ms White. She was definitely missing something.

It was nearly five o'clock by the time Ros finally made it back to Ilkley. She decided to drop the car at home and change out of her work clothes before she went to collect the girls from Diana's. Diana wouldn't mind. But first, she wanted to have a look at her website and see if she could work out what Ms White was talking about.

She shouted hello to Adam, who was pacing up and down the lounge, then made herself a cup of tea and headed upstairs to log on. She sipped her drink as she clicked through to her company site and waited for the front page to load.

Ros gasped. The mug crashed to the floor at her feet, spilling a spreading pool of hot tea across the carpet. She didn't move to pick it up. Her eyes were riveted to the screen.

No. It isn't possible.

A shiver ran down her spine, one of horror and fear.

39

ROS

Ros realised she'd let out a cry because, a moment later, Adam was there in the doorway, taking in the mess on the carpet, the anguish on her face.

'What?'

She couldn't speak. All she could do was stare at the screen.

The logo of her company was still intact, with the neat thumbnail picture of Ros at one side. It was her website, clearly. But it looked very different. Before, the large, main picture had been an anodyne shot, posed by a photographer, of Ros sitting in an interview room, a pen in her hand and a folder on her knee, smiling thoughtfully at a young woman in a trouser suit who was playing the part of a candidate.

That picture had disappeared.

Instead, the image jumping out of the screen in its place was vibrant with blurred colour, criss-crossed with falling shafts of artificial light. In the centre, hemmed in by whirling, twisting bodies, a young man, his body hard with muscle and slick with sweat, leered at the camera. He had one hand clamped firmly around the breast of a woman who was slumped in his arms, facing away from him. His other hand was on her crotch, pinning her hard against him.

The woman's head lolled to one side, as if she'd lost control of her neck. Her face was streaked messily with make-up, her mouth hung slightly open, her eyes had fallen closed.

Ros stared in horror at her own distorted features. How was it possible? It was clearly her. And she recognised the young Spaniard. He was one of the men who'd checked them out at the start of that night with Lotte in Majorca, the men Lotte had dragged her over to, unwillingly, to dance with.

Had he assaulted her? She had absolutely no memory of that happening. None at all. Had she really been as drunk as she looked?

She felt herself flush with shame. All the contacts she'd emailed, all the companies she'd contacted, pitching her corporate services. What must they have thought when they googled her and checked out her website? No wonder they hadn't been responding. It was hard to think of anything more unprofessional.

She remembered the disapproval she'd sensed from Ms White. Now she understood. *Image matters*, she'd said.

Ros bit her lip. As if she'd have posted anything so humiliating on her website herself. Of course she hadn't.

'What is it?' Adam headed across towards her desk, his eyes searching out the screen.

'Nothing.' She reached quickly and, fumbling, managed to close down the page just before he bent beside her to look. 'Just the stupid website. Crashed again.'

Adam blinked. 'You want me to have a look?' He stretched his hand towards her keyboard.

'No, it's fine.' She shoved him away, forceful in her determination to stop him looking. 'No need.'

He frowned, then shrugged. 'Suit yourself.' He turned and headed out of the room and downstairs.

Ros sat stiffly, staring at her laptop, her shame slowly mixing now with rising anger.Someone had deliberately hacked into the site and doctored the front page to damage her, to destroy her reputation, just as she tried to build her business.

And she had no doubt in her mind who that person must be.

40

ROS

Ros decided not to take the car to Diana's. She didn't trust herself to drive.

She strode there instead, fuelled by anger, hardly aware of her surroundings as she crossed the old bridge over the churned waters of the Wharfe, then headed up the steep hill into the smart residential area of Middleton.

She hoped Diana would ask her in for a chat while the kids finished playing. She needed to sit down with someone sympathetic and figure out what to do. She was tempted to go to the police. Maybe they'd investigate. They must have the technology to find out exactly who'd hacked the site. If they could prove it was Lotte, maybe then they'd believe her and see that she was a stalker, that she'd made up that pack of lies about Adam out of spite.

She felt her face grow hot as she thought about Adam. *What if he saw that awful photograph?* He'd be so hurt. She just hoped he didn't decide to check the website before she could get it taken down. Hopefully he was too preoccupied with his own problems.

She was panting by the time she turned into Diana's drive.

The front of the house looked deserted. They must all be round the back, in the sunny kitchen with its views across the valley. She rang the bell and heard the chimes echo through the hall. When no one came, she lifted the ornamental brass knocker and let it fall with a crash. They wouldn't miss that.

The only sound, in the silence, was the chirp of birdsong in the surrounding trees and bushes.

She pulled out her phone and dialled Diana's mobile. Her friend picked up almost at once.

'Where are you?' Ros stepped back from the front door and started to walk towards the side gate as she spoke. 'Shall I come through to the back?'

'Ros? Look, I can't talk long. We're just going in.'

'Going in where?'

Diana let out a messy breath which crackled down the line. 'The doctors. Max isn't well. He's wheezing and the inhaler isn't helping.' Ros heard her turning away from the phone to speak to the children, hurrying them along. 'He wasn't well at school, apparently, but the first I knew about it was when he came out at pick-up, pale as a ghost and gasping for breath.'

A woman's voice interrupted her. The doctor, perhaps.

'Look, sorry, I've got to go. Speak later?'

'Wait!' Ros was struggling to make sense of what was happening. 'Are the girls with you? Shall I come to the surgery?'

There were footsteps and a door closed. For a moment, Ros thought she'd ended the call. 'Di?'

'They're fine.' Diana sounded flustered. 'They're at Lotte's.'

'At Lotte's?' Ros felt something twist in her gut.

'Well, I couldn't bring them here.' She sounded mad, as if she were already in crisis and expected Ros to be supportive, not to make a fuss about nothing. 'Lotte offered. She was there to get Caitlyn.'

Ros was instantly suspicious: 'She offered?'

'She was trying to help out.' Diana sounded impatient. 'Sorry. I've got to go.'

The line went dead.

Ros turned and started to run down the hill, her heart pounding, clutching her phone in her hand. Her anger had melted away in a moment, squeezed out by panic. This woman who was trying to ruin her husband's career, to ruin hers, now had Sophie and Bella.

Hurrying, she lost her footing on the steep incline and fell, skidding, grazing her knee through her tights.

'You alright?' A stout woman in a waxed jacket called to her from across the road. 'Careful.'

Ros picked herself up, brushed off the loose gravel clinging to the broken skin and limped on as fast as she could. She hobbled back across the bridge and, reaching the edge of the Riverside Gardens, ignored the paths and cut straight across the grass, heading towards Bridge Lane.

As she drew nearer, her breath burning now in her chest, she tipped back her head and squinted up at the large picture window in Lotte's kitchen. The evening light glinted on the surface of the glass, turning it into a mirror which reflected the darkening sky back at itself. Whatever secrets were inside, they were hidden from view.

Ros scrambled up the grassy bank towards the road, panting hard. She paused on the sidewalk, waiting for a break in the passing traffic so that she could close the final distance to the front entrance.

A sudden flash at the side of the building caught her eye. It was high, at the same level as the apartment. Lotte's bedroom, perhaps. She blinked, staring, trying to make sense of what she'd seen. As she looked, it came again, a flicker of reflected light. A window was open wide, moving a fraction.

She narrowed her eyes, craning to see. Something small and

dark appeared there, silhouetted against the pale glass. It was in the shape of a large doll, facing out into the gathering darkness.

Ros opened her mouth to scream but the breath stopped in her throat. The glass gleamed as it shifted position again. The window was wide open now, and, *Oh, no!*

Her body started to shake. Her eyes fixed on the child as if she could pin her there by sheer force of will. A full, cotton skirt swelled and flared around her legs. The little girl's thin, white arms, spread wide, paddled the empty air as she pitched forwards and plunged towards the ground.

A moment later, she disappeared from sight. Her final impact was screened by trees and bushes.

Ros was left, staring, standing alone on an empty sidewalk, choking, her arms stretching forwards, as if she might somehow have reached all that way, have caught her, have saved the little girl as she plummeted to the earth.

41

ROS

For a moment, Ros couldn't move.

She stood, quivering, staring at the empty air, her arms still uselessly reaching, unable to comprehend what she'd just witnessed. *Had it been real?* The light was fading rapidly around her. Had it been a trick of the eye, an illusion in the deepening shadow?

She had to be sure. Ros threw herself into the next gap in the traffic, her breath hard in her throat, forcing her way around the side of the building through a tangle of bushes and weed-thick soil. Sharp branches scratched at her arms and legs, catching on her torn tights. Her nose filled with the heavy stench of leaf mulch and damp earth. Moisture bled through her shoes to dampen her feet.

She emerged in a rush onto a narrow gravel path and started to run. A moment later, she stopped abruptly and let out a cry. A small, crumpled figure lay motionless on the grass, face down.

Sophie.

One arm was twisted to the side at an odd angle. The cotton skirt she'd seen balloon and swirl in mid-air lay still across slim white thighs.

'No!' She rushed forward and stooped to her child, touched her back with gentle fingers, frightened of hurting her. She heard her own high-pitched voice shrieking: 'Sophie, can you hear me? Sophie!'

No answer. Her body was warm, the ribs lightly fluttering as they rose and fell, but she didn't make a sound, didn't move.

'Help!' Ros lifted her head and shouted, as loudly as she could into nothingness. 'Please, someone, help!'

Above her, the wide-open window on the first floor twitched and a face appeared. Lotte. She peered down, blinking, at the scene below, then let out a cry. 'Oh, my god!' She looked horror-struck. 'Is she OK? What happened? How did she—?'

'You!' Ros screamed at her, shaking with rage. 'How could you?'

'But what—?' Lotte shook her head, as if in disbelief. 'Hold on! I'll call an ambulance. I'm coming down.'

'No!' Ros clenched her jaw. 'Keep away from her.' Her hand batted the air, swatting at her, defending her motionless daughter. 'You did this to us. You hear me? Leave us alone!'

Ros heard the emergency siren from a distance.

She could almost see the ambulance, threading its way along The Grove, turning down towards Skipton Road, on its way here. She imagined the passers-by stopping and falling silent for a moment, following the ambulance with their eyes as it nosed its way through the arrested traffic: children, pressing their small hands against their ears and shrinking against the legs of a mother or father, waiting for the noise to pass; adults, wondering whose emergency it was, mentally ticking off their own loved ones, knowing them safe and feeling thankful that, that day at least, the crisis wasn't theirs.

She crouched, stiffly, at Sophie's side, stroking her hair and murmuring to her. 'It's alright, poppet.' They were the same words she'd whispered to her little girl since she'd been a baby. They'd never felt so impotent. 'Mummy's here.'

Finally, a pulse of blue light flashed across the bushes. There was a scrape of tyres and slamming of vehicle doors. From around the corner of the building, heavy footsteps pounded. The front door buzzer sounded.

'Here!' she shouted. She wanted to jump up, to fetch them, but she couldn't leave, she couldn't tear her hand from Sophie's inert body. 'Round here!'

They appeared at last, hurrying moonwalkers bulked out by heavy gear. The reflective strips on their clothing shone in the half-light as one led the way with a torch in hand. The one behind, a shorter, slighter figure, carried a stretcher.

They saw Sophie, ran to her, knelt by her side. All the time they talked, their eyes stayed on Sophie, their careful hands busy with her, checking for broken limbs, for bleeding, for wounds.

One, a man, asked: 'What happened?'

Ros hunched down on her heels. She was taut with adrenalin, not ready yet to let go. She swallowed. What she'd seen, the horror of it, was too big for the words she had.

'She was up there.' She pointed. The window was closed now. 'I was crossing the road. I saw her. The window, it opened and she' – she faltered as she remembered the horror of the sight, her child, plummeting through emptiness – 'she fell.'

She thought of the outstretched arms, the billowing skirt.

The crew, the older man and a young woman, exchanged words in a low, deliberate tone. She wanted desperately to understand, to know what they were finding, but she was too frightened to interrupt and slow them down. They needed to save Sophie. That was all that mattered.

'Do you know this child?'

'Know her? I'm her mother.'

The young woman lifted her head, as if she were seeing Ros for the first time. The man lifted his shoulder to speak into a radio fastened on his jacket. He was calling it in. She didn't understand the code he was using, the jargon. She didn't know what story it told about Sophie's injuries.

'What's her name?' The young woman spoke over her shoulder as she stretched forwards and fitted a neck brace.

'Sophie. Sophie Crofter.' Ros paused, choking. 'She's only eight.'

The crew worked together, their hands deft and efficient.

The young woman said loudly: 'Right, Sophie. We've got an ambulance and we're going to take you to hospital now, OK? Your mum's here too.'

They reached under Sophie and strapped her body, fragile as a bird, onto a hard board.

'Here we go, love,' the young woman said, as if Sophie could hear her.

The man said, 'Nice and steady.'

The two of them gently turned the board and placed it onto the stretcher. Sophie lay on her back, pinned there firmly by straps and brace, ready to be carried.

The young woman reached to secure Sophie's limply hanging arm against her body. Ros felt bile rise in her throat. The arm looked so wrong, the bone protruding at a peculiar angle. Sophie's face was white, her eyelashes long and dark against her skin. There was no movement in the closed eyes. A red weal stretched down the side of her face. Her cheekbone was grazed and speckled with earth.

'Is she—?' She didn't know how to say it. 'Is she OK?'

No one answered. Ros followed as the crew lifted her and carried her carefully out to the ambulance. Ros pressed as close as she could, trying to keep sight of her daughter's pallid face.

They emerged from the bushes to find a lightshow of strobing blue flicking back and forth across the front hedge. A police car was parked at the kerb, behind the ambulance. On the far side, a young couple stood on the sidewalk, hand in hand, watching.

The crew opened the back doors and secured the stretcher inside. As she climbed out again, the young woman pointed Ros to a flip-down seat in the back, alongside the stretcher. Her colleague secured a transparent, moulded mask over Sophie's face and busied himself with wires and monitors.

Ros was just about to sit down when she caught a glimpse, through the open back doors, of a uniformed police officer on the top step, notebook in hand. She peered harder. Lotte was standing there, just inside the communal front door, answering his questions. Her face was white and strained.

'It was her!' Ros's voice came out as a shriek. 'She did it!'

The paramedic glanced over his shoulder at Ros, then followed her pointing finger.

Ros hovered, torn between her determination not to leave Sophie's side and the furious impulse to jump down and confront Lotte.

The paramedic shook his head. 'Later.'

Behind them, his young colleague secured the back doors, ran round to the driving seat and set off at speed, lights flashing and sirens on, the sound oddly muted to those inside.

Ros hurriedly buckled up her safety harness. She thought of Bella, left behind, still in Lotte's apartment. *No. Bella mustn't see Sophie like this.* Someone else needed to rescue her.

'My husband,' she said. 'I need to call him.'

The paramedic glanced at her, reading her expression.

Ros was already steadying her phone and dialling his number with a trembling finger. As the ringtone sounded, she asked the paramedic, 'Where are we going?'

'Airedale.'

She nodded. Of course. Her mind was numb with shock. Adam's phone went to voicemail. She imagined him, slumped on the sofa or back in bed. She took a deep breath and left as calm a message as she could, saying Sophie had had an accident and he needed to call her back at once.

She sat, rigid, bracing herself against the sway and swing of the ambulance as it careered through the streets and onto the dual carriageway. In front of her, Sophie lay still, her neck pinned in position by the brace, her damaged arm fixed to her side, her eyes closed.

42

ROS

Once they entered the hospital, time seemed suspended.

As soon as the ambulance arrived, Sophie was swallowed by a silent tidal wave of activity. Men and women in white coats descended on her as soon as she was lifted out of the back of the ambulance and carried inside, all working with brisk efficiency. They strapped the stretcher onto a wheeled trolley and rushed it down a grey, brightly lit corridor, as Ros, almost forgotten, struggled to keep pace. Voices, low and brisk, gave orders and read out numbers.

The details blurred. A nurse took Ros by the arm and led her away, into a poky, airless room. She proceeded to ask endless questions about Sophie: her full name and date of birth, her blood group, their home address, details of their family doctor and her short medical history.

All Ros wanted to talk about was the accident and whether Sophie was going to be OK. But the nurse impassively wrote all the answers on printed forms, barely looking Ros in the face, then turned the clipboard and handed it across for Ros to sign consent to treatment.

'But how is she?'

The nurse rose to her feet and ushered Ros back into a waiting area. 'Take a seat. The doctors will be out to see you as soon as they can,' she said, then squeaked away across the corridor's polished floor.

Ros sat in limbo, dully staring at her phone. She jumped when it rang.

'I just got your message.' Adam sounded frantic. 'Are you alright?'

Of course she wasn't alright. She felt a sudden rush of emotion. Relief at the sound of his voice. She was no longer alone with the burden of it now. But his tone softened her defences a fraction too. Her jaw trembled as she tried to explain.

'I'm at Airedale. Not much news yet. They're doing tests.'

'But what happened?'

For a moment, Ros couldn't speak. She sensed the danger of letting herself go. She took a deep breath and straightened her position in the hard chair. 'She fell, from the window.' She swallowed hard. 'It was her. Lotte. She was at her apartment.'

'Her? But why? What was she doing—?'

Ros, hearing his anger, cut him short. 'Diana was going to take them for the afternoon. Then Max was ill and she couldn't and, well, apparently Lotte stepped in.'

Adam breathed heavily down the line. 'She fell out of a window?'

Ros whispered, 'Yes.'

Adam swore under his breath. She sensed him imagining what had happened to Sophie, visualising the drop from the apartment window. 'But how? I mean—'

'I don't know,' Ros said. 'I just don't know.' She hesitated, feeling her way. She wanted to soften the blow for him, to protect him from the hurt. He adored Sophie. He always had. 'Maybe it was an accident.' She thought about Lotte, standing there on the doorstep, feigning shock as she talked to the police. Ros's body clenched.

There was a tense silence.

'So how is she?' Adam's voice sounded strangled. 'Have the doctors, I mean—'

'I don't know yet. Her arm.' She paused, thinking of the sickening way it had twisted out of place. 'That looked bad. And I don't know, she was unconscious.'

'I'll come straight in. Where are you exactly? Can I bring anything?' He was thinking aloud, panicked, recalculating.

'No. Don't come, not yet.' Ros looked sightlessly at a long dark stain running down the wall in front of her. 'You need to get Bella.'

Adam sounded alarmed: 'Isn't she with you?'

'She's still with her.' She couldn't bring herself to say Lotte's name. 'I don't want her seeing Sophie like this. You need to go and get her. Now.'

Adam faltered. 'But I'm not allowed, the police thing... I'm not supposed to—'

Ros felt her voice rise. 'Go and get her, for heaven's sake. Don't even speak to that woman, don't make things worse, just get Bella away from her. OK? Call me as soon as you've got her safely home.'

'Shall I bring her with me, to Airedale?'

'No.' Ros looked around at the hard light, bouncing off the sterile corridor. This was no place for Bella. She'd be distressed enough. 'Stay home with her, will you? She needs you. Let's try to keep things as normal as possible for her. There's nothing you can do here. I promise I'll let you know if there's news.'

'What about you? Do you think you'll be there all night?'

'I don't know.' Ros shrugged. 'Maybe.'

A doctor appeared and stood in front of her, waiting. She was a middle-aged woman with tired eyes and greying hair.

'Gotta go. Tell me as soon as you've got Bella.' She rang off.

'Mrs Crofter?' the doctor asked.

Ros followed, her heart pounding, as the doctor led her into another bare room, dominated by a hospital bed with raised sides.

Sophie lay, white and still, her neck and back still supported by a brace, her crooked arm strapped to her side. Her eyes flickered without opening, then became still.

Ros's breath caught in her throat. She reached over the high sides to brush Sophie's hair from her face with her fingertips, then gently held her hand. 'Hello, beautiful,' she murmured. 'Can you hear me? It's Mummy.'

She bent over Sophie, looking down into the expressionless face, willing her to respond. Ros's eyes suddenly filled with tears, which gathered, then dropped onto her daughter's cheek, exploding and trickling down into her hair.

Ros pulled a tissue from her pocket and dabbed at first Sophie's face and then her own.

'Sorry, lovely. Did that tickle? Silly Mummy.'

Ros's back was rigid with tension, her shoulders like iron, but she struggled to keep her voice calm. She needed to imagine that Sophie could hear her and tried to give her daughter the impression that this was just another tumble that would soon mend.

On the side wall, a large screen showed coloured photographs of animals, each image dissolving quietly into the next. A blue whale became a lion. The lion morphed slowly into a butterfly.

The doctor started talking in a low voice about the need for further X-rays and an MRI and concerns about the extent of the trauma. Ros didn't understand, not really, but nodded as if she did and thanked the doctor repeatedly. There was talk of an operation to reset Sophie's shattered arm.

'Of course,' she heard herself saying. 'Whatever you need to do.'

Ros found herself wanting to tell this kindly doctor about what she'd witnessed, about the nightmarish horror of the fall and also all about Sophie – such a wonderful girl, so bright and funny and full of determination, the clever way she used words sometimes, the unexpected things she'd say that had always made them laugh, about the fact she wasn't just an ordinary girl, that she wanted to be an astronaut or maybe a famous film actress.

She wanted to explain: *Sophie has just had a strange time of it recently. Problems at school, that's all.*

She was about to speak when an orderly appeared, a thick-set man in green cotton overalls. He bustled around the bed, clicking the brakes off the wheels and turning the bed into a trolley. He pulled it away from the wall and put his weight behind it to push it out of the room.

Ros followed the doctor as the orderly wheeled Sophie down the squeaky, echoing corridor. Ros tried to press against the side of the trolley, leaning in so she could look down on Sophie's still, upturned face.

They pointed Ros to a new place to sit and wait – a short row of chairs bolted to the floor – then wheeled Sophie through plastic flapping doors.

Ros sat down, her hands grasping each other in her lap, her knuckles white.

Sometime later, Adam phoned her.

His tone was curt. He didn't say much about his visit to the apartment, only that Bella was safe at home again, tearful but unhurt and already settled in bed.

Ros gave him a brittle update on Sophie and promised him more news when she had it.

She pressed her spine into the hard back of the chair as if it could keep her upright. She imagined Bella, tucked under her brightly coloured duvet, her arms wrapped tightly around a cuddly bear or rabbit. Ros's own arms ached with the need to hold her, to rock her. At least she was safe, back with Adam, away from that woman.

Slowly, the hospital quietened. Ros sensed a shift change. Day staff bustled home to spouses and children. Night staff, languid in their movements, slipped in to take their places.

At around eight thirty, a nurse paused to speak to Ros as she hurried past. 'Mrs Crofter?'

Ros sat up straighter. 'Yes?'

'Has anyone been out to see you?'

Ros blinked. 'No. I mean, yes, but not for a long time.'

The nurse nodded. 'I'm sure the doctor will be able to update you soon.' She considered Ros. 'Have you eaten? The café's shut but there's a drinks machine just off the ward' – she pointed the way – 'and you can get something from the vending machine outside Maternity. They might have a sandwich left. Or a bar of chocolate.'

Ros felt too sick to eat or drink anything, but she nodded her thanks anyway. She folded up her jacket and set it on the wooden armrest of the chair as a pillow, tilted her body awkwardly sideways and drew up her knees. She closed her eyes and tried to let go, but images from the last few hours swirled in her mind. As her body started to surrender to tiredness, it jolted, making her gasp, as if she too were dropping into nothingness with her daughter.

After that, she stayed awake. She thought about Lotte. She thought about the allegations against Adam and the damage they were already causing his reputation. She thought about the way her website had been hacked and her image as a professional tarnished. *All of this,* she thought, *I can live with. All of this we can repair.*

But not Sophie, not our sweet, wonderful daughter. She imagined Sophie becoming paralysed, a wheelchair user for the rest of her life. She imagined her child with brain damage, the course of her life fundamentally altered forever. Ros's head swam with memories of the baby she'd carried, the little girl so full of fun and curiosity, the child who had already grown from an infant to a young girl.

She clenched her hands so hard that her nails cut half-moons in the soft skin of her palms. She squeezed her eyes shut and prayed: *Please, God, please, if you grant me anything in this life, look after my little girl, make her whole again. Please.*

But soon afterwards, as the long hours of waiting stretched out, a darker voice rose in her head, fuelled by rage and revenge. *No one hurts my little girls,* she thought. *You did this. I know you did. I'm going to get Sophie through this crisis and, once I have, I'm coming for you. Whatever it takes to make you pay the price for this, that's what I'll do.*

43

ROS

'Mrs Crofter?' A soft male voice.

Ros snapped open her eyes and bolted upright. Had she dozed off? It was late in the evening now. Her mouth felt dry, her eyes crusted.

A man of around thirty-five was stooping over her. He was wearing round black-framed glasses and his white coat looked crumpled. She blinked, disorientated. *He ought to hang it up*, she thought, *as soon as it comes out of the wash. Someone should tell him.*

'What?' She could hardly speak, his face looked so solemn. She froze. Was Sophie—? *Oh no, dear God, you wouldn't—*

'I'm so sorry.' The man sounded gentle and well-spoken. He pulled up a chair and sat close to Ros, their knees almost touching. 'I know you've had a long wait. We're short-staffed. One of the radiographers... well, you know.'

Ros stared at him, waiting, her heart aching.

He cleared his throat, suddenly awkward. 'It's early days,' he said. 'But so far the indications are very encouraging.'

Ros stared at his mouth as he spoke, seeing the changing shapes of his lips and struggling to understand. He started using medical terms she barely understood. Sophie's arm was badly broken, she knew that. It sounded now as if the operation to reset it had gone better than expected. They hadn't needed to insert pins. That was good news, surely?

He paused. His eyes were on hers and he seemed to read her uncertainty.

She said, 'So will it be OK? I mean, she'll be able to use it again, normally?'

He nodded, thoughtfully. 'That would certainly be my expectation, yes. For a child of her age, the outcomes are usually very positive.'

She frowned. 'What about her head? She was out cold. Do you know how far—?'

He gave a slow nod. 'Well, there's always an element of watch and wait, Mrs Crofter, when it comes to cranial trauma. There are indications of concussion. But, the results of the MRI, the brain scan – they haven't suggested any significant abnormalities so far.'

'So—' Ros hesitated, hardly daring to ask, 'are you saying that basically, apart from breaking her arm, she might be alright?'

'Well, generally, the prognosis for a head trauma of this nature—' He broke off and inclined his head to one side and considered Ros, as if he were deciding whether or not to disappear down another cul de sac of medical language. He paused. 'Basically, yes, from a clinical point of view, I'm optimistic that she may make a full recovery.'

For a moment, Ros was completely immobilised. Then, just when she tried to open her mouth to say thank you, first to the doctor but also, inside, to God, she found herself incapable of doing anything apart from bursting into noisy, messy tears.

44

ROS

Once Ros had called Adam to tell him what the doctor had said, she was led into a small, bare room.

Sophie was lying, inert, on the same bed. Her face was deathly pale and her position, on her back, her arms at her sides, stopped the air in Ros's throat. Sophie never slept like that. She looked lifeless, as if she'd been laid out.

Ros reached over and gently stroked her hair from her forehead. 'Hello, beautiful.' She looked over the medical apparatus, noted the changes to her girl. The cannula attached to the back of one hand, secured with tape, was dispensing clear liquid from a bag on a stand. The far arm was straightened, bulky in a plaster cast. 'Oh, my love.' Ros bit hard on her lip to stop herself from crying.

The doctor with the crumpled coat was watching her. 'She's doing well.' He lifted a padded chair from the far side of the room and set it beside Sophie's bed for Ros. 'You can sit with her, if you like.'

Ros looked anxiously at Sophie's still face. 'But she's still unconscious?'

A nurse, busy with the drip, said briskly, 'She's just sedated, that's all. Nothing to worry about. She came round briefly after the general anaesthetic.'

Ros spent the rest of the night dozing on and off by Sophie's bed. She leaned forward, one hand resting on the crisp white sheet that covered her daughter and the other reaching towards Sophie's face, cupped so that her knuckles skimmed the warm skin of her pale cheek.

The only sounds through the night hours were the low, intermittent whirrs and clicks from the drip that was feeding fluid into the back of Sophie's hand, underpinned by the soft hum of the machines that monitored her heart rate, her oxygen levels.

At around five thirty, just when Ros was squirming in her chair, trying to revive stiff muscles, Sophie stirred and let out a low moan.

'Sophie?' Urgently, Ros leaned over her. 'Are you OK? It's Mummy.'

Sophie's eyes flickered, then bunched as she tried to open them against the light. Her dry mouth spoke thickly. 'What is it?'

'You're in hospital, sweetheart.' Ros gazed down at her daughter's face. 'You're OK now but you had a nasty accident. Remember?'

Sophie's eyes closed again. A moment later, tears shone in the corners, swelled and burst down her temples, running into her hair.

Ros felt her heart tighten. 'It's alright, Sophie.' Her voice was a gentle song. 'You're safe now. The doctors and nurses are looking after you.'

Sophie's mouth compressed into a tight line. She didn't speak, just moved her head from side to side as her eyes continued to squeeze out tears.

45

ROS

'Stop calling it an accident.' Ros glared across the stained wooden table at Detective Wright, who regarded her impassively. 'SHE did it. I don't know how. I wasn't there. But Sophie's eight years old. She's a very sensible girl. She wouldn't open a second-floor window and lean out. She was in *her* care.'

An elderly man at the next table, hunched forward over a jacket potato and cheese, lifted his head and glanced across at them, frowning. It was mid-morning. Ros's head ached from worry and lack of sleep. The hospital café was subdued, the air cloyed with the smell of fried food and cheap coffee.

Detective Wright waited for a moment before she responded. The uniformed constable, sitting at the far end of the table, looked awkwardly from one face to the other as if he were trapped alongside a distressing tennis match.

'Mrs Humphries insists it was an accident. According to her statement' – she flipped back through her notebook – 'the children were all playing together in the lounge. She left them and went through to the kitchen to prepare food.'

Ros snorted. 'Of course she did.' She wished Adam were there. Maybe he'd do a better job of keeping calm. She'd had so little sleep. She took another sip of the hospital's bitter coffee. 'What about the window? Have you examined it?'

Detective Wright returned her gaze, coolly. 'We have attended the scene of the incident, Mrs Crofter, yes.'

'And?'

The detective looked weary. 'The catch seems perfectly secure. The windows were recently renovated, along with the rest of the property. There's no evidence that they're faulty or otherwise unsafe.'

Ros leaned in, her eyes flashing. 'So why wasn't it locked, when she's got small children in the apartment?'

'Apparently, most of the windows were secured by locks. But this one, inside Mrs Humphrey's bedroom, was an exception. She likes to keep it open at night, she said, for fresh air.'

Ros said, 'That's another thing. Why would Sophie be in that woman's bedroom? No reason at all. She must have lured her in there. An eight-year-old girl wouldn't suddenly get up from playing, leave her sister, go on her own into a strange adult's bedroom and then open the window and fall out.' She brandished her finger at the detective, feeling her temper rise. 'She did this to my daughter. And she's not getting away with it.'

Detective Wright didn't answer for a few moments. She looked back over her notes as if she were checking something. The elderly man had stopped pretending not to listen and was openly staring across at them as he chewed, waiting to hear the next line of the drama.

'The testimony which may prove central to this dispute is that of your daughter, Mrs Crofter. Would you or your husband raise any objection if we were to interview her about the events that led to her fall? Only, of course, once the medical team deems her well enough.'

Ros hesitated. She thought about Sophie, still so pale and fragile. She didn't want to subject her to any more stress than was strictly necessary. On the other hand, that woman couldn't be allowed to get away with this. Who knew what other vindictive acts she might stage?

She took a deep breath. 'That's fine. But I'd like to be present.'

The detective nodded. 'Absolutely. As long as you don't compromise or in any way hinder proceedings.' She paused. 'And just to clarify, so far, your daughter hasn't been able to tell you anything about what happened?'

Ros shook her head. She had tried, once or twice during the morning, to ask Sophie what she remembered about her time in Lotte's apartment. So far, she'd just been met with a blank stare, then, when she tried to coax her, more tears. Ros was reluctant to distress her daughter any more until she seemed less traumatised by what had happened.

The detective took a brave gulp of the foul coffee, glanced at the large industrial clock on the café wall and moved on. 'Now, Mrs Crofter, this other matter you mentioned, about malicious damage to your company website. What grounds do you have for accusing Mrs Humphries of that?'

The elderly man craned forward for a look as Ros pulled out her phone and brought up her website to show Detective Wright the doctored front page. She saw the police officer's eyes widen a fraction as she looked at the lewd picture.

'And you believe this image was falsified? Photoshopped, perhaps?'

'I don't know.' Ros felt her cheeks flush. 'Not necessarily.'

The uniformed police officer lifted his head from his notebook. 'She must have taken it.' Ros stuttered slightly as she explained, aware of how dreadful it all sounded. 'We went out drinking when we were away and I, well, I had a bit too much and I don't remember everything. But clearly it's her photo. How else did it get there?'

Detective Wright's eyes widened. It was hard to imagine

her being sympathetic to a woman of nearly forty getting legless in a club in Majorca and losing control of her faculties. 'This was when you and Mrs Humphries first met, on vacation?'

'Yes.' Ros pressed on. 'She was the one who asked me to go out for a drink with her, then pushed alcohol into me. I think it was all planned. She set me up, took the most embarrassing photo she could and then hacked into my website and posted it on the front page. It's sabotage.' Ros pointed again to her phone screen. 'I've lost business because of that. I'm sure I have. She's out to ruin our family.'

'May I?' Detective Wright took Ros's phone from her hands and photographed the page, with the website address, with her own phone. 'Well, we'll certainly add it to the file.'

Ros wasn't sure if the detective was being sincere or sarcastic.

As the two officers scraped back their chairs and heaved themselves to their feet, Ros said, 'I know it's nothing compared with what she's done to my daughter. Even what she's done to Adam. But it's still illegal, surely, hacking into my website and damaging my reputation? That's still a crime, isn't it?'

The detective nodded. 'We'll be in touch, Mrs Crofter, about arranging to talk with Sophie, once the doctors give permission.' She was obviously trying to be reassuring, but Ros's stomach clenched as she added: 'Perhaps then, we'll find out what really happened.'

46

ROS

'You don't think you'll be home this evening?'

Adam sounded stressed out. Ros could hear the strains of
the television in the background. She concentrated hard,
picking up indistinct phrases until she identified the song and,
with it, the Disney film Bella must be watching in the lounge.
She smiled tightly to herself. Her need to hold Bella throbbed
like a physical hurt. She'd only dropped her daughters off at
school the previous morning, but already it seemed like
weeks ago.

'No one's said anything yet about discharging her,' Ros said.
She was pacing back and forth on the lift landing outside the
entrance to the paediatric ward. The hospital's general visiting
hours hadn't started yet and the foyer was deserted, the acoustic
echoey. 'They want to keep monitoring her, after the concussion. I get the feeling nothing much will happen anyway over
the weekend. We may have to wait until Monday morning now
for a more senior doctor to see her.'

'Monday?' Adam sounded horrified. She could understand
why. Making it this far, Saturday afternoon, already felt like a
marathon.

He pressed on: 'Look, why don't I come in with Bella this afternoon? She'll be quiet if she's got the iPad. It might do her good. She's dying to see you. We could swap. I could sit with Sophie and you could bring Bella home and get a decent night's sleep.'

For a moment, Ros was tempted. The thought of lying in a clean bed and getting some sleep was intoxicating. She took a deep breath. 'No, that's OK. I'd rather be here.'

'Well, just for a few hours, then? I could bring Bella to the hospital with me. You could drive back and grab a shower and a change of clothes, then we could swap back. How about that?'

Ros frowned. She missed Bella terribly. She wanted so much to wrap her arms around her and give her a cuddle, to make sure she was fine. But she didn't want her there. She didn't want her to see Sophie in her present state. It was all too frightening for a four-year-old.

'Thanks, but I'd rather just see Bella at home, once Sophie's discharged.' She took a deep breath. It wasn't easy for Adam either, she knew that. He was doing his best. 'Take her out to the park or something, would you? Take her mind off what's going on. I'm hoping to get more rest tonight, now we're on the ward.'

A few hours before, Sophie had been moved out of emergency and onto a small paediatric ward. It was light and airy, and Ros had graduated from a hard chair to a padded armchair by her daughter's bed. Sophie's colour was slowly coming back too and, at lunchtime, Ros had helped her to eat some tomato soup and bread. They were incremental steps forward, but they felt like giant's strides.

Adam, always concerned, said, 'Have you eaten anything?'

'A bit.' Ros thought about the dry toast she'd forced down in the café while Sophie was being moved. Just the smell of it had made her stomach heave but she'd kept it down. 'Don't worry. I'm fine.'

She sensed his hesitation, before he said, 'Did I do the right thing, telling the police? I thought I'd better get in first. You know, in case she reported me for going round there.'

'Quite right.' Ros imagined how much he must have agonised about calling Detective Wright and reporting the accident. He must have felt terrified when he went around to Lotte's apartment to rescue Bella. He wasn't a person who ever broke rules, let alone a legal injunction. And he was in enough trouble as it was. 'Look, she didn't say a thing about that. I think she knows you had to go round. You didn't have much choice, the way things were.'

Adam let out a breath. 'Maybe that means she hasn't been in touch with them to make a complaint.'

Ros nodded to herself. 'Which speaks volumes,' she said, thoughtfully. 'It's not like her to miss a chance to put the knife in. She must really be worried if she's suddenly keeping a low profile.' She looked out across the empty foyer, mulling it all over, and added. 'Maybe she knows we're on to her.'

Adam didn't answer.

Even now, after all that had happened, Ros still wasn't sure if he believed her.

47

LOTTE

It was blisteringly hot that summer. The air had been thick with the close, oily smell of molten asphalt, the crackle of parched grass and the sharp, shrill notes of ice-cream vans.

Some of my earliest summer memories were of being fielded out for the day to other families, an experience I remember as both exciting and bewildering. I was dropped off with all sorts of people. I never quite became used to the unnerving strangeness of being plunged – all alone at first, until my sister, Emma, was old enough to join me – into differently furnished homes with peculiar toys and unfamiliar routines. I didn't understand why until years later, when I finally understood my mother's need to stitch together a creative patchwork of childcare to cover the gaps between her annual leave and my long summer vacation from school.

There was the cleaner who snoozed in an armchair all day. She had two cats that I chased determinedly all over her apartment each visit, trying to coax them out from under dressers and down from the tops of wardrobes, fancying myself a cat whisperer.

There was a neighbour down the street with two older boys who part-fascinated, part-frightened me as they made me join in their games of spies or cops and robbers. The neighbour, a big-waisted, cheerful woman, wore her hair in a bun and cooked up hearty food of a kind I'd never eaten before, like toad-in-the-hole and bubble and squeak. I still can't catch the smell of greasy fried mash without being transported back to her kitchen.

Somewhere in the middle of all this, in August, I'd be packed off to stay for a week or so with my mother's older sister and her husband in Ilkley: Aunt Rose and Uncle James. My uncle worked in a building society in Skipton and wasn't often around, but I remember running to the door when I heard him coming home, knowing there was a good chance he'd have brought me a treat from the newsagents on the corner – a white chocolate mouse or liquorice sherbet or an elasticated necklace of multi-coloured sugar beads to suck and snap. Unlike my own father, he indulged me with horseplay, rolling me around on the floor, tickling, while my aunt shook her head and smiled at the two of us and told him not to get me overexcited before bed.

Aunt Rose was a school teacher in a primary school in Addingham. She wore flowery dresses and flat shoes and kept a large wooden box under the sideboard, filled with scraps of coloured paper and felt, sequins and threads. Some of my happiest afternoons were spent kneeling up at the kitchen table, its surface carefully covered by spread sheets of the *Ilkley Gazette* or the *Telegraph and Argus*, following her movements as we made jewellery from uncooked pasta or monsters out of old cereal packets.

I knew very few adults like them. They didn't have children of their own but, nonetheless, they understood what children wanted and took care to make their home not only safe for young children but a happy place for them. Aunt Rose's house was modern and tidy and could have been boring to a child. No attics or turrets or cellars to explore. But she made up for it with baking and painting and imaginative games that had me fishing for sharks from the banisters or rowing across the carpet to a desert island in a cardboard box.

Then there was the garden. It had an old plum tree with a thick rope swing, created by Uncle James, and a stubby platform, made of several planks nailed into the wood at the height of about ten feet, just high enough to be dangerously thrilling to a young child. Once I was confident enough to climb up there, I called it my own special lookout, a place to perch with my back against the trunk, munching a snack or reading a comic.

The house was close to the river and the grassy garden tumbled downwards from the house to a wooden fence with its own gate. It gave on to the muddy footpath which ran under the trees along the bank of the Wharfe, along the Middleton side of the river. Beyond the footpath, there were steep mud tracks, worn by generations of children, to the edge of the water, through slopes peppered with nettles and wild grass and gnarled, ivy-hung trees.

At the time, I accepted their love for me without question. It was just the way of things that my mother had children, but Aunt Rose and Uncle James did not. Since then, I've wondered if they were really childless by choice or if they'd been heartbroken not to have any of their own. Whatever their disappointments, they certainly loved children and I loved them.

That particular sweltering summer, I was seven and Emma, my little sister, was five. My mother was always more protective of her than she'd been of me. In her early years, Emma refused to sleep away from home without our mother and no one forced her. So I knew it was a milestone for everyone when my mother left us together with my aunt and uncle for the first time.

I was certain she'd left me in the past with barely a backwards glance but, on this day, she seemed loathe to wrench herself away. She waved a hand out of the car window all along the street until she finally turned into the main road.

As the car disappeared from view, Emma promptly burst into tears. It was as if they both knew, my mother and Emma, what a terrible mistake it was to prove for them to be parted.

I took charge of Emma at once. I was embarrassed, worried even at the age of seven, about how it would make our aunt and uncle feel if she didn't seem happy. It could spoil my visit too. I felt a veteran of their home by then, and was still adjusting to the fact I was expected to share it all with Emma. My sense of ownership made it fair, in my view, for Emma to take second best. I gave myself the first choice of where to sleep – taking the narrow single bed with the feather pillow and leaving Emma to a sleeping bag on a blow-up mattress next to me, under the sloping roof. She was a shy girl, used to living in my shadow when we were together, and, if she minded, she didn't complain.

It was Uncle James who unveiled the dinghy that afternoon. He'd borrowed it from a work colleague and, at first, we used it as a paddling pool. Emma and I had danced around him in our bikinis in the garden as he rolled up his sleeves and, red in the face and sweating hard, he set about inflating it with a modest foot pump.

Once it was firm, Aunt Rose carried out buckets of warm water and filled it and we spent the rest of the afternoon shrieking and splashing each other and churning the surrounding grass to slippery mud.

The next day, Sunday, I came across its heavy plastic oars, propped up at the back of the garden shed and started begging our uncle to take us out on the river. The day was sticky with heat and a panting heaviness lay over the town. As the sun rose, even the playground on the other side of the river fell silent.

Aunt Rose lathered us both in sun-cream and put floppy hats on our heads and told us to keep, as much as we could, to the shrinking line of shade beneath the trees.

When the worst of the day was over, Uncle James finally gave in. Yelling and whooping, we ran ahead and back like overexcited puppies as he heaved the dinghy onto his shoulder and carried it out of the garden and, gingerly shifting sideways, manoeuvred it through the trees to the edge of the river. He tied it to an overhanging branch and lifted us both in.

Nowadays, of course, people worry about lifejackets for kids when they take to the water, and helmets when they ride bikes. There was none of that with Uncle James. He prided himself on being from another generation, when kids had more freedom to be independent but also ran more danger. We'd both been taken to the swimming baths since we were babies and we weren't afraid of the water. Even if we should have been.

My memory of that afternoon is tarnished by hindsight but at the time, it was an amazing adventure. In places, the water was still and languid under the trees and when we drifted into these calm pockets, it became a game to shove ourselves away from the shore again, pushing back on tree branches, spurring ourselves back into motion.

In other areas, in the centre of the river, the bright, clean water was fast flowing, foaming as it tore downstream towards the weir. We shrieked and swayed, leaning back to brace ourselves when the current caught the dinghy, spinning us to one side, then back again, or tossing us off course while Uncle James plied his plastic oars to regain control.

At the end of the afternoon, he headed for a natural stone beach, revealed by the river's mid-summer shallowness, and dragged the dinghy out of the water. We paddled and splashed in the shallows, curling our toes tightly against the poking sharpness of the stones and feeling the drag of the current on puckered skin.

Later, my aunt made hot chocolate. When I closed my eyes in bed, my body still rose and fell with the motion of the water.

When I think back now, I want to wrap my arms around that child, who slipped so happily into sleep, and save her from the future. She had no idea of the horrors to come.

48

LOTTE

'Don't be a scaredy cat.'

Emma hung back, watching me with large eyes as I lifted one end of the cumbersome oar and gestured to her to grab the other end.

'Come on.' I pulled a face at her. 'If you don't help, you can't come.'

She took a reluctant step forward and hoisted it up into the air, hugging it close to her side as she wrapped her arm around it. We set off towards the river in a jerky, awkward rhythm, knocking each other off balance if we moved too fast.

The second oar was easier. We stowed them both under the trees, out of the river's reach, then went back for the dinghy itself.

The inflatable, so agile on water, was a dead weight on land. Uncle James had left it leaning upright against the side of the shed, drying. It was easy enough to push it sideways, so it fell flat onto the grass, but it was much harder to force it across the dry grass. We slipped and slid and panted as we strained, tried pushing and pulling and even kicking it.

When we finally got it through the gate and across the path, we slid it through a patch of nettles towards the water's edge, freeing it now and then from snagging tree branches.

'There!' It dropped with a satisfying smack onto the surface of the water and turned, caught at once by the current. I hung on to the rope.

'We'll get into trouble.' Emma's face was red with exertion.

Aunt Rose had tipped us out into the garden to play while she caught up with housework. Did she tell us to stay away from the river? She usually did. It was a long-standing house rule. But this was different. We'd never had a dinghy at our disposal before. It was our big chance to have an adventure and I didn't want to miss out.

'No, we won't.' I tried to sound more confident than I felt, showing off in front of my little sister. 'Anyway, they needn't ever know.' I gave her a stern look. 'Unless you tell. You've got to promise you won't.'

Emma nodded but still made no move to scramble down to the shoreline to join me.

I beckoned to her. 'Well, come on then.' I felt the steady pull of the dinghy on the rope. It was a wild stallion, bucking and straining, one only I could tame. 'Or I'll go without you.'

She slithered down, grabbing roots and branches to slow her descent, then grabbed my hand. I held the dinghy steady as she clambered in. Between us, we managed to get the oars in after her, then I jumped in, releasing us to the tug of the water.

'Paddle harder! Not like that, like this!'

Uncle James, with his muscles, had made it look easy to control the dinghy. It wasn't, not for two small girls. Even so, the struggle was fun at first. I was the captain of my own boat, out on the wild water. Finally, I was having the kind of madcap adventure I'd read about in books. When Emma dropped her oar and I leaned over and grabbed it just before it floated away – a violent move which set us both rocking – we giggled helplessly.

In the centre of the river, hard sunlight shattered into shafts. Along the banks, it mellowed, streaming greenly through the trees. Even Emma, lounging on her back, gazing at the cloudless sky, seemed awed by the magic.

Thwack. Something hard bounced off the side of the dinghy. Emma sat up, startled. A solid plop in the water near us made me twist around to look. For a moment, it seemed to be something rising from the river. A fish, maybe. I peered down, seeing nothing but the ripples of light on the stony bed far below. Another splash made me turn and shield my eyes, peering at the bank.

Two lads, much older than us, were standing on the stony beach, chucking pebbles at us.

'Hey!' I shouted. 'Stop it!'

One said something to the other and they laughed. An arm drew back and another stone flew through the air towards us. It landed smack on the bottom of the boat. Emma, frightened, drew in her knees and looked to me, certain I'd know what to do.

I picked up the stone and angrily threw it back. It fell far short, dropping into the water.

The lads hollered and jeered at me. 'Want a fight?' one called. 'Come on, then!'

Emma's lip trembled. 'Don't, Lotte, please.'

'They're just stupid little boys.' I tried to sound defiant, to bolster Emma's confidence, but inside, I was scared too. 'Stupid, stupid, stupid!'

The current was drawing us closer to where they stood. It felt as if a giant invisible hand under the water had grasped the dinghy and was steadily bringing it in, delivering us into danger. I felt helpless, powerless to stop it.

As the gap narrowed, the stones flew more often, striking the rib of the boat and falling back into the water. Then Emma let out a howl and gripped her ear. A stone had clipped her.

The howl turned into a low moan of pain. She bent forward, nursing her injury. Her oar slid from her hand, into the water, and drifted away. This time it happened too quickly for me to think about retrieving it.

Emma, curled forward, was crying. Blood pounded in my ears. Frantically, I shoved my single oar in the water and tried to pull us back, to stop our inexorable passage to the shore. The current was too strong, and I was too weak. The dinghy turned lightly on the surface of the water, twisting this way and that in the flow, but there seemed nothing I could do to change its course.

The boys, sensing victory, jumped and jeered. Panic bubbled up through my body, making me nauseous. As they grew nearer, the boys loomed, bigger and more menacing. They were teenagers, twice my size. The older one was thick with muscle. I knew I couldn't fight them. I knew they were too strong for me. I didn't know what else to do, how to drive them off, how to make them leave us alone. My hands shook as I stuck the end of my oar deep in the water and I leaned back, both hands gripping the handle, uselessly trying to slow down.

I was too small and too late. As we approached the rounded edge of the stone spur, the older boy took a step or two into the water, leaned out and grabbed hold of the rope that ran around the outside of the dinghy. He stepped backwards, bringing us closer still. The bottom of the dinghy bumped and scraped against the outlying stones.

I clambered across, making the dinghy pitch and sway, and hit uselessly at his arm, trying to beat him off. My blows seemed to make no difference to him.

'Temper, temper.' He grinned, showing wolfish teeth. His shoulders were as broad as a man's and his upper lip was tufty with the first growth of a moustache. 'We've got you, you naughty girls.'

I screamed, 'Let go!'

Emma, her face streaked with tears, lifted her face to stare at him, horror-struck.

'Got you!' He puffed and panted as he tried to heave the boat closer to shore.

The other boy, his face and body thinner, splashed into the shallows to join him.

'Stop it!' I screamed at them, beside myself, both frightened and furious. 'Leave us alone!'

The second boy, scrawnier and, I could see now, younger than the first, said, 'They're not very polite, are they? Called us stupid, didn't they?'

The older one said, 'I think they need a lesson in good manners. Don't you?'

Emma, her knees drawn up, crept closer to me in the boat and pressed against my side. I looked around desperately for help. This was an ominously quiet section of the river. The stony beach was hemmed in by a high mud bank, dense with trees and bushes.

'Help!' I tipped back my head anyway and screamed, as loudly as I could: 'Help!' My voice sounded puny and weak, dispersing into nothingness in the open air.

The boys just laughed.

The older, stronger boy reached in and grabbed me under the arms, hauling me out.

'Stop it.' I kicked and flailed, trying to twist around to land a blow on him but he was too big, too strong for me. 'Put me down!'

'Lotte!' Emma's cry was so pitiful, it stabbed my heart. 'Help me!'

'Kick him, Em! Fight!'

It was useless. The bigger boy pinned my arms behind my back and marched me onto the stones. He dug a knee in my back. The wrench sent a hot jolt of pain through my shoulders and I cried out.

Emma, sobbing, too frightened to put up a fight, let herself be captured. She stumbled out of the boat, caught her foot and pitched forwards onto the pebbles. The second boy grabbed her arm and heaved her back to her feet.

Outraged, I jerked back my elbow and dug my attacker as hard as I could in the chest.

He swore, winded, then tightened his grip on my arms. He lifted his knee again and bashed me hard in my lower back. His breath was hard in my ear. 'Want to fight, do you?'

I twisted my head and tried to bite him but he was too quick for me. He dragged me ahead of him over the uneven stones to a ridge of sandy earth at the base of the overhanging bank, throwing me down onto the ground. I struggled up and tried to bolt around him, to get away, but he reached out easily and recaptured me, laughing at the feebleness of my attempt.

'Nice try, shrimp.' Then he called over his shoulder to the other boy, who was approaching with Emma.

His job was easier. She was already submissive, her nose running miserably, her face meek and defeated.

'What shall we do with them, little bro?'

The younger boy shrugged. 'Walk the plank?'

'Not a bad idea.' The older boy nodded. His eyes were on mine, watching for my reaction, playing with me.

'That's my uncle's boat.' My voice sounded shrill and childish, even to me. 'He'll be looking for us.'

'Oh, he will, will he?' The boy made a show of looking out at the empty river. 'You sure about that? I can't see him.'

The other boy sniggered.

'He will. And he'll call the police, when he hears what you've done.'

Emma, hopeful, raised her eyes. I could see her frowning as she considered whether this might be true. I tried to look confident but I knew I was lying. Uncle James was at work. He had no idea we'd taken his boat, without permission. We'd be the ones in trouble.

'Ooh, the police!' The older boy's tone was mocking. 'I'm so scared.'

He gave me a hard shove in the chest and, caught off guard, I found myself propelled backwards, landing on my bottom with a thud. I winced as a sharp stone stuck into me.

The teenager took a step closer and stood over me. I shrank back. His skin had a greasy sheen. A cluster of red pimples ran down one side of his nose. I lay, panting, too terrified to move.

'Maybe we'll keep 'em as slaves for a bit first.' He was speaking to the other boy, but his eyes were on mine. 'Put 'em to work. Good plan?'

'Sounds good to me.'

Somewhere behind, Emma squealed, 'Lotte!'

I bit my lip, tying not to cry. The panic in Emma's voice was infectious. I made my hands into fists. I had to be strong. I had to handle this for both of us.

'Lotte!' The younger boy mimicked her. 'Aw, how cute. Little Lotte.'

'Let us go!' I tried to stand up, but the boy shot out a hand and shoved me back again, sending me sprawling.

'We're going to teach you a lesson,' he said. There was meanness in his look that made me shiver. He was working himself up to anger. 'You've no business being here.'

'Yes, we have.' I squirmed on the stones. 'It's not *your* river. Our aunt and uncle live here. We've every right.'

'You hear that?' He shook his head. 'Fancy. Her ladyship's family owns the Wharfe. Who knew.'

I swallowed. 'I didn't say they—'

'Shut up!'

I tried to peer past him, to see what was happening to Emma.

She was sprawled, face down, on the stones. The younger

boy was sitting astride her, lazily pinning her to the ground with his body weight.

I shouted to him: 'Get off! You'll hurt her!'

He just shrugged and didn't move.

Emma managed to lift her shoulders enough to turn her face towards me. It was swollen and red with crying. Mucus bubbled around her nostrils as she gulped air.

'So, as we were saying,' the older boy carried on, 'you owe us an apology.'

I didn't answer.

'You want us to let you go, you'd better say sorry.'

I took a deep breath and mumbled, 'Sorry.'

He cupped his hand behind his ear. 'What was that? I didn't quite hear her. Did you?'

'Nah,' said the other boy. 'Not me.'

'Go on then.' He lifted his leg and prodded my chest with his dirty foot. 'Speak up.'

I opened my mouth to speak again but the unfairness of it all stopped my breath. We hadn't done anything to them, so why should I say sorry?

He seemed to sense my struggle and raised his eyebrows in a questioning look. 'Well? We're waiting.'

Emma, flattened on the ground, whimpered. She was such a tiny thing. She had the bones of a bird. He must be hurting her.

I took a deep breath and said loudly: 'I'm sorry. OK?'

'Nope.' The older boy grimaced. 'Didn't catch that either.'

The young boy laughed, enjoying the sport.

I shouted: 'I said I'm sorry, didn't I? Let us go.'

My voice faltered and for an awful moment, I thought I was losing it, cracking into tears.

There was an awkward silence. The older boy turned, as if he were sounding out the other, deciding how much further to push it.

I seized my moment. I jumped up and flung myself at him,

catching him off guard, hitting him with everything I had. My only advantage was surprise.

His arm reached for me, his eyes widened, and I grabbed his hand and bit down on it. It was one of the few weapons I had. He yowled and swore, pulling his hand away and bending over it.

I pushed past him, on my feet but propelled unsteadily forward, and flung myself into the other boy, knocking him sideways off Emma.

'Em! Run!'

For a second, no one seemed to move. Then suddenly Emma was scrambling to her feet in a flurry of stones and staggering towards the dinghy. I kicked out at the smaller boy, catching him in the face, and surged after her. I grabbed the dinghy with both hands and together Emma and I dragged it back to the water.

Already, the older boy, nursing his injured hand, was closing the gap between us, his eyes blazing with fury.

Fuelled by panic, I threw myself full length into the dinghy, sending it skimming, then twisted back and reached out a hand to Emma. She was splashing messily through the shallows, sending up fingers of spray.

I tried to steady the boat as it rotated on the current, feeling itself afloat again.

'Come ON!' I screamed. 'Jump!'

Emma hurtled towards me and I seized her hand, trying to pull her up over the rim and into the safety of the boat. Her feet slipped on the plastic sides and she fell back again.

'I've got you.' I tugged as hard as I could on her hand, trying again to heave her up and over, even as the dinghy swung out into deeper water, into the fast-moving river.

Behind, the bigger boy was splashing towards us, fuelled by anger, shouting: 'I'm gonna get you!'

Emma, twisting back to see, whimpered, her grip on my fingers slipping.

'Hang on!' I closed her fingers around the rough rope which ran around the outside of the rib and fell to paddling frantically with our single oar, trying to get the dinghy further out into the river, away from the boys, desperate to catch the fast-flowing current that might sweep us away from the shore. It was our only hope of escape.

I peered over the side, grinding the end of the oar into the stones on the riverbed.

Bang! Something solid crashed onto us. The dinghy bounced and tipped into the air. One side rose crazily from the surface. I felt my feet jump through empty air as I fell backwards, dizzy and disorientated, then I smacked, the back of my head first, into cold, rushing water that closed over me.

The sunlight streaked away into a blurred mass of ripples and foam as my head and shoulders crashed against stones. My lungs burned.

I kicked out wildly, panicking, and felt my body right itself, then whoosh upwards through the churn. My head broke the surface not in the open air, as I'd expected, but in a dim yellowish pod, dappled with amber light. I gasped. I focused on coughing and filling my lungs with air again.

A moment later, I realised what had happened. The older boy, pursuing us, had somehow hurled himself at the dinghy and flipped it upside down. I was now underneath it in the air pocket, being carried away downstream.

I grabbed the rope and hung, suspended there, my legs curled up under me, as the dinghy drifted on, gradually gathering speed as it drew me away, off into the flow.

49

ROS

'What is it, sweetheart?'

Sophie was pale and exhausted. All night, she'd hardly slept. Ros, lying beside her on a lumpy fold-out hospital chair, had reached over every time she heard another of her daughter's distressed moans and murmured to her.

In the small hours, just as Ros had dozed off again, Sophie let out a sudden shriek, jolting her mother awake.

'What, Sophie?' Ros whispered.

Sophie's eyes were wide and glassy.

'Is it hurting? Your arm?' Ros looked past her down the shadowy space between the set of six beds, towards the dimly lit nursing station. 'Do you need some more medicine?'

Sophie didn't yet seem clear where she was. She was struggling to focus.

'You're in hospital, remember? Mummy's right here. You're safe now, Sophie.'

Sophie frowned to herself.

'Was it a bad dream?' Ros kept her voice low, sensitive to the rest of the ward. 'It's gone now. All gone.' She sat up properly, pushing aside the blanket the hospital had given her. She swung down her legs and went to perch at the top of Sophie's bed near her pillow. 'It's strange here, isn't it?' she whispered. 'I know. It's been an awful shock, hasn't it? But you've been so lucky. The police and everyone say so. If the bushes hadn't broken your fall, well, it could have been much worse. But they did, didn't they? Clever bushes.' She paused.

Ros sensed Sophie's stillness. Her breathing had slowed to become steady and even again. 'I'm hoping we might be able to go home tomorrow. Wouldn't that be great? Daddy and Bella will be so excited. They're dying to see you. They miss you so much, petal.'

She bent lower to kiss her daughter's cheek.

Sophie screwed her eyes tightly closed. Tears leaked in a sudden stream from the outer corners, meandering down her temples to dampen the pillow below.

'Oh, Sophie.' Ros plucked a tissue from the box on the bedside locker and dried them. 'I know. But the worst is over now. You're young and healthy. Your arm will soon mend.'

She stayed close to her daughter, stroking her hair. Sophie's muscles slowly slackened as she relaxed and slipped back into sleep.

Back on her fold-out chair, Ros lay quietly, her eyes on the dark squares of the ceiling tiles above them, thinking hard.

Sophie was withdrawn when the police tried to talk to her the next morning.

It wasn't their fault. Even Detective Wright managed to show a gentler side of her brisk personality when she bent forward, lowering her voice and doing her best to encourage Sophie to open up.

Ros sat beside Sophie, holding the hand of her uninjured arm. Across from them, a young female officer took notes.

They'd chosen the playroom on the children's ward for the

interview. It was a poky side room made palatable by cartoon stencils on the walls and a jumbled assortment of plastic toys in brightly coloured toy bins. A stack of leaflets hung in a pouch by the door, suggesting ways of supporting the local charity that had provided it.

Detective Wright led up to the time of the accident with general questions about school and the weather that day and how Sophie might have been feeling.

Ros listened, trying hard not to interrupt. Sophie had always been such a bright, chatty kid. The monosyllabic answers she was giving the detective, the silent nods and shakes of her head, that wasn't at all like her. Was it the concussion? Or was it something else?

Detective Wright was calmly continuing: 'So you were playing with Bella and Caitlyn in the lounge, Caitlyn's mummy says, and she went off to make the tea. Is that what happened, Sophie?'

Sophie just looked at her with big eyes.

'Or was it something else?'

Ros squeezed her hand and prompted: 'Can you tell us, petal? Tell us what you remember. You're not in trouble. They're just trying to understand.'

Sophie shook her head.

'What happened, Sophie?' Detective Wright's gaze was intent, reading her face. 'Why did you go into Caitlyn's mummy's bedroom? Was there something there you wanted to have a look at? It's OK. You can tell us.' Pause. 'Or did someone tell you to go in there?'

Sophie turned her head and looked at Ros, her eyes fearful.

'It's OK.' Ros tried to smile reassuringly. 'The detective is on our side. She wants to help.'

Sophie bit down on her lip and closed her eyes, shutting them out.

Detective Wright lifted her gaze to meet Ros's and raised a questioning eyebrow.

'Maybe we'd better leave it for now,' she said.

Ros nodded. 'Maybe in a few days' time,' she said in a low voice. 'When we're home, and she feels a bit better in herself.'

A short time later, once the police officers had left, Ros crouched down by Sophie's side.

'You do remember, don't you?' She rested her warm hands on Sophie's legs and looked straight into her daughter's eyes. 'What is it, Sophie? What happened?'

Sophie's eyes flickered and filled with tears.

Ros's gaze didn't falter. 'Whatever it is, you won't get into trouble. We just really need to know.' She hesitated. 'Can I tell you what I think happened? I think Caitlyn's mum did something. Maybe she asked you to go into her bedroom with her, so she could show you something? Maybe she asked you to go across to the window so she could point something out to you, something fun? Am I right? Can you remember?'

She watched her daughter for the slightest flicker of reaction. 'You can tell me, can't you? Please, my love. You won't get into trouble. Is she the one you're worried about? Did she threaten you in some way, say something terrible would happen if you told? You know that's wrong, don't you, Sophie, if she did say that?'

Sophie lifted her hand to her face and began to sob. 'I can't tell you, Mummy. I promised.'

Ros leaned in and wrapped her arms around her daughter. She held her tightly and rocked her gently, kissing the top of her head.

When the sobbing finally subsided, Ros whispered: 'I need you to be very brave, Sophie. Please. I really need you to tell me about this. Sometimes, if someone else has done a very bad thing, a dangerous thing, grown-ups need to know. Even if it's frightening, telling someone you trust is the right thing to do.'

Sophie shuddered. Her eyes were red and bright with tears, her face wretched.

'Please, Sophie. You know you can trust me.' Ros sensed that Sophie was listening keenly and, finally, wavering. She was getting through to her daughter at last.

'Good girl,' Ros carried on, carefully. 'That's it. You'll feel better if you tell me, Sophie. I'm sure you will.' She held Sophie tightly in the circle of her arms, keeping her safe, and put her cheek close to her daughter's.

'Now then, my love,' she murmured. 'You be a brave girl and tell me what happened.'

50

LOTTE

A man, walking his dog along the riverbank, pulled me out.

He didn't realise he was saving a child. He'd just waded in after his barking, splashing dog, which had been leaping round the strange yellow floating mass. He discovered me as he heaved it to the bank. I had been clinging on underneath, inside the air bubble, my skin blue with cold, my numb fingers still clamped determinedly to the rope.

I heard about the rescue later. I don't remember the man or the dog or being found.

My memory only restarted later. A scratchy blanket around my shoulders and a strong man hoisting me up into his arms and carrying me into the back of a vehicle. An ambulance, as it turned out. Inside, he stripped off my sodden clothes. I remember feeling mortified at being naked in front of him, a stranger, even as he rubbed me down, called me Tiger and handed me a vast blue T-shirt, no doubt his own. It smelled of laundry soap and reached almost to my knees.

Later, there was sweet, warm milk in a ceramic mug and a piece of chocolate, then the sight of Aunt Rose, eyes swollen with crying, jumping out of Uncle James's car and running to me, throwing her arms round me and saying, 'Praise the Lord!' I hadn't even known she believed.

But then she'd my face in her hands. 'Where is she?' She'd looked me hard in the eyes and I saw the fear there. 'Where's Emma?'

I opened my mouth to tell her about the teenage boys and everything they'd done to us, and I thought about Emma, lying there sobbing on the stones, pinned down by that boy, calling my name, needing me to save her. She'd trusted me when I rushed her to the water and fastened her fingers around the dinghy rope and told her to hold on.

I found I couldn't speak.

Apparently, the search went on all night. Divers and flashlights and shouts across the water.

They found her body in the small hours, becalmed in a deep, still section of river, her billowing clothes caught in the stooping branches of a tree. My little sister, dead at the age of five.

51

LOTTE

It is a terrible burden to be your parent's less-loved child.

I think I felt it, deep down, even when I was little. My mother certainly loved me but her love for Emma had been of different stuff. I remember, at the age of three or four, lifting my head from a toy and seeing the two of them together, lost in each other: my infant sister, locked in my mother's arms, her eyes fixed on my mother's face with a look of utter devotion; my mother, smiling and dreamlike, gazing down on her, besotted. My world had shifted and never fully righted itself again.

When my mother's car had drawn up outside my aunt and uncle's house, I had run and hidden in the garden shed. It smelt of wood shavings and varnish and I was frightened of the dark with its cobwebs and scuttling woodlice. I waited, huddled in a corner, my face pressed into drawn-up knees. I longed for my mother to hurry out to find me, to wrap me in her arms and comfort me.

She never came.

Later, much later, my aunt coaxed me out. My legs were stiff and she put her arm around me as she led me back into the house.

My mother was a hunched shape in a shadowy corner of the lounge, wearing a black dress I'd never seen before. Her face was puffy and lined with grief and sleeplessness.

I crossed the room to her and stood there, trembling, willing her to open her arms to me. She turned away. I tugged at her dress and tried to scramble up onto her knee, desperate to be hugged.

She glared at me. 'You did this!' Her voice was a spiteful hiss. 'You wicked girl.'

I shrank back. I couldn't speak.

'Helen!' My aunt lay a warm hand on my shoulder, steadying me. Her tone was soft. 'Don't. Don't take it out on her.'

My mother's eyes flashed. 'Why not? It's her fault. If she hadn't—' She broke down and wept.

My aunt took me into their pristine kitchen and sat me up at the counter. She warmed some milk, mashed a banana with a fork and spread it in a sandwich, then sat close beside me as I tried to eat.

'Grief does funny things to people,' she said, quietly. 'She doesn't know what she's saying, Lotte. You're just a child. I know that's hard to understand.'

The bread was thick in my throat. I did understand. I understood completely. If one of us were to have been saved, my mother would have longed for it to have been Emma, not me. Now I would serve as a constant disappointing reminder of the perfect little girl she'd lost.

I took a big breath and blurted out: 'But it wasn't my fault. There were these big boys. Brothers. They attacked us. We were trying to get away.'

My aunt looked down at her clasped hands. For a moment, she didn't speak. I didn't know what power my revelation might have. Perhaps it would shift the spotlight onto the boys. Perhaps it would change everything, stop even my mother blaming me.

In fact, my aunt seemed unmoved. 'It's nobody's fault,' she said, finally. 'It was an accident. A terrible accident. That's all.'

For the next few days, I spent a lot of time hiding, alone, in the bedroom that Emma and I had shared. I lay on the blow-up bed and drowned in my own sorrow and guilt. Maybe my mother was right. It was my fault. *If only I'd let Emma choose the single bed. If only I'd believed her when she said it was wrong.* I'd called her a scaredy cat when she didn't want to take the dinghy out on our own, frightened we'd get into trouble. *If only I'd listened.*

My aunt served me sandwiches or fish fingers in the kitchen, and sat with me while I ate. It felt wrong, eating when Emma couldn't. Still living when she wasn't. My mother, a bowed, motionless figure in the lounge, seemed too mired in grief to notice me.

I remember the house humming with the doleful murmur of adult voices as they answered telephone calls, received sad-eyed visitors and made arrangements for the funeral, back home in south London.

Once, late in the evening, after I'd been put to bed, the voices from the lounge became raised. I gripped the top edge of my eiderdown, shaking.

It was my mother. She was screaming: 'Where *were* you? You said you'd look after them. You lied to me. You *lied.*'

'Come on now, Helen.' Uncle James's voice. 'Don't say things you'll regret.'

'She's always been jealous of me!' My mother sounded out of control. 'Always! Is that why, Rose? Is it? You couldn't stand the fact I was so happy?'

'Stop it!' Uncle James was losing his temper. 'That's enough! She's in pieces, for God's sake. Can't you see?'

I had huddled further under the eiderdown, rounded into a ball and pressed my hands to my ears to block them all out.

52

LOTTE

The next morning, Uncle James, taking pity on me, I suppose, took me out with him when he walked briskly to the local shops to buy groceries. As we strode along Denton Road, ready to turn right over the road bridge and into the centre of Ilkley, I gazed aimlessly over the houses with their neat gardens and brightly painted doors.

I saw him. He stared out at me from behind the picture windows of the house on the corner. Him. The older boy, the heavy one who'd straddled and hurt me, the one who was almost a man.

I froze, pulled back hard on my uncle's hand as if it were a brake. My uncle, stopped in his tracks, looked down at me. 'You OK?'

I pointed. Sun suddenly burst through the clouds overhead flashed on the surface of the window and turned the glass into a mirror for the dappled sky, hiding the boy from view as if he had never been.

'They live here,' I said. 'Those big boys.'

I looked up into my uncle's face. He frowned, confused. 'What boys?'

I blinked. *Surely my aunt has told him?*

I tugged at his arm to get him to stoop lower. 'That day, on the river,' I whispered. 'We were trying to escape two boys. Teenagers.'

He shook his head at me and just said sadly, 'Oh, Lotte.'

He moved forward, and hurried me on.

When we reached the corner, I twisted, peering back, but the face at the window had gone.

The following day, we packed up the car and left.

My mother sat stiffly in the driving seat, tight with grief and anger. She didn't say goodbye to my aunt and uncle, didn't wave. I didn't either. I tried not to see my aunt's tired, haggard face as I pulled away from her.

I didn't really understand but I sensed that a deep division had been created amongst the adults and I was desperate to show my loyalty to my mother, hoping I might still win back her affection. I had no idea at that age that my mother's feud against her sister would last for the rest of their lives. I had no idea that, as a result of the bitterness and blame, I'd never have the chance to see them again.

Afterwards, everything was different in our lives. My mother cleared away all traces of Emma. Photographs disappeared overnight. The only one I salvaged, of the two of us, I kept carefully hidden from her. Emma's crayoned drawings went in the bin. Her clothes and shoes, picture books and even her teddies and rabbits and all those other soft toys vanished. All at once, it was as if my little sister had never been.

After that first time, she never accused me again. Emma was never spoken of. But I knew, I always knew, that in her heart it wasn't only her sister she held responsible, it was me too. She saw me as a cuckoo in the nest, a second-best daughter who had destroyed the most precious person in her life. And I knew too that she would never forgive me for it.

53

ROS

The house was silent.

Shaking, Ros unlocked the front door and helped Sophie inside and settled her in an armchair in the lounge, surrounded by cushions. Sophie still looked pale and seemed drowsy from the painkillers, but the doctors seemed optimistic that she'd recovered well from the concussion. Her arm, encased in its cast, would take time to heal but she was young and her bones should mend quickly.

'Keep her quiet at home for a day or two. You may find she sleeps a lot in the next few days,' the doctor had advised when Sophie was finally being discharged. He handed Ros a factsheet on concussion with a list of possible symptoms. 'If you're concerned, bring her back into emergency. But if not, if she seems bored at home and ready to go back to school next week, I'd have no objection. Just take it slowly at first.'

Ros warmed up some milk for Sophie and sat with her until Sophie's eyes closed and she started to doze. Ros sat on a little longer, watching her daughter sleep, thanking God that she'd had such a narrow escape.

Finally, she took her phone into the kitchen and forced herself to make the call she was dreading. 'Where are you?'

'Out.' Adam sounded breathless. 'You're home? Already? I didn't think... How is she?'

'Tired but OK. She's asleep.' Ros tried to keep her voice normal. It wasn't easy. She heard the sound of passing traffic in the background. 'Where are you?'

'Walking.' Adam suddenly let out a torrent of words, seemingly pumped up with rage. 'They didn't speak to me! At school, when I walked Bella in.'

Ros frowned. 'Who didn't?'

'The other parents. None of them. Morons. It was like I was a nasty smell. They saw me, I know they did. I smiled at one or two of the dads. They looked right through me.'

'What did you expect?' Ros said. 'People talk.'

Adam's voice was hard with anger. 'She did this. All of it. I'm finished. Even if I win the case, even if she can't prove it, you know what they'll say: No smoke without fire.'

He was talking so quickly, she could hardly get a word in. She just held the phone and listened to him speak, sensing the way he was working himself up. She imagined him pounding down the sidewalk, pouring his fury into his body, panting with effort.

He went on: 'You were right. I knew it already. I mean, I knew what she'd done. But this morning, seeing the way they shunned me. In front of my own daughter. Lowlifes.' He broke off for a moment, trying to control himself, trying to find the words. 'And Soph. That poor kid. When I think what that woman did to her, how she's hurt her. My God, she could have killed her. It's a miracle she didn't. She can't get away with it, Ros. She can't. And don't tell me to wait for the police to do something. I don't trust them. I know who's side they're on and it's not ours.'

'Stop it, Adam.' Ros finally managed to cut in. 'Just be quiet a minute.'

Adam didn't seem to hear her. 'She deserves what's coming to her. I don't care what happens to me. She can't keep hurting us like this. She's evil, pure and simple.'

'Listen!' Ros took a deep breath, trying to keep her voice steady.

'You listening?'

'Well, go on, then.'

When she spoke, her voice was slow and deliberate. This was important. She wanted to be certain he caught every word. Their daughter's safety depended on it.

Diana sounded flustered when she answered Ros's call.

'Ros! Oh, my goodness, are you OK? I've been trying to call you since Friday but your phone was off. Did you get my messages? Darling, I am SO sorry. She told me. Lotte told me what happened to Sophie. I mean, how is she? I feel so responsible. Really, I've hardly slept. If we hadn't been in crisis ourselves, with Max, well, none of this would have happened. Can you forgive me? Where are you? What can I do?'

'Listen.' Ros cut in. 'There is something. Please. Where are you? Could you possibly get over here and sit with Sophie for me? She's fine. She's asleep. I just need to—'

'Of course!' Diana seemed to jump at the chance to have something practical to do. 'I'll bring her card. Posy made it for her. She's been so worried. Give me five minutes and I'll be there.'

Ros felt relief flood her. 'Thank you.' She didn't have time to explain. 'It's just, well, it's Adam. He's in a real state.' Her voice shuddered with emotion. 'I'm worried sick. I'm scared he's going to do something. Something terrible.'

54

LOTTE

I sat at the big kitchen window, cradling a cup of coffee in my hands, and looked out over the wide expanse of green.

The sky was heavy with rain. The playground had emptied. The shapes of the slide and of the climbing frame shone in the watery light. The roundabout was still. The swings hung, lifeless, on their chains, waiting for children.

The trees, denuded of leaves, made dense scribbles with their branches along the paths that lined the riverbank. I pulled myself away from the view and went back to the kitchen counter, plucked a sharp knife from the drawer and started to slice carrots for later.

As I fell into the steady rhythm of chopping, I let my mind roam. I thought about Aunt Rose and Uncle James and the house they'd once owned, many years ago now, on the far side of the river. I thought about the shadows in the shed and the sloping lawn to the path on the far bank. And I thought about my little sister, Emma.

It was strange to be back in Ilkley, after all this time. Being here had brought me something I'd never expected: along with my anger and determination to exact revenge, it had brought me closer too to Emma, to the last days we'd shared together before her death.

Two young girls, not so very different from Sophia and Bella. From my own daughter, Caitlyn.

And it had brought me closer to someone else too: a long-buried version of myself. A child who was not yet warped by guilt, not yet suffocated by her mother's bitterness, a child who was still full of adventure and hope. A child who was still innocent.

The downstairs bell sounded. I set down my knife and went to press the button. 'Hi. Who is it?'

A man's voice. 'Delivery for Mrs Humphries? Number 5, Apartment 2?'

The image on the screen was fuzzy. All I could make out was a thick-set man with his collar turned up and his head bowed. 'OK. Come on up.'

I went back to chop the last carrot, giving the delivery guy time to come inside the building and take the stairs. As heavy footsteps sounded, I headed for the door of the apartment and pulled it open.

I didn't recognise him at first. He only lifted his head to reveal himself as he reached the open door and shoved his foot out quickly to jam it as I, slower than him, tried to slam it on him.

'Adam? What the—?'

He pushed me roughly backwards into the apartment and closed the door behind him with a click. 'I thought it was time we had a little talk.' His breath smelled sour.

I tried to square up to him, to pretend I didn't feel intimidated. 'Really? Have you forgotten? You're not allowed to come anywhere near me, and you're especially not allowed to come barging into my home.' I was desperately playing for time, trying to think where I'd left my phone. On a counter in the kitchen? Or in my bedroom. I wasn't sure which way to lead him.

'Oh, please.' He shook his head. There was a madness in his eyes which I'd never seen there before. A menacing fury. 'Is that really the best you can do? We both know those were false charges. I never laid a finger on you or anyone else.'

'Or anyone else?' I narrowed my eyes. 'Well, we both know that's a lie.'

Something flickered in his face. He looked taken aback, wrongfooted, just for an instant. It was as if he realised that perhaps I did have something on him, after all. As if I could see through the surface to his darker side.

I took a deep breath, taking advantage of his flash of unease, and turned, striding purposefully back to the kitchen.

He recovered quickly. By the time I reached the kitchen door, he was there too, so close I could feel the warmth rising from his body as he barrelled into me.

He shoved me forwards, propelling me ahead of him into the kitchen. I pulled quickly away from him and span round to face him, my face defiant, my back to the kitchen counter.

I'd never seen him enraged before. There was a thuggery about him that made me wary of antagonising him any further.

'You are going to stand there and shut up.' He stabbed a finger at me. 'I'll do the talking. Got it?'

I tried to force my expression to be neutral. Maybe, if I let him say what he'd come to say, that would be the end of it. That way, I might stay safe.

'Why?' He glared as he started on me. 'Why did you do this to us? First me. Then Ros. And now Sophie. A little girl who never hurt anyone. What kind of person—' He paused and for a second, I sensed that he was on the brink of losing control. He shuddered and reined himself in more tightly. 'I can't even call you a person. What kind of *monster* does that to a child? Did it make you feel big and brave, luring her to the window? Did you lift her first or just push her out, head first?'

I tried to stay rational. 'I didn't—'

'Shut up!' Flecks of spittle flew from his mouth as he spat out the words. 'You thought she'd die, didn't you? Falling from a height like that. Well, you were wrong. She didn't. And you know what? When she's ready, she's going to tell everyone exactly what happened. In court, if she has to. And you'll be finished. For good.'

He paused for breath, and I interrupted, trying to calm him down.

'You're wrong,' I said, levelly. 'Some of it, yes. But about Sophie, I never—'

'Right.' He let out a mirthless laugh. 'You never laid a finger on her. She just decided to stop playing and march into your bedroom, wrench open the window and fall out of it, all on her own. And you knew nothing about it. Of course.' He sneered. 'What kind of idiot do you take me for?'

I didn't know what to say. His hands were clenching and unclenching at his sides. The look in his eyes was unhinged.

I knew about anger. I knew about vengeance. I just wasn't used to being on the receiving end of it.

I said softly, 'I'm telling you. It's not what you think. I never hurt Sophie.'

He shook his head as if he were tired of hearing it. 'We both know that's a lie. Same as we both know I never assaulted you. But you haven't answered my question. Why? What did we ever do to you?'

As well as anger, I saw a need in his face, as if this were something he'd been wrestling with, struggling to understand. Our eyes locked. My heart was banging so loudly in my chest, I feared he could hear it. I took a long, deep breath.

Maybe it was time.

'You killed my sister. You and your brother.' I heard the

words coming out of my mouth but I could hardly believe I was finally telling him. I'd rehearsed this so often in my head, imagining a moment of reckoning.

'That's insane.' He stared. 'What are you on about?'

'Oh, please.' My tone was caustic. I didn't have the patience for this. 'Spare me the drama. You know exactly what I'm *on about.*'

He looked dazed and wary, as if he'd been caught off guard and had no idea what might come next. He opened his mouth to say something, then seemed to think better of it and closed it again.

I carried on, speaking slowly and carefully: 'Your brother didn't die of a heart attack. I killed him. I was there, with him, in that seedy hotel room.'

His eyes widened in shock. For a moment, he looked lost. Finally, he said, dully, 'That's impossible.'

I carried on, speaking evenly. 'You want to know why? That's why. That's why I searched you out. He died too easily. I wanted something worse for you. Ruin. Pain. Humiliation. And don't think about trying to pin it on me. You haven't a shred of evidence. No one would believe you.'

He shook his head. 'You're mad. What are you—'

'I was with my sister that day, on the river.' The words were coming faster now. It was a relief to say it out loud, to force him to hear. 'I was there when you and Charles attacked us. For what? For nothing. For the fun of it.' I paused, finding fresh breath. 'My sweet little sister. She was five years old.'

'No.' His voice had fallen to a shocked whisper. 'I don't know what you're—'

'We were staying here for the summer, with my aunt and uncle,' I went on. 'We took the dinghy out, even though we weren't supposed to. It was bright yellow. My sister drowned because of you. Because you and your brother thought two little girls, out on their own, were fair game for big, strong teenagers like you. Ring any bells?'

Something stirred. I saw it in him. A memory.

'Remember now?'

His look was one of horror, not denial. 'It's not what you think!' he said. 'Charles, yes. But not me. I wasn't there. He despised me. He thought I was weak. Stupid.'

I gazed at him, disgusted. He was a born liar. Ros had confirmed to me that he was involved, without even realising what she'd done. That evening in Spain, when she'd made her drunken confession about Adam and Charles. It had all poured out. The fact she'd overheard the argument between the two brothers, late at night, years ago, when she and Adam had been staying with Charles and his wife and their young daughter, Cassandra.

Ros had been lying awake in the bedroom, she'd said, and the men's voices had drifted up through the open window from the patio below. She hadn't meant to eavesdrop.

But then they'd accused each other of having done something terrible. Not just terrible, criminal. Something that could put them both in prison.

Ros had described it so vividly.

Charles's voice, malevolent as he challenged his brother: 'Keep away from us. Was that your idea, that sweet invitation to Cassandra to come and stay with you during the vacation? She doesn't know the truth, does she, your little wife? She doesn't know what she's married. Shall I tell her?'

Adam, his voice tight: 'You wouldn't dare.'

'Try me.'

Silence. Ros, startled, had sat up and strained to hear.

'If I go down, you're going with me.' That was Adam's voice, she'd said, full of malice. 'Don't give me that look. You know exactly what I mean.'

Afterwards, when she confronted them, they'd colluded to

make Ros believe she'd been dreaming. They must have persuaded her that her paranoia was another reason their families could never reconcile.

But I'd recognised the truth, at once. Of course, Ros hadn't imagined what she'd heard. She'd chosen to believe that she had. It was easier for her to blame herself, easier than accepting that her husband and his brother had a criminal past, that they were capable of doing something unforgiveable.

For me, it was the final nail. The extra evidence I'd been looking for to be certain that Adam was indeed the second boy, the one who'd held down my little sister on the stones and been part of the bullying that led to her death. Just as I'd already suspected. It was the last piece in the puzzle that strengthened my resolve to go after him.

Now, I glared at him. 'You're lying. Ros told me. I know she heard you and Charles arguing about it. You accused each other, threatened that if one of you blabbed, you'd both suffer.'

'She told you?' Adam's eyes widened. He looked shaken as he took this in and tried to work out how to respond. 'Charles was a bully. I knew, as soon as he came home that evening, that he'd done something dreadful. He was white as a sheet. He'd shocked himself. And then I heard they were searching the river, looking for a little girl. My dad went to help.' He blinked hard. 'But I had nothing to do with it. I wasn't there.'

I almost laughed. 'Right! So why did he turn on you? Ros heard him. He threatened to tell her the truth.'

'You don't know what you're talking about.'

'Fine. Play it like that.' I tried to turn away from him, my eyes scanning the kitchen surfaces for my phone. 'I'm calling the police. I'm reporting you for forcing your way in here and threatening me in my own home.'

'No!' He reached out, grabbed me by the shoulders. His eyes, hard on mine, were frightened. 'He did warn me off.

That's true. He despised me. But it was nothing to do with what happened to your sister. Nothing at all.'

'Let go of me.' I tried to knock his hands away but he just gripped me more tightly, pinning me back against the counter.

'It was something else.'

'Something else?' I squirmed, trying to get away. 'What?'

An awkward grimace made the corners of his mouth buckle. 'He wanted me to keep away from his daughter, Cassandra. That was what the row was about. Ros had asked, you see, if maybe Cass could visit us—'

I shook my head. He was trying to deflect me. I wouldn't listen. 'It was you,' I repeated. 'I heard him, on the stones. He called you "little brother".'

'Little brother?' He frowned. 'He never called me that. He hated me, I told you.' He hesitated. The look in his eyes shifted. 'Did he say "little brother", or was it "little bro"? Was that it?'

'Maybe. What difference does it make?'

Something seemed to dawn on him. 'Him. The other boy.' He seemed to be talking not to me but to himself. 'It was him—'

I seized my moment, raised my fists and shoved him in the chest, as hard as I could, away from me.

He lunged for my throat. His fingers, used to pummelling limbs and manipulating spines, were strong. I choked, gasping for air. I felt myself rise, straining for air, as if he were lifting me off my feet.

Everything in me struggled to loosen the pressure on my windpipe, desperate for breath. I kicked out uselessly, meeting nothing but air.

55

LOTTE

It felt as though my eyes bulged in their sockets as he squeezed my throat.

Spangles of light bobbed and danced in front of me.

Pictures flashed through my mind.

Emma, her small face puckered with worry, her eyes saying: *We shouldn't do this. We'll get into trouble.*

Emma again, pinned under that boy, her eyes swollen and cheeks tear-stained, silently begging me to do something, to save her.

My fingers scrabbled behind me on the counter. I tried to press myself higher, as if straining might give me a precious extra breath. My fingertips touched something firm. Something solid. The sharp kitchen knife, abandoned there on the side.

My hand closed round the handle. I dug deep and drew on the last whispers of strength I had left in me. In a single, desperate movement, I pulled it forward through the air, twisted the blade to face him and plunged it into his chest.

It penetrated between the ribs with a visceral sucking noise and stuck, quivering, there.

The world stopped.

His hands hung round my throat, barely loosening.

A look of surprise registered in his eyes, as if he were slowly realising what I'd done. He tilted his head and looked down, fixed his eyes in disbelief on the handle protruding from his shirt and the rapidly spreading dark stain surrounding it.

His hands fell away from me.

I ducked to the far side of the counter, making it a barrier between us. I scrabbled in the drawer, pulled out a breadknife and brandished it. My neck throbbed with pain. I could still feel the imprint of his fingers, sense the tightness which had almost crushed my throat. I was afraid to swallow. Saliva pooled in my mouth.

Adam staggered backwards, grasping at one of the tall kitchen stools and steadying himself against it. He looked stunned, as if he still couldn't quite make sense of what was happening. His blood was pumping out steadily, soaking his clothes, dripping down onto his shoes, making sticky pools on my pristine kitchen floor. He opened his mouth, as if he were about to speak, then gasped and slid, slumping to the floor, exhausted.

A sudden shrill note sounded in the quiet, stopping my heart. Someone was downstairs, at the door.

I couldn't move. My body was rigid with shock, with adrenalin. My eyes were fixed on Adam, motionless on the floor.

What had he said? That the row had flared because his brother was determined to stop his daughter visiting Adam and Ros. *Why?* I blinked. A second later, something slid silently into place in my mind. It was as if an opaque curtain were suddenly ripped away and I saw clearly, for the first time.

My god. Of course.

The buzzer sounded again. I ran in a panic to answer, peering at the lit screen. A woman filled the blurred square, a woman I knew at once. Ros.

'Lotte? Are you OK?' She stared into the camera.

'Yes, but—' I swallowed hard. 'Get an ambulance. It's Adam.'

'You're OK?' she said again.

She can't have heard me. I pressed the buzzer to release the front door and ran down the stairs to meet her halfway. She looked tense but determined.

'You can't go up there.' I spread my arms to bar her way, realising in a rush what she'd find, how the horror of it would never leave her. 'Go back. Just call an ambulance. Tell them he's been stabbed.'

A curious look passed over her face. I'd expected shock or horror, but it was neither. I shook my head. She can't have understood.

'Quickly.' I clenched my fists, urging her to listen, to do something. 'Or it might be too late.'

She said, calmly, 'Stabbed? Where?'

I shivered, pointed to myself. 'Here. In the chest. I didn't mean...' My hand rose to my throbbing, bruised throat. 'He attacked me.'

She gave me a long, steady look. Still, she didn't move.

I reached out and gripped her arm. 'He's bleeding.' My voice had become shrill. 'He needs help. Now.'

She nodded thoughtfully and put her warm hand gently on mine. 'Not yet,' she said, quietly. 'Let's just leave it a while, shall we?'

56

ROS

Once again, the lounge felt crowded with police officers.

Detective Wright sat, solemn faced, on the sofa, flanked by the young constable, his notebook open on his knee, and the earnest family liaison officer who was helping Ros and the children deal with the aftermath of Adam's death.

'So, Mrs Crofter.' Detective Wright craned forwards. 'You say your husband seemed mad when you spoke on the phone that morning.'

'Very mad.' Ros pulled out a tissue and wiped her eyes. 'He was ranting about Mrs Humphries. "That woman," he called her. He blamed her, you see, for everything. He felt humiliated by the allegations she'd made against him. And then I suppose I made it worse. I blamed her too, you see, not just for that but for Sophie's accident. I was wrong, I know that now. Sophie's talked to me about what happened.'

Detective Wright raised a questioning eyebrow but didn't interrupt.

'But at the time, we were so upset,' Ros went on. 'I was out of my mind at the hospital. We didn't know at first how badly injured she was. If there was' – she shuddered and took a deep breath – 'if there might be brain damage.'

Detective Wright nodded. 'So your husband was very angry when you spoke. Did he say where he was going? What he was intending to do?'

Ros hesitated. 'He did say something about teaching her a lesson. I warned him. I told him to keep away from her. That we should leave it to the police to investigate. We both knew he wasn't allowed near her because of, you know, the other thing.'

'And what was his response, when you told him to keep away from Mrs Humphries?'

Ros sighed. 'I don't remember his exact words, but he wouldn't listen. He said something like he didn't care what happened to him. That she deserved what was coming to her.' She paused, thinking back. 'He called her evil. I remember that. I thought it was a peculiar word to use about someone, whatever they'd done. You know, sort of extreme.'

There was a silence. The young constable stopped scribbling and looked up at her.

'So then what happened?'

'Well, I called my friend, Diana. That's her in the kitchen, the one who made the coffee just now. She said she'd come over and stay in the house with Sophie. I wanted to stop Adam, you see. He was in such a rage, I didn't know what he might do. I was frightened.' She dabbed again at her eyes.

'So your friend came over?'

'Yes. Straight away. She's amazing. She always drops everything to help out.' Ros glanced back over her shoulder towards the kitchen. Diana was sitting at the kitchen table in the quiet, sipping her coffee. If she'd heard her friend's tribute, she didn't react.

'And what time was that?'

Ros shook her head. 'I'm not exactly sure. Half past nine, maybe? A little after? She might remember.'

'Did you leave the house as soon as she arrived?'

Ros nodded. 'At once. I was sitting, ready, frantic about Adam and what he might do. I ran round to Lotte's place – she's just round the corner, there.' She pointed vaguely towards the end of the road. 'The downstairs door wasn't properly closed,' she lied, 'so I ran upstairs and hammered on the door of the apartment. I thought Adam must already be there. I thought he must have been the one who hadn't shut the main door properly, because he was in such a state.'

Detective Wright prompted gently: 'And then what happened?'

'Lotte let me in. She was shaking. I heard Adam as soon as I went inside. He was shouting at her. Accusing her of ruining our lives, of trying to kill Sophie.' She dropped her gaze to her hands, which were crumpling the tissue into a ball. 'It was my fault. I'd thought that, you see. Now I know it really was an accident. Nothing more than a terrible accident.'

'Where was your husband at this time?'

'He was in the kitchen. He was so out of control, he barely seemed to see I was there. Lotte was crying. She was obviously frightened. But she went back into the kitchen, maybe to tell him I was there or maybe to tell him to leave, I don't know. That's when he lunged at her and grabbed her. Here, round the throat.'

Ros put her hands to her neck, demonstrating.

'I screamed. I flew at him and tried to pull him off but he didn't even seem to notice me. He was so intent on her. And her face, her eyes, I thought she really was dying, that he really was strangling her, right in front of my eyes. And that's when she grabbed the knife. I don't think she meant to stab him. It didn't look like it. She looked as if she wanted to brandish it in his face, to make him back off, but then he sort of stumbled forwards against her and that was it. It stuck right into him.'

She buried her face in her hands and her shoulders shook.

The family liaison officer said, 'If you need a minute, Mrs Crofter. That's quite alright. We know how difficult this is for you.' She raised her voice slightly and directed it toward the kitchen. 'Maybe your friend could get you some water?'

Ros heard the slap of the kitchen cupboard doors as Diana rummaged, then the whoosh of water from the tap. Diana hurried through with the glass and perched on the arm of the chair. She steadied the glass as Ros drank, her other hand resting on Ros's shoulder.

Detective Wright waited until Ros had composed herself again, then said, 'Are you OK to continue?'

Ros nodded.

'I believe you were the one who called for an ambulance?'

'There was so much blood. Everywhere.' Ros took a deep breath. 'I didn't know what to do. The knife, it was sticking out of him. It was horrible.'

Detective Wright prompted again: 'So you called emergency services?'

'Yes. On my mobile. Lotte seemed to be in shock. I mean, she could hardly breathe. He nearly killed her. If she hadn't—' She broke off, looking at the row of impassive faces. 'You've seen the bruises?'

'Mrs Humphries has received medical attention and her injuries have been documented.' Detective Wright flicked through her notebook. 'How long would you say it was, Mrs Crofter, between the stabbing and making the call to emergency services?'

Ros widened her eyes. 'I don't know. I mean, it's all a blur. It was such a shock and everything happened so suddenly. A minute, maybe? Two? I'm not sure.'

'One or two minutes?' Detective Wright frowned.

'About. Maybe more. I couldn't move at first. I was frozen. Adam was on the floor and Lotte was just standing there, shaking, staring at him. Maybe three minutes. I don't know.' She sounded puzzled. 'But you can find out the time, surely? From my phone records.'

Detective Wright gave her a wry look. 'We can indeed. But it's harder to be certain of the exact time of the stab wound. The ambulance crew seemed to think some time had elapsed between the injury and their arrival at the property. Valuable time.'

Ros looked stunned. 'That's awful,' she said. 'I did everything I could. I just keep thinking, if only I'd managed to calm him down on the phone, if only I'd got there sooner, maybe he'd still—' She sank her face into her hands again. 'Poor Lotte. I didn't believe her before, when she accused him. I hated her. Adam knew that. But he tried to kill her! She was fighting for her life.'

Her words tumbled out through the web of her fingers. 'She isn't in trouble, is she? It wasn't her fault. I'll testify to that, if I've got to. I loved Adam. He was everything to me. But I can't see an innocent woman go to jail. I can't.' She gulped, her mouth shuddering. 'It won't bring him back. Nothing will.' She burst again into sobs.

Diana leaned in and snaked an arm around her shoulders. 'Is that all, Detective? You can see how upset she is.'

Detective Wright heaved herself to her feet. 'We'll be in touch, Mrs Crofter. Thank you for your cooperation.' She paused as she prepared to leave and added, stiffly: 'I'm sorry for your loss.'

The family liaison officer, rising too, said breathily, 'Anything you need, Mrs Crofter, you or the girls, just call. You've got my number.'

Ros sat quietly, following the sound of the women's footsteps as Diana followed the police officers into the hall, then the soft click of the front door as she closed it behind them.

When Diana returned, she hovered in the lounge doorway. 'I can take the girls, if you need some space,' she said. 'Anytime.'

Ros managed a rueful smile. 'Thanks, Di. What would I do without you?' She swallowed hard. So much had happened in such a short time. She felt utterly exhausted.

She thought about Adam. The husband she'd adored. The father now lost forever to his children. She wiped her eyes with an already sodden handkerchief.

Diana slipped onto the sofa beside her. 'I don't know what to say.' She reached for Ros's hand. 'It seems so unreal.' She paused as if she were searching for the right words. 'I keep expecting him to walk in through the door, don't you?'

Ros didn't answer. She couldn't. She was heartbroken. Her family was in tatters.

But, as for her husband, well, she was just glad she'd never have to set eyes on him again.

57

ROS

The next few days passed in a blur.

During the day, while Sophie rested upstairs and the other children were at school, Diana was a constant presence, flitting in and out of the house. She answered the telephone and the front door and managed the visitors who spoke in hushed voices in the hall and handed in bereavement cards and arrangements of flowers. *We won't stay,* they whispered. *Don't want to intrude. But how is she?*

Otherwise, Diana kept an eye on Sophie, who was still mostly in bed. She dozed on and off during the day and complained of being drowsy when she was awake. Downstairs, Diana tiptoed through the rooms, bringing Ros cups of tea and plates of tiny sandwiches, trying to tempt her to eat.

After school, Diana collected Posy, Max and Bella from school and took them all to her house for tea, only bringing Bella back home when it was almost bedtime.

There were telephone calls back and forth with the detectives, a daily visit from the earnest family liaison officer ('just checking in') and an appointment with a solicitor to discuss

Adam's will. Ros couldn't bring herself to start thinking about a funeral yet. She had no idea how long it would take for the police to release Adam's body for burial.

Otherwise, she spent the hours sitting alone in silence in the empty lounge or in their bedroom, her bedroom now, thinking about Adam and the years they'd shared. The memories crowded into the room around her, demanding, intense and often suffocating.

In the evenings, once Ros had soothed Bella and Sophie to sleep, she went to stand at the window in the darkness of the study they'd shared and peered across the back gardens towards the rear of Lotte's apartment.

Lotte and Caitlyn were in there. Ros could tell. The curtains in their lounge were closed, fringed by bright light. Those black windows, those ever-staring eyes, seemed finally at rest.

Detective Wright returned.

Diana, primed for the visit, hurried around to give support. She ushered the detective and her constable into the lounge to join Ros, then rushed to make them tea and coffee.

Detective Wright brought out a file of documents and opened it on the coffee table. 'If you could just read through your statement, Mrs Crofter.' She fished out a printed sheet and handed it across. 'Any amendments need to be witnessed and initialled. Otherwise, once you're satisfied that it's a full and true account, please complete the final section and sign and date where indicated.' She pointed to the final lines.

Ros signed, hot under the detective's severe gaze. She hoped any wobble in her writing would be put down to grief, rather than guilt.

Once it was done, Detective Wright slotted the sheet back

into her file. 'Anything you wanted to ask, Mrs Crofter?' She put her head on one side in a rather studied gesture of concern. 'I realise this must be a difficult time.'

Ros took a deep breath. 'What's going to happen now? I mean, to her, to Mrs Humphries?'

'That will be a decision for the CPS.' Detective Wright's face gave nothing away. 'The first step is that we complete our investigations and submit a report.'

Ros blinked. 'It was self-defence, though. You've said that, haven't you, in your report? I saw it. I saw what happened.'

Detective Wright's eyes barely flickered. 'As I say, that's a matter for the CPS.'

They sat for a moment in the quiet. Blood pounded in Ros's ears. She didn't know what else to do, what else to say, to help Lotte.

'In the light of your husband's death,' Detective Wright went on, 'the investigation into allegations of sexual assault, made by Mrs Humphries, will be closed.'

Diana, carrying in the tray of mugs, said tartly: 'I should think so.'

Detective Wright, ignoring her, focused only on Ros. 'And, just to be clear, Mrs Crofter, you are withdrawing your previous allegation that Mrs Humphries was responsible for your daughter's injuries. In your statement, you say you're now satisfied that these were caused accidentally.'

Ros nodded solemnly. 'Absolutely. I was wrong about that. I know that now. I was in an emotional state, that's all. Distressed about my daughter.'

'Indeed.'

Diana handed around a plate of ginger snaps as the detective and constable sipped at their drinks, then settled herself in a chair, close to Ros's side.

'There is one final outstanding issue I'd like to address, if I may,' said Detective Wright after a few moments.

Ros nodded, nursing her mug.

Detective Wright took a deep breath. Her eyes moved from Ros to Diana and back again, as if she were considering something. 'Previously, when we met, you voiced another allegation concerning Mrs Humphries.'

Ros stiffened, waiting.

'It was about the malicious doctoring of your company website.'

Ros let out a breath. 'Well, yes. I did. Lotte took that picture, clearly. She's the only person who could have. I have thought about that. I think I know when she did it, too. She brought her children round for a playdate, you see, and she disappeared upstairs. I thought it was odd at the time because the downstairs toilet was free. But going upstairs would have given her access to my study, to my computer.'

She shook her head. It seemed such a long time ago and suddenly trivial now. 'Diana was here. She saw. But now, after everything else that's happened, I don't really think—'

Detective Wright held up her hand to silence her. 'Mrs Crofter, we believe she did indeed take that picture. We've found the original on her phone.'

Ros shrugged. 'Yes, but even so, I... It doesn't seem to matter now.'

'But that's not all we've found.' Detective Wright was in full flow. 'When our IT people examined your website, they found something rather strange.'

'What?'

'It turns out that Lotte wasn't the person who posted it there at all. They've traced the IP address, you see. It leads to someone else.'

Ros stared, baffled, waiting.

Detective Wright's gaze shifted subtly from Ros's face back to Diana, who was still perched there at her friend's side. 'In fact, it leads to a device registered in your friend's name.' The detective's gaze was piercing. 'It was posted from your phone, Mrs Thompson, wasn't it?'

58

ROS

A low, soft puff of air.

Diana didn't speak but Ros sensed her friend crumple in her chair, bending slightly forwards as if she'd been punctured.

Ros turned to stare at her. 'You? But—' She shook her head, uncomprehendingly. 'Di?'

Diana's face was turned away from her, her eyes dipped to her shoes, to the carpet.

Detective Wright took a final gulp of coffee, gathered together her papers and heaved herself to her feet. Beside her, the constable put away his notebook and rushed to follow.

'I can see this comes as a shock, Mrs Crofter.' Detective Wright addressed Ros, but her focus was on Diana, whose neck was reddening. 'Maybe we should discuss the matter further tomorrow? I appreciate that you might need some time, in the light of this information, to decide whether or not you'd like to pursue your complaint.' She paused. 'I realise it's delicate.'

Once the police had left, Ros headed back into the lounge and shut the door behind her. She was glad that Sophie was asleep upstairs. This was not a conversation she wanted her daughter to hear.

'Diana?'

Diana was standing at the window, looking out.

'Well?' Ros felt her initial shock and disbelief slowly giving way to anger. 'Is it true?'

Diana gave a half-shrug. She was trying to look nonchalant, to suggest it didn't really matter to her, but Ros knew her better than that.

'But why?' Ros stared. 'I thought we were friends.'

Diana addressed the window, her voice sarcastic. 'Oh, yes, great friends. Call Diana if you want someone to run over at no notice to act as a free babysitter. Good old Diana will collect them from school if you're too busy with your terribly important work. Ask Diana to make up the numbers if it's an awkward playdate, she won't mind being used, will she? What else has she got to do, anyway?'

Ros's legs buckled. 'Di?' She sat down abruptly on the arm of the chair. 'Why didn't you say? I never meant – I never thought—'

Diana turned on her. 'No, you never *did* think, did you? You were too obsessed with yourself. You never thought how I might feel, watching you setting up your precious little business – which is on the brink of bankruptcy from what I can see. Just because your darling Adam was happy to indulge you, to bankroll the whole thing.' Diana poked a finger bitterly at her own chest. 'What about *me*? Don't you think I've got a brain too? When Posy was born and I gave up work, Phil promised me it was just for a few years. Then Max came along and it all got pushed back. Now look at me. Phil won't even consider helping me pay for childcare so I can get back to work again. It's all snack boxes and sticky fingers. That's all I'm good for, apparently. But you, oh, you're Mrs Perfect, wonderful mummy and entrepreneur extraordinaire! That's all I bloody get from Phil. He thinks the sun shines out of your backside.'

Ros listened in silence, suddenly exhausted. Diana. Her

best friend. The woman she had most trusted. She was seeing a side of her that she'd had no idea existed: jealous, petty and frustrated. She said, sadly: 'You should have said. Adam could've talked to him.'

'Oh, please. What – ask for your help in dealing with my own husband? Do me a favour!'

Ros shook her head slowly. 'But how did you do it? That was Lotte's photograph. It must have been.'

Diana looked suddenly sly. 'Too right it was.'

'So, what happened? Did she put you up to it?'

'I took it.' She pulled a face. 'You might as well know – you know all the rest now. It was when I was in the practice for an appointment with Adam. She was looking at her phone – I saw her – and then Sam called her, and she went into his room to see him and left her phone on the desk. It was just a fishing expedition – I wasn't sure what I'd find – but I grabbed it while the screen was still live and took it with me to the toilets.

'She's got quite a few photos of you tanked up on vacation, by the way. That one was the worst, or should I say, the best. I emailed it to myself, then deleted the sent email. Then I just walked back in, all apologies, saying I was SO sorry, I'd picked up her phone by mistake, thinking it was mine, and handed it back. She didn't suspect a thing.'

Ros took a deep breath. 'You went to all that trouble, just to try to damage my business?'

'Not as stupid as I look, right?' Diana smirked. 'I knew that when you finally did clock, you'd blame her.' She pulled a simpering face. 'And poor little best friend Diana would be there to pick up the pieces and comfort you.'

'I think it's time you left.' Ros got to her feet.

Diana reached for her bag and followed her out into the hall.

At the front door, Ros hesitated and turned to look Diana in the eye. 'You're not even sorry, are you?'

Diana didn't answer, her mouth tight.

Ros stood for a few moments, considering. She took a deep breath. 'You've been a good friend to me, Di. In lots of ways. I'm grateful, I really am. I had no idea—' Ros broke off. She thought about the way Diana had brushed her off when she'd tried to talk to her about getting back to work, about the dismissive comments Phil had made about Diana and the hurt in her friend's face as she'd turned quickly away.

Ros had never much liked Phil. She'd only made an effort with him, all this time, because he'd been Adam's mate and her best friend's husband. But there was something selfish about him, something controlling. She could see that. Yet, all this time, she'd failed to realise how unhappy her friend had been, a friend she now barely recognised.

'I'm sorry,' she said at last. 'Don't worry about the police.' Ros nodded to herself. 'I'll tell them to forget it. Put it down as a prank gone wrong.'

Once Diana had gone, Ros headed up the stairs, her limbs leaden.

In her room, Sophie was still asleep. Her hair was messy, stray strands slick against her cheek. Her face was pinched and pale. Her broken arm, heavy with plaster, rested on top of the duvet. Ros stood for a moment, watching over her, then touched her lips gently to her daughter's damp forehead.

A book, which had slipped off the bed, lay abandoned on the carpet. Ros picked it up, smoothed out a crumpled page and set it on the cluttered bedside table.

Closing Sophie's door softly behind her, Ros went into their study – just her study now – the air thick with silence. She dropped into her chair and sat for a little while at her desk, staring at her laptop. She didn't have the energy to power it up. She felt light-headed with shock.

In a matter of days, her whole life had changed. Two of the people who'd been most important in her life, some of those she'd most loved, had turned out to be monsters. A best friend who'd secretly plotted to betray her. And Adam, her husband.

His was the worst betrayal of all.

For a moment, weighed down by everything that had happened, she felt utterly defeated. How would she survive this? How would she carry on?

She blew out her cheeks and shook her head. She didn't know how, not yet, but she would survive. She would rebuild her life. Not just for herself but for her daughters.

Just thinking about them, she felt herself bolstered by new strength. Her wonderful, beautiful girls. A lot had changed, that was true. But not everything. Her love for her daughters was more powerful than ever. She'd do anything to protect them. She'd always known that. However far she had to go.

She pushed herself back onto her feet and crossed to the window. Her eyes fixed at once on Lotte's apartment and the weak fall sunlight glancing across the windows there.

Diana had been precious to her. Ros knew she'd need time to grieve for their broken friendship. She'd need longer still to grieve for her husband. But already she sensed a new alliance emerging, a new friendship, one that would sustain her, one that had been forged in a most dramatic and brutal way.

EPILOGUE

'It's a hard life.'

Ros turned to Lotte, lying next to her on the poolside sunlounger. They raised their glasses, each one brimming with a coconut cocktail, decorated with a curly plastic straw and a paper umbrella. A single, plump cherry floated on the surface.

'But someone's got to do it, right?' Ros finished for her.

Lotte winked and they smiled at each other.

Ros took in Lotte's long, slim legs and skimpy bikini. Even if she really worked at it, Ros knew she'd never have a figure like that and, finally, she felt just fine about it. She was fitter now, though. She'd really started feeling the difference since Lotte had started getting her out for a run three or four times a week. They jogged along the river, sometimes, through the cemetery and back on the far bank or, if she could face it, through the town and right up onto the moors. That was plenty for Ros. Life was too busy.

Besides, her gorgeous girls still told her she was perfect. That was good enough for her.

Ros shifted her position on the sunlounger, angling herself more fully into the shade thrown by the parasol.

It was even hotter in Majorca this August than it had been the previous year, when the two of them had first met. She spent half her day smothering the girls in sun-cream and shoving wide-brimmed hats on their heads.

She shielded her eyes with her hand and watched them now. The early afternoon sun shimmered on the moving water. Sophie, Bella and Caitlyn were screaming as they splashed each other in the shallow end of the hotel pool. It was happy shrieking. She thought about last year and the concerns she'd had about Sophie. The aggressive outbursts that seemed so out of character. The toilet accidents.

She shook her head. Despite all the sessions she'd had in the past year with the therapist, she still felt guilty. She was Sophie's mother. Her job, more than any other, was to protect her daughter from harm. She'd failed as a parent. She should have known what was going on.

There were still nights, although fewer now, when she woke with a start in the small hours and lay, wide-eyed, reading the spidery patterns of the shadows across the ceiling and feeling her head race as she thought about it all. How had she missed the signals about Adam's special relationship with Sophie? How had she failed to see that the closeness she'd seen as loving had actually been sexual abuse?

The realisation had been devastating. She'd thought she was supporting Sophie through a troubled time by encouraging her to spend more time alone with her father, hiking on the moors and picnicking and going off cycling on Sundays; in fact, all she'd been doing was unwittingly giving him more access to her, giving him more opportunities to molest her.

She knew now that he'd threatened Sophie with terrible consequences for the family if she dared to tell.

No wonder her little girl had felt so tormented and so trapped that she'd decided to throw herself out of Lotte's window that day. It was the ultimate cry for help. Thank goodness she'd been lucky and the bushes had broken her fall.

Thank goodness she'd finally decided, that day in the hospital, to risk letting Ros in on her deep, dark secret and trust her mother to keep her safe from her father.

That was another question she'd asked herself a thousand times in the months since Adam's death: *What would I have done to Adam if Lotte hadn't got there first?*

Ros was glad he was dead. That was the truth. In all her anguished churning about the way events had unfolded, she had never found herself imagining an alternative life in which Adam was still alive. That was an outcome she couldn't bear to contemplate.

She still carried her own secret burden of guilt, though. She'd told the police that she and Adam had spoken on the phone that fateful day, before he'd stormed round to confront Lotte in her apartment. That part was true. They had the phone records to prove it.

But she'd lied when she'd told them that she'd begged him to come home, to keep away from Lotte.

The opposite was true. She'd been the one who'd sent him round there.

She'd expected that, at the very least, he'd be arrested for harassment. In fact, it had turned out far better than she'd hoped. If Lotte hadn't stabbed him, Ros might have been the one to wield the knife. And if that had happened, she'd be in prison now and who knows what would have happened to her wonderful girls.

'You're brooding, aren't you?' Lotte raised her sunglasses a few inches and leaned in.

'How can you tell?' Ros shook her head at her friend wryly. 'Am I that obvious?'

Lotte shrugged. 'Yep.' She put her straw to her lips and drew on it, then nodded across at the children. 'They're doing

OK, aren't they?'

Ros focused again on the girls. Bella and Caitlyn were sitting side by side on the edge of the pool, feet in the water, arms raised and pressed to the side of their heads, bending forwards, ready to topple forward in a beginner's dive.

Sophie was in the water, coaching them. 'Put your head lower. Yes, like that. Then just slide in. You can do it!'

There was a nervous pause followed by two messy splashes. Sophie hopped up and down and clapped her hands as the younger ones surfaced, spluttering and coughing.

Bella twisted towards her mother, her face lit with pride, and hollered, 'Did you see, Mummy? Did you see?'

Ros sat up and put her hands together in an exaggerated gesture of applause.

'Well done you!' Lotte, sitting up too, waved her hand at Caitlyn in a high arc. 'Go, girl!'

Caitlyn jumped up and down and beamed, revelling in her mother's praise.

A moment later, Sophie called to the two girls again, urging them out of the water for another go. The two women settled back on their loungers to watch.

'You're right,' Ros said. 'They're doing more than OK.' She paused, looking. Caitlyn and Bella were splashing and giggling, racing each other back to the steps in an excited scramble. 'They really are.'

She turned back to Lotte and the two of them exchanged a thoughtful look. There were so many questions they'd never asked each other, and Ros sensed now that they never would. There were some answers it was better not to hear. Had Adam sexually abused Lotte in the practice? Ros thought he probably hadn't. Like many bullies, he'd been a weak man, lacking in confidence. She suspected that a woman like Lotte would have intimidated him, rather than tempted him.

But then she'd never have thought him capable of abusing his own daughter.

Lotte had gently hinted to her that, perhaps, when Ros had heard the two brothers arguing all those years ago, she hadn't been deluded. That perhaps what she'd heard had been Charles voicing veiled suspicions about his little brother's warped sexuality. That Charles had long been sickened by something unsavoury about Adam's relationship with Charles's young daughter, Cassandra, including the way he doggedly sought her out and pressed her to go with him for adventures on the moors, just the two of them. Ros thought of the look she'd caught between Charles and Alexandra when she had innocently suggested that Cassandra, then a ten-year-old, might come and stay with them. No wonder they'd wanted no further contact between their families.

Ros shook her head. *Perhaps you never truly know what another person is capable of doing, however well you think you know them, however long you are married to them.*

As for Lotte, Ros knew that something painful lay in her past. It wasn't only the fact that Lotte had been widowed so young, a loss which Lotte even now had found it difficult to discuss. Ros sensed that there was something else, long buried, that had prompted her to seek out Ros and her family, to pursue them and to make that allegation against Adam. Ros didn't know what had caused that darkness. She also knew she'd never ask.

Lotte had told her only that her aunt and uncle had lived in Ilkley once, kind people who'd loved her, and that her little sister, Emma, had drowned in the River Wharfe in a tragic accident when the two girls had visited them as children. It wasn't the whole story, Ros sensed that, and yet it was enough.

It was as much as she needed to know.

'Ice-creams?' Lotte set down her empty glass and checked her watch. 'My turn?'

Ros smiled. 'I'll get them.' *Hang the expense. I can afford it now.* Her business was thriving at last and, besides, she relished the fact that Adam's life insurance had left them with enough money for poolside treats. After all they'd been through, the girls deserved them.

Lotte swung her long legs down from the lounger, pulled on a wrap and headed off towards the children to cheer on Caitlyn and Bella as they braced themselves to attempt another seated dive. Several men lifted their eyes surreptitiously from the books they were reading, checking Lotte out as she stalked past.

Lotte seemed oblivious. She only had eyes for one person nowadays, and that was her daughter. Ros smiled to herself. It was a delight to see the two of them together. It was as if Lotte and Caitlyn had both finally mended some fissure inside themselves, some profound damage caused by the sudden death of Lotte's husband and Caitlyn's father. They seemed set free from their grief at last.

Ros saw the difference in them both. No more after-school club, no more breakfast club. Lotte always found a way of escaping work in the afternoon so she could be at Ros's side at the school gates at the end of the children's day; the two of them stooped together, eyes bright, arms open wide, ready to scoop up their daughters when they came running out to them. For her part, Caitlyn had lost that shy, anxious look which had always worried Ros. She was a happier child, finally blossoming.

Later, when the girls had finished their ice-creams and jumped back in the pool, Lotte's phone pinged with a message. She rummaged for it in her bag and checked the screen.

'Do you think you'll ever forgive Diana?' Lotte said, looking up.

Ros tutted. 'Is that her? Again?'

Lotte nodded. 'Another begging one. She's so sorry, blah, blah, blah. She knows you won't talk to her but if I could just tell you how sorry she feels, how much she'd like to make it up to you. Usual stuff.'

'Not yet.' Ros sighed. She would find a way of forgiving her old friend, but it wouldn't be easy. She needed time. 'I wish she'd find a job and make a life for herself. She's got too much time on her hands.'

Lotte looked thoughtful. 'I thought her husband wouldn't let her? What's his name?'

'Phil.' Ros settled herself more comfortably on the lounger. 'They deserve each other. Honestly. I never liked him. He's so controlling. I only ever invited him round for Adam's sake.'

Lotte was listening keenly. 'They were childhood buddies, weren't they, Phil and Adam?'

'Kind of.' Ros considered. 'Actually, Phil was mates with Adam's big brother, Charles, more than with Adam. I always got the feeling Adam was jealous because Charles treated Phil more like a brother than he did Adam – you know, his partner in crime. Adam told me once that Charles even called Phil "little bro". It was just a nickname, but I think he was sort of rubbing Adam's nose in it, making sure he felt as excluded as possible. I wouldn't put it past Charles.' She shrugged. 'That was my impression, anyway.'

Lotte's expression had shifted, then stilled. She stayed silent for a while and her breathing seemed to quicken.

'What?' Ros frowned. Lotte seemed suddenly preoccupied, as if she were wrestling with something.

'Just thinking.' Lotte hesitated, then took a deep breath. 'Now Caitlyn and I have decided to stay in Ilkley, at least for a while, I really ought to get to know more people.' She turned to Ros. A strange, secretive look had come into her eyes. 'You wouldn't mind, would you, if I invited Phil and Diana over? You're welcome to come too, obviously. I don't want you to think I'm being disloyal.'

'I wouldn't think that. Feel free. As long as you don't mind if

I steer clear.' Ros paused and gave her a searching look. 'What? You're up to something, aren't you?'

'Me? Up to something?' Lotte's careful smile gave nothing away. 'I just think it's time I got to know Phil, that's all.' Lotte paused, her eyes distant as if her mind were already elsewhere, making plans. As Ros watched, a shadow seemed to pass over Lotte's face, her features darkening.

'Lotte?' For a moment, Ros felt thrown, as if her new friend had once again become a stranger to her. 'What is it?'

'Nothing.' Lotte adjusted her sunglasses. The moment passed. 'I was just thinking about Phil. And you know what? I will ask them over. I think it's time I got to know him a whole lot better.'

A LETTER FROM JILL

I want to say a huge thank you for choosing to read *The Mother at Number 5*. If you enjoyed it and want to keep up to date with all my latest releases, just sign up at the following link. Your email address will never be shared and you can unsubscribe at any time.

www.bookouture.com/jill-childs

Have you ever shared an intense, intimate conversation with a complete stranger?

I have. I can still vividly remember talking many years ago with a kind, sympathetic woman who happened to sit beside me throughout a long train journey. I was in my twenties at the time and recently bereaved and the woman, perhaps sensing my grief, gently prompted me to talk and patiently listened. I opened up to her more candidly than I could at the time to close friends and family, precisely because it felt anonymous. We never exchanged more than first names but, all this time later, I still think of her, wherever she is, with gratitude.

Talking with a stranger, especially if our lives coincide in a place outside our everyday life, can feel very liberating. We can share confidences, even secrets, assuming that they'll be safe. We can unburden ourselves with fewer reservations that usual, imagining that we'll never encounter this kind listener ever again.

But what if a chance encounter of this sort with a sympathetic stranger turns out not to have been accidental at all, but deliberately contrived? And what if that stranger, with whom we've shared our darkest secrets, subsequently appears in the midst of our lives, armed with information which could prove damaging, even toxic?

In exploring this rather alarming idea, I realised I wanted to write about a close-knit community which I know well, a relatively small town where families were intertwined, where people put down roots and shared history, somewhere where reputation matters.

Ilkley, in West Yorkshire, is where I grew up and where members of my family still live. In writing this novel, I've revisited many happy memories, from careering across the school playground to my own waiting mother, to paddling a dinghy in the River Wharfe through long, hot childhood summers. Any darkness in the novel is, of course, my own invention.

It was out of these thoughts about dangerous strangers and their impact on a close community that *The Mother at Number 5* was born.

I hope you loved *The Mother at Number 5*. If you did, I would be very grateful if you could write a review. I'd love to hear what you think, and it makes such a difference in helping new readers discover my books for the first time.

I love hearing from my readers. You can get in touch on my Facebook page or on Twitter. Thank you!

All best wishes to you and yours,

Jill

facebook.com/jill.childs.71

twitter.com/author_jill

ACKNOWLEDGEMENTS

Thank you to my delightful editor, Maisie Lawrence, for your creativity and enthusiasm. It's a pleasure to be working with you again.

Thank you to the rest of the amazing Bookouture family for everything you do, from outstanding covers to passionate publicity. I'm grateful for the team's support for this book and all my previous ones.

My thanks to Jo Penton of the charity Victim Support for kindly talking me through the police and legal procedures in allegations of sexual assault.

Thank you to my brilliant agent, Judith Murdoch, the best in the business.

Thank you, always, to Nick and the rest of my family for their love and support.

And, finally, a particular thank you to Ilkley itself. It's a very special place.

Made in the USA
Monee, IL
18 July 2023